A DANGEROUS
MISCONCEPTION

Chapter One

Where it all began – 2012

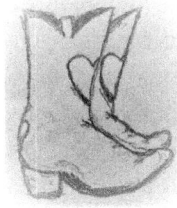

November 23rd, that was the day that my life changed. I started my day as I usually would by getting up and going to work with a black coffee in hand. I worked in Rose's café' six days a week. I've worked here since I was fourteen years old, Starting first on weekends and now full-time and I absolutely loved it. it always kept me out of trouble, plus there weren't very many other career choices in our little town. Rose's café was a small, quirky café right in the centre of our little town, it had a couple of ornate wooden tables outside the front of the stone wall building, that were all different from each other, these could be found under the awning that had a string of white fairy lights along it. which made it look quite quaint when they lit up in the evenings or I thought so anyway. Rose's café really stood out from all of the other shops in town. There were beautiful purple and yellow potted plants, that could be found out on the window ledge and in a couple of pots that were on either side of the door.

Inside it was very colourful, the walls were white with solid stone bits showing in places and around the room, you could find posters up on the wall of Marilyn Monroe and Audrey Hepburn and various other movie stars too, on the back wall there were signed polaroid photographs of people that had come and gone to Nashville and tried to "make it" and dotted around the room were lots of beautiful, colourful paintings of scenery from around our local area. Every chair in here was designed differently, some were made out of wood, and were very ornate, others were covered in different coloured and textured fabric and were more like armchairs. The counter to the right was long and silver with various bar stools sat around it, the coffee machine sat just in behind, and the old-fashioned till which was to the left of the counter and just in behind that was where you could visibly see the food being prepared and cooked, by the chef, Ben who was also Rose's son. The atmosphere was always jolly just like Rose herself. She was a plump, dark, short-haired lady, she was the kindest and sweetest person but also a very strong character, the type that didn't take any trouble from anyone, you would occasionally catch her and Ben having strong words in the kitchen and then laughing it off a while later, whilst making small digs at each other throughout the day.

When I wasn't there I was up at Pops and Mama's ranch helping with the horses and keeping the work on the Ranch up to date, this place was where I grew up and it really was home. My parents were the kindest people, I mean the definition grumpy old man would probably be the best way to describe my father, but he had a good heart and would do anything for his family, he's never been afraid of hard work, which I think he's installed in my brothers and me, but he would do anything for anyone if he thought it would make a difference to their lives, he's a cuddly built man, has a full head of hair which is unusual for someone of his age and he always has stubble on his face which Mama is forever nagging him to shave. My Mama is just amazing, she's sweet, funny and she doesn't take any crap from anyone, I love to sit there and watch my brothers wind her up or Pop's try his luck and she's back with a sarcastic comment or telling them off almost instantly. The best thing I've ever seen is my Pop's playing a trick on my Mama by asking her if the cream in the fridge smells off and him pushing it into her face, I've never seen him run so fast, ever since that happened they tend to play tricks on each other every so often. It's safe to say they really do have a playful relationship and are very rarely serious until they need to be that is. It's amazing to think they have had us, children, because they're just like big kids themselves, but in this family, we were always taught that family comes first. I think it's safe to say these people are the people that I can definitely call home and also the people that I can always depend on. Home is a funny word isn't it, because I believe that home isn't just somewhere you live but it's who you actually build your life with, and these people I love with all my heart and if they weren't my family I'd pick them over and over again. Life is one big adventure and there's no other family I'd rather go on adventures with.

Living here in Franklin, I guess I always thought that my life was perfect, I was engaged to one of the most career-driven men around. Nathan was never home because he was in the United States Navy and served as a Lieutenant, I was proud to be his, but he was away a lot and had a lot of responsibilities. We spoke occasionally or when he had the time and obviously when he was back from sea. He came home when he could, but I knew what I signed up for, this was normal for us and it kind of suited me. I've always been very independent even as a small child, I mean I had to be, I had three big brothers to contend with.

I really thought life was perfect. I had the nice green coloured house, with the porch, a little garage, and driveway, that you would find in our charming neighbourhood on the outskirts of town. Where everyone was really friendly and seemed to know things about you that hadn't even happened yet. I had the fancy Mitsubishi warrior, twin cab, pick-up truck white in colour to be exact complete with the chrome bits and I loved nothing more than to take her out and put the tailgate down and sit with a blanket watching the stars and reading a book or even sunbathing, she's sturdy and never lets me down, listens to my problems and has been known to get me out of some sticky situations, my truck is kind of like my child or so my family tells me. I had the job that I enjoyed, working for Rose wasn't really like work at all, Rose was in her late fifty's, and she was a good friend of my mother's, so she was fairly easy going just like the rest of this town. I had great friends although I had very few, I kind of lost touch with most of them after high school because they went off to different universities, travelled the world, and some even moved away but I heard from the odd few every now and then through those social media sites, I was always taught to keep your friends close, but hey I grew up with three amazing brothers so there was always someone around to hang with or talk to, Which meant I was never really alone.

I had an amazing family that always gave me all the love and support I could ever ask for; family is so important. They're the only ones, really that will see you at your worst and accept you for who you truly are. so, as you can see, I basically had everything I could ever want or need in my life. But the night of the 23rd of November made me feel as though the carpet had been pulled from beneath my feet and my life had changed forever, kind of like I had lost it all in such a short space of time.

I had just come back from a long night out, along with my three brothers, Spencer the eldest, Clay in the middle, and Dawson the youngest, and where there concerned there's always trouble, and being the youngest out of the four of us and being the only girl, they were always very protective of me, sometimes a little too overprotective. The bar had closed and herding them into my truck was proving a little bit of a challenge but that's when I had seen him standing there and I will never forget what was unfolding right in front of my eyes, I had to lock the doors to stop my brother Clay from getting back out the truck (not that he was in any fit state to do anything, but I knew he would try) and trying to stop Spencer and Dawson reacting to what was happening was hard too.

After a lot of shouting, tears and then driving them home, I tried hard to digest what had just happened, I decided to stay with my brothers and stay at our parent's house on the ranch that night, there was of plenty shouting when we got in but after a lot of convincing from Mama, the boys eventually calmed down and passed out or went to bed. I made my way up to my old room and just laid there on top of the covers staring up at the ceiling, the room smelt so familiar to me, like a musky cotton smell, and looking around I could see all my childhood things left untouched from the day I moved out and in with Nathan. The room was still baby pink in colour, and the curtains were still all white and frilly, old toys and dolls lay around the room untouched, even an old pair of cowgirl boots sat under my bed, I must have forgotten to take those with me I think to myself, and I briefly wonder if they still fit. I laid there for what seemed like hours, thinking the night's events over in my mind trying to clear my thoughts, taking several deep breaths, and wiping the make-up off my face. That's when I decided it was time for me to make a change and make a fresh start and find out who I really was, I had to do this, do this for me but right now I felt broken, numb, and sort of scared of what my next step was, but someone once told me like a glow stick sometimes you have to break to shine.

   I grew up in a small town in the south known as Franklin which isn't too far from Nashville. it's the type of place where everyone knows your name and even your grandparent's names, but here they all know everything about everyone, newcomers really stick out like a sore thumb, but you can understand why they would want to come here. Everyone is so friendly, and it really is the most beautiful place, the countryside is just stunning which is where Pop's and Mama's ranch is. They're surrounded by fields which gives you the feeling like you're in the middle of nowhere, it's the type of place that you wouldn't know was there unless you were told, the views from the ranch really are very beautiful and you would have to drive for miles around to see anything else like it, fields and hills are all you can see and then in behind the house you can just see our little town in the short distance.

There are a few small, quaint shops not far from here, that can be found down in the town, little gift shops, groceries stores, a bakery, a few bars, cafes, a salon, a couple of cute clothing stores, a high school that's not too far from here, and a florist. You see we live just on the outskirts away from all the hustle and bustle not to mention away from the gossip. To most people, it's not much but to me, it's definitely home.

I looked at my clock on the wall it was 2.47 am, everything was quiet, and the night's events were wildly running through my head, I assumed that everyone was now asleep and laying on my bed I started to let out the sobs that I had been holding in for so long, by the morning everyone in town would know what had happened.

For the next five days, I didn't leave my bedroom, I couldn't, I was totally humiliated. I didn't want anything to eat either, much to everyone's trying. I just wanted to hide under that blanket forever, away from the world. My mother had taken to checking on me every few hours and bringing food and drink that I would just pick at, she would sit and talk to me, begging me to eat, asking if she could get me anything, and seeing if I would just get up and take a walk with her around the ranch, every time I declined. I couldn't, I felt numb and exhausted all the time and I really just wanted to be on my own and left to sleep.

It was a Friday night or at least I thought it was, I had lost all track of the days and times, my brother Dawson gently tapped and opened my bedroom door, slowly he entered my room, and sat himself on the end of my bed looking at me.

"Right, you, that's enough of this, please stop moping around and feeling sorry for yourself, you need to get up" taking a deep breath he pleaded with me, but I could always trust Dawson to tell me straight

I couldn't, I didn't want to, I sat up in my bed and looked at him with a tear-stained face

"Am I that bad?" I mumbled, "Am I that unlovable?"

I could feel the tears coming again and he just held me for a little while, while I sobbed, I had lost everything within the space of five minutes and my world felt like it was completely empty like someone had punched a hole right through my stomach.

"You know what you need" he paused pulling me into a hug "A fresh start and no you're not that bad…. Don't get me wrong you could use a shower and put a bit of meat on them bones but no you're not that bad at all Darlin"

he always knew how to put a smile on my face and for the longest time we sat and neither of us said anything. Silently I agreed with him, he was right, I needed a fresh start, and I might need that shower.

"Maybe you need to get away for a little while, go on holiday or something, take some time away, find yourself and maybe one day you'll find a man that's worthy of you, not a boy that's going to play those silly games," he told me

He was right, I knew he was, I needed to do something, I couldn't sit here all my life and hide in this little room. He told me to think it over and that he would help me in any way he could, making his way to the door he closed it and leaving me sitting there. I sat there for a few moments and knew what I had to do, I would leave franklin and give myself the break I needed. I don't think I could take the drama that would surround my life, I was sure to be the talk of the town by now. So, it was decided, I packed the few essential things, clothes, toothbrush, wallet, and my

cell phone into a bag and started by leaving a note for
Dawson.

Daw,

I've taken your advice and decided to leave, not
sure where I'm headin. Needed to get away for
a little while, as we discussed.

I'm going to need your help please, firstly with
Nathan and the sale of what once was our
home, could you please retrieve my belongings
that are at the house, I've left you the keys.

Secondly, make sure that Pops and Mama are
okay.

Also, I just want to thank you for always
having my back and looking out for me, I'll call
as soon as I hit a rest stop and I'll be home
again soon.

Bea xx

I left another note for Mama and Pop's on the kitchen side
by the coffee machine, knowing that's where their first
stop is every morning.

Mama & Pops

I need some time away, things have become a little too much lately and I need a break, I hope you both understand, please don't worry about me, I'll be fine, and I'll call as soon as I can. I love you both dearly and I'll be home again soon, I just need some time away and some space.

I love you both so much

Beatrice xx

Putting the pen down I looked over at the clock seeing it was 3.21 am, I picked up the keys to my truck, placed the key to the house that I once shared with Nathan with Dawson's note, and with that, I left.

I got in my truck and just kept driving; I couldn't take all the trouble that surrounded me in my little town. By 5.01 am, I noticed I had five missed calls from Dawson and two from my mother, I know they would be worried and standing around the kitchen drinking coffee, discussing my decision. Ignoring my phone, I turned the music up and just kept driving, I would call and explain when I hit a rest stop but as for now it was just me and the open road, I wasn't really sure where I was heading but after driving a day and a half with few rest stops, I found myself in the city of Chicago.

That was seven years ago now and I now work as a waitress in a little Italian restaurant, which is in Streeterville, Chicago. It's really lovely here although it's a little different from home, the restaurant is situated so it looks out across the water, it's very much the classic style Italian restaurant with the round wooden tables and fancy red and white chequered tablecloths and the very fancy pizza oven to the back of the room, where the owners and locals watched me make and burn my first pizza when they tried to convince me that I could cook. They serve the best wine in town which comes from Carlos's uncle's vineyard in Italy, As well as the best Italian dishes, I mean I might be slightly biased, but the food here really is delicious.

My boss Carlos and his family are the most amazing people. They took me in and have treated me like one of their own since I arrived here in Chicago seven years ago. They helped me find somewhere to live and even helped me with meals before and after my shift when they knew things were a little tight, they have given me people to depend on and are kind of like my family away from home. If I needed the extra cash, there would always be extra shifts (even if they didn't really need me) and thanks to them I can now comfortably stand on my own two feet. Within my first few months of meeting them they told me that their family is rather large so what would one more person do, they have treated me like one of their own ever since I got here. Where Christmas and birthdays were concerned, they would always make sure I would attend with them so I wasn't on my own and when it was my birthday, they always made sure I would have a cake and that they would do something special for me at the restaurant. There was never a dull moment with this family. They have five children all between the ages of ten months and twelve years, so it's safe to say they have their hands full. The restaurant is family run which included Carlos's cousins, Aunts, and even his grandma Nera helps out occasionally, so I got to know them all pretty well. There eldest Sophia would sometimes help out in the kitchen, so I got to know her best. She's a very pretty young girl with very long, thick black hair and beautiful olive skin and she's very intelligent, I always tell her she'll grow up and go extremely far, she'll probably grow up to be a surgeon or an accountant or do something amazing with her life, I know she'll do this family proud because I've never met a child so young to know so much and actually be enthusiastic about it all, sometimes she'll tell us facts that we wouldn't even dream of knowing.

Alongside this I have gone back to school to study publishing in the hope to become a publisher someday, I love to read, the stories people come up with can just be incredible, I guess I like the idea that one book can change the way you look at life, sometimes rescue you, change your mood and even make you travel in time, you can travel anywhere within a book.

I study at the University of Chicago - Graham School in the day and I work here in the restaurant in the evening or whenever I don't have to attend the university. Carlos and his family really have been so good to me fixing my shifts whenever I'm not studying.

I walked into the restaurant just like I do any other night, saying hello to Carlos and his wife Gabrielle who's holding their ten-month-old, Marcel. I walk into the back by the lockers, pulling out my apron and putting on. I was just about to pick up my pad and pencil to head out to start taking orders when an excitable Willow comes bouncing in.

"Gooooood evening Beatrice, it looks busy out there tonight" she smiles a wide-tooth grin "Sooo…….., tell me…..how was your date with Dan? I want all the gossip," she says as she ties her apron around her waist

Willow is originally from California, and you can really tell because she's roughly 5ft 7, long blonde, straight hair, piercing blue eyes, petite, with a bubbly personality and basically looks like a supermodel. The total opposite to me with my long wavy black hair and green eyes, curvy figure, and short 5ft nothing in height.

Willow has been my most loyal friend since I moved here. We met when I started working for Carlos, she kind of took me under her wing and where she's concerned nothing's ever too much trouble, but she loves to know all the details on everything, my best friend but a total gossip however I'd trust this girl with my life.

"Oh god, don't even get me started" I replied "What a total bore, he kept droning on about his ex, I swear to god I know everything there is to know about his Millie and how she left him for her boss"

Willow starts to laugh "I did wonder if that would be the case," she says smiling at me "He did give the not completely over my ex-vibe but at least it got you out of the house for a few hours and a free meal, but don't worry I'll pick better for you next time"

"Oh no, no, no, I don't want to hear about any more ex's or other people's problems thank you, plus with this last one I picked up the bill, He forgot his card, after that experience I'm definitely done with this whole dating thing, I'm done searching for Mr Right, I think I just want to focus on myself right now, I can't disappoint myself and who knows maybe Mr Right will come and find me when I least expect it"

Willow starts to grin at me "Nooo way, forgot his card, that old trick, I can't believe it…. Okay, okay no more blind dates then but when you're ready you let me know and I'll wave my magic wand and find prince charming for you"

"Thanks," I say with a laugh as we leave the locker room with a smile and make a start on our shift.

The shift goes quickly tonight, we laugh, we smile and once again Willow tries to set me up on yet another date.

"What about Mr. Tall, dark and handsome over there?" she nudges me as we're stood at the till and I start to log the meals under each table.

I look up to see where she's looking "God no…. Willow he's far too young and I'm pretty sure his dates in the restroom" (I had clocked that when I served them earlier)

"Ahhhh" she pauses for a second, "I thought that was his mother…………." she goes quiet like it's only just dawned on her "Eww he definitely likes the older woman doesn't he" she giggles "Na…. I don't think you're old enough for him," she tells me with a nudge

I laugh at the look on her face "Plus I said no more dates" I lower my voice to a whisper "and stop staring at them"

"Oh… okay… yeah" she stutters then says "Okay you're the boss Beatrice, god I can't believe that's his date, yuck man that's gross," she tells me as she leaves me to go and serve another table.

The guy looked around his early twenties, whereas the woman was definitely in her late fifty's early sixties. They could have passed for mother and son until we saw them making out across the table. We both stand there watching and I laugh at the grossed-out, look on Willow's face.

The customers were out in full swing tonight, and we don't seem to catch a break, the regulars keep us going with their cheeky remarks, giving us a glimpse into their daily lives. One of my regulars, Albert, always books the same table, Table eight by the door (just so he can see out the window clearly, or so he tells me), every night for one, for 7 pm, it was always for two but ever since he lost his wife about eighteen months ago, he comes by himself.

he tells me "She would want me to still enjoy myself and it saves the washing up" he jokes. "Plus, I like Italian food"

She was only seventy-eight when she died of lung cancer due to being a smoker, he himself is eighty-four and use to be in the marines and he was pretty high up he once told me. He's full of lots of fun and interesting stories that he would always share with me and the girls that work here. he used to come here once a week with his wife Josie until she passed away, it was kind of their thing and she was just so beautiful and kind, however ever since he lost her it has been more of a regular thing for him, I always make sure that he has a pint of Guinness waiting for him and he always brings a framed photo of Josie to dinner with him to sit it on the table, while he enjoys his meal. We always talk for a little while because he's usually the last one here and I'm not sure that he sees many people or gets too many visitors, he tends to sit here till just before closing then he goes on his way, I wave him off "Thanks for keeping me company" he tells me smiling.

I smile back "Your welcome Albert, do you need me to call you a taxi?"

"No thank you, dear, it's just across the way"

It's almost midnight when Carlos tells me to head on home, I hang up my apron, wave goodbye to Willow and the girls, and leave the restaurant. I start to make my way back to my little apartment which isn't too far from Sak's fifth avenue, it's a cold night so I quickly head-on into the small, dark, green-tiled foyer first checking my mailbox on my left and picking up my Amazon parcel, As I start making my way up the metal railed staircase to my apartment, Suddenly I hear that cranky voice that I know oh too well from behind me.

"Your late again Beatrice" it calls

I carry on walking up the staircase not bothering to look in the direction of the voice and I roll my eyes, here we go again I think to myself taking a deep breath I reply "Got to work hard to play hard Mrs Moyle" I tell her

Mrs Moyle is a mature lady, that wears large thick glasses, has curly, grey hair, and is a very skinny woman and I swear she has spent most of her life in that beige, woolly cardigan. She lives two stories below me, she's been here for absolute years, since it was built I think, but she clearly thinks she has a claim on the building and anyone who enters it. She is the type of person that has her large, crooked nose in everyone's business and loves nothing more than to complain about everything and anything, I swear she even keeps track of when I use my toilet as well as my work shift patterns. She keeps informing me in full detail about John at number six and his "fancy woman" and how she could hear them giggling above her, and that she thinks it's disgusting at his age (bearing in mind he's only sixty-two) she then goes on to tell me I'm overworking myself and that I will overdo myself causing myself to have a breakdown when she's finished having a moan, she finally lets me carry on up the stairs to my apartment. I get to my red door at number nine. I walk through into the old, small, dated apartment. I hang up my coat, looking around noticing it's in need of a lot of love and care. I've hardly done anything since I moved in here and now I'm starting to think it would do well to have a fresh coat of paint, I've only had it three years, but I was in such a hurry to get everything in that I didn't have time to redecorate anything. The blue second-hand, soft couch is the first thing I come to in the middle of the room in the small open plan living room, and the kitchen area is a little dated, it's bright yellow in colour and looking a little tired, I make a mental note to redecorate when I have a few days off and have finished my final for uni. I make my way to my emerald, green coloured bedroom (not my choice of colour) and head into the en-suite, firstly washing my face and then making my way back into the bedroom, pressing play on the answering machine beside my bed as I go, I sit on my bed and start to take off my ugly, black flat shoes and begin to listen, a voice plays, and I instantly recognize it to be my mothers.

Chapter Two

The Call

"Hey Beatrice, it's your mother here, just wonderin how you are…….would be nice to have a coffee and catch up with you soon, I'm thinking maybe I could visit, call me"

I smile hearing her voice before hearing the beep and it cutting off, I mean we've never been terribly close, but she has always tried her best for us as mothers do and she was always there for me through the rough and the smooth, believe me, there's been a lot of rough but not so much now. she usually calls once or twice a week just for a catch-up, making sure I'm doing okay and keeping me informed about everything and everyone back home, I'm not sure she dealt with me leaving very well but she comes to visit me here in Chicago every so often, which we both enjoy, and I speak to my brother Dawson at least once a day, sometimes more. so, family is never that far away.

"Beatrice, it's your mother here, I tried calling your cell a couple of times, I need you to call me as soon as you can, it's kind of urgent, we kind of have a problem here" and I hear the panic in her voice and then the machine cuts off with another beep.

She sounds worried, I'll call her in the morning it's late and she's probably worrying about the local fate that's taking place at the weekend, and what she should bake for the event. We already had this conversation last week I think to myself and I'm sure we agreed she'd make pumpkin pie and various cheesecakes, maybe she's changed her mind again or Mrs Hinds has asked her to make something else.

Another message comes through on the machine and it's my eldest brother Spencer. Which I find rather odd because we have never been too close, Spencer's the one I clash with, I think maybe we're too much alike and he's always been the wild card.

"Bea, it's Spence, I've tried your cell a few times, call me asap, we're at the hospital, we could really do with you here, you've got my number" and with that, it cuts off again.

At the hospital why would they be there I wonder, I then search into my handbag for my cell, I find it at the bottom and realize it's been on silent all day, which is why I haven't noticed anything all night. Thirteen missed calls and eight text messages from all three of my brothers and my mother, all asking me to call, telling me it's urgent. My stomach drops and I begin to feel sick, I phone my mother first, but it goes straight to voicemail. Darn it I say to myself there really must be something wrong as she usually answers my calls on the first few rings, I phone my brother Spencer, I try five times, but it just keeps ringing, So I phone Dawson and on the second time, he finally answers.

"Bea! I'm so sorry I didn't realize you were calling, there's been so much going on here"

"That's okay, what's been going on? What's the emergency? Is Mama worrying about the local fate again? we only spoke last week and agreed that she'd make a pumpkin pie and a few cheesecakes" I ask my voice full of urgency but also trying to make light of the situation.

"No….. no, Bea I wish it was….. listen I don't know how to tell you this but It's Pops……" he starts

"Okay, what's happened?" my father is my world, to me, there is no greater man, he's the head of our family, the one that's the glue that holds us all together, the one that makes us laugh with his not so funny jokes, the biggest kid but ultimately my hero.

"Pops is in the hospital Bea, he collapsed at the ranch this morning, they think he's had a severe heart attack, I found him in the barn, it's touch and go at the moment and we think you really need to come home, he's on machines and everythin Bea…It'd ahh… it's pretty bad," he tells me

I'm speechless, I feel like my head is spinning as I process all this new information, my poor Pop's how could this have happened, he's always been so strong, our rock and I don't know why but I always believed him to be invincible, but I guess that's just not the case and that thought hits me like a ton of bricks. Plus, I haven't been home in seven years, what would people say or think, the thought terrifies me, but my Pop's and family need me….

"Bea you still there?" Dawson jolts me from my thoughts

"Yes, I'm still here Daw… Okay I've got to make a few phone calls and I'll be there as soon as I can," I tell him

"Okay Bea, thanks…. Hey, listen, I know this is a big thing for you to do and it must be really hard to come here but I think you really need to be here, drive safe, and get here soon yeah" and with that, he hangs up

I lay there on my bed for a few moments feeling numb, the anxiety rising, I tell myself not to be so stupid and that I've got this, as my father would have said, I take a deep breath, get up and start to pack as much as I can into the big black gym bag that I rarely use and when I say rarely what I really mean is I used it once and then never went back to the judgemental gym again. Quickly leaving the apartment and closing the door as quietly as I can, I swiftly make my way down the stairs to the foyer. As I get to the bottom floor entrance hall, I can hear is Mrs. Moyles once again

"Dirty stop out, going out at this hour can only mean one thing, up to no good, must be a man involved, it's disgusting" she shouts "People in this building have no respect for themselves or anyone else who lives here"

I roll my eyes, leave the building, and choose to ignore her, I walk across to the parking lot, reach my truck and start the engine to warm her up, it purrs into life, I pull out my cell, taking note that it's nearly midnight and then make my first call to Carlos to explain the situation. He answers pretty quickly (I think he must be up with the baby, Marcel) he wishes me a safe journey, reassuring me that my job is still there when I return and to take as much time as I need. The next person I contact is Willow I choose to send her a text message to give her a brief idea of what's going on and promise to call her in the morning to explain everything.

With that, I put the truck into drive, leave the parking lot and start my journey to the place that I once called home,

As I do my mind drifts back to the moment that caused me to leave.

I was working on the ranch with my brother Dawson that day, Dawson was 23 years old at the time, he had dark hair, was lean, always had a tan, and was and still is a true cowboy, but also a proper nerd, we're always teasing him about his marvel and superhero obsession, telling him that it's so unhealthy for a man of his age to still love superheroes the way he does and that it would be totally acceptable if he was a five-year-old boy or even had a girlfriend.

It was a Friday, and we were busy working at the ranch, the sun was high in the sky and the heat was about twenty-seven degrees, I love the feeling of the heat on my skin and being out in the fresh air. The views from the field were phenomenal, all you could see were high hills and green fields for miles around. To the back of the house, you could see in the short distance franklin, our little town. The horses were out in the fields just over to the right by the stables and the sheep were in the next one over, it was so peaceful, all you could hear were the birds chirping and the smell of the freshly cut grass filled my nose – Spencer must be cutting it again I think to myself. Dawson and I were working hard, moving hay bales, I sat down by one of the last ones placing my head back against it and the smell of fresh hay filled my nose, then I realized I felt totally exhausted.

"Your slacking Bea" Dawson teases me as he walks towards me and bends down offering me a hand to help me back up onto my feet.

I start to smile a wide-tooth grin and hit his brown cowboy hat off his head as I stand and think to myself here we go again with the witty remarks.

"Like you could do better Batman"

"I'll have you know Batman would have had all this done in about 4.2 seconds" he states

I roll my eyes and I listen to him rattle on about different superheroes, Iron man and the Avengers like I have so many times before, and then he starts to compare himself and tell me all about their superpowers, and how he has the outfits, I can't help but laugh, thinking to myself he'll never get a girlfriend at this rate. It's 6 pm by the time we've finished. We turn and head back to the house where we find our brother Clay standing out the front with three cold beers in hand. We took a seat on the swing seat on the front porch with Dawson choosing to sit on the floor not too far from us, it's hot and I wipe the sweat from my brow, I start by taking a swig from the bottle Clay has just handed me, the taste is refreshing, and we sit and discuss the day's events.

"You made good time today, that was a lot of hard work," Clay tells us as he takes a swig from the bottle he's holding then goes on "So what's the plan for tonight?" he says looking to both of us, he'd been in with the horses all day, Clay was tall, fair-haired with blue eyes, with a beard that he had only just been able to grow and he was medium built and was really good with computer systems and technology, he loved to learn anything new, so he did as many courses as he could and now he could hack into almost anything if he wanted to.

I shake my head "Nope nothing for me just a chilled night in I think, a film, a gin and tonic and maybe a hot bubble bath, yep that's my plan for the evening"

Dawson looks over to Clay and rolls his eyes and then gives me a big grin

"No it's not, don't be silly….. that's not the plan……...lets hit the bar"

"Umm no thanks, you guys can hit the bar, but I refuse to come along, you guys always cause way too much trouble wherever you go, plus I'm shattered, and Nathan comes home next weekend, I need to sort the house before then and actually get myself looking presentable," I tell them, but I know I'm going to get bullied into going out with them.

"YES!!!, now were talking" shouts Clay excitedly

Dawson jumps up "Oh, C'mon Bea, it'll be fun"

Clay now jumping up beside Dawson says "Ohh C'mon Bea it'll be awesome, and I've got some new moves you need to see"

They both stand there doing the worst dance moves I have ever seen, wiggling their bums, and moving their arms around and I'm pretty certain Dawson just did a bunny hop and I couldn't help but stand there and laugh at the sight of them both and how ridiculous they look….. and, there not giving up easily. Spencer appears from around where the barn is with a bottle of bud light in hand and when he notices them he can't help but wear the biggest grin I've ever seen, which is followed by a laugh.

"What's going on here then?" he asks still trying to contain his laughter

"We're going to the Hideaway" Clay and Dawson say in unison still jumping around like the idiots they are

I smile "Ohhhhh……no,no,no …..We're not….. they are" I protest, pointing my fingers between me and them

"Oh, C'mon don't be a wet weekend and a bore, let your hair down baby Bea" Dawson teases using my childhood nickname. "Nathan will be back in no time and then you can be boring as hell with him then, but tonight you're out with your big bros"

"But it's been such a long day and I'm exhausted" I protest

"You never want to spend time with us anymore" Clay moans at me putting out his bottom lip and giving me his best fake sad face and puppy dog eyes "C'mon it'll be fun"

And I've got, to be honest, that hit a nerve.

"They just don't like the thought of you being on your own" Spencer whispered so that only I can hear, as the other two carry on with their so-called dance moves, and the next thing I know they've all stopped and looked at each other and then I'm being picked up and carried in the house and forced against my will to get ready, but I'm wearing my biggest smile.

Chapter Three

Home

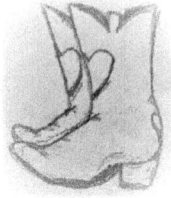

The sound of a horn brings me back from my daydream. I find myself sitting at a green light not realizing it had changed, it's almost 8 am and I need to stop for a coffee and something to eat. I'm six hours through my seven-and-a-half-hour journey, only an hour and a half from the place I once called home.

Pulling up, I find myself at a diner on the freeway, it looks like a sweet wooden hut type of building with the sign reading "Emma's place" above the door. getting out of the truck, I walk in and find myself a table near the window. The diner is cute with little red and white booths all along by the windows, on the opposite side of the booths is the metal counter where a few other customers are sat, and in behind them, you can clearly see the chefs cooking this morning's breakfast. As I sit down a blonde waitress, I notice by her name on her badge that her name is Tiffany, comes over to take my order.

"What can I get for ya sugar?" she smiles at me chewing her gum, not really looking at me just at the notepad she's holding.

Looking up at her, all I can notice is the amount of makeup that's caked on her face, in particular those eyebrows and the way they look way too much like upside-down Nike ticks that have been glued to her face, but she seems nice enough, wearing her pink and white apron, I do a double-take at her eyebrow's again and I kind of want to make a suggestion, but I don't want to embarrass her or seem like a bitch, so I settle on ordering an expresso coffee and some waffles.

"Coming right up," she says as I watch her walk back to the kitchen and then to the counter where she starts refilling the other customer's coffee cups, looking around I notice that it's not very busy in here and that there are only around five or six people dotted around the room, a couple of them look like truckers that have only just got off shift. looking at my watch I notice that it's just gone 8 am so it's fairly early.

I sit back with my coffee and waffles, that's when I realize how exhausted I am, it's been a long night, but I would never let them down and I needed to see my Pops and make sure for myself that he's doing okay. I briefly wonder if he's been too stressed about things or overdoing it, maybe he wasn't getting much work or maybe he needed more help, but I guess the only people that can answer my questions are my family. finishing my coffee and waffles, I order another one to go and then hit the road again on my journey to the place I once called home.

Finally, I arrive at Williamson medical centre, parking the truck in the biggest space I can find, I get out and make my way inside, everything is so clean and white and it's really busy in here today, there are people everywhere. I make my way to the reception desk and when I start speaking to the receptionist, I find out my father is on the 10th floor. I take the elevator up and then make my way down the corridor. I rush up to the receptionist on level ten and as I'm about to ask her in which room I could find my father. I turn to my right and notice my brother Dawson walking down the hall with his head buried in his phone.

"DAWSON!" I shout as I run up to him

"BEA!" he says pulling me into a hug "I'm so glad you're here, god it's been too long," he says as he takes a step back to look at me.

"How's he doing?" I ask my voice full of urgency

"Not so good but he's talking away like nothing's happened and keeps telling us not to worry, to head on home, and that he'll be there soon. He's had open-heart surgery and it's going to be a long road to recovery, he's going to need help at home and everything Bea, but you know he'll get…..."

"Frustrated," we both say in unison

"But mainly with Mama but that's supposed to be a sign of a heart problem" he informs me

"Well, we know she won't take any crap from him, Has he been overdoing it? Or not getting enough help? Or stressing about things Daw?"

"No, we don't think so, he has been a bit on edge about things at the ranch, we've been doin most of the manual work, although he has been snappy and short-tempered with us, the doctors have said that's also a sign" he informs me

With that Spencer and Clay come around the corner both with a coffee cup in each hand, spotting me Spencer pulls me into a big, unexpected, long hug.

"Ahhh….. it's good to have you home stranger" he states in a southern drawl

"It's good to see y'all too," I say as I try to catch the lump in my throat before it can escape, before the tears come, seeing them all after so long is just very overwhelming and they've barely changed, apart from they have all become more muscular and Clay has finally been able to grow that long beard he always wanted.

Clay pulls me into a hug too "Hey baby Bea, when did you get so big? C'mon let's go see Mama and let her know you're here" he smiles "She'll be so pleased to see you; she didn't think you'd come"

I follow them down the corridor, the next thing I know Dawson comes up beside me taking my hand, it's like he can almost sense that I'm nervous and that I'm a little scared of what I might find behind that door.

"It's okay Bea, he's okay" he whispers "We're just going to need to help him every now and again, you know, when he lets us that is" he smiles and I nod.

Rounding the corner, we go into a small room on the right, my brothers head in before me, I watch as Spencer hands Mama a coffee cup and takes a seat across from her, I just stand there in the doorway not really knowing what to do with myself and taking her in. she hasn't changed much, she's still tiny, with dark wavy hair like mine that's been cut into a bob and there's a hint of grey in there now, her piercing green eyes look tired and red like she hasn't slept in days and hasn't stopped crying either, but she looks like the same Mama she's always been.

"Well, this is crowded," I say "Not what I had in mind for a family reunion though"

This startles my mother, as she jumps up from her seat and greets me with a hug and starts to cry again "Oh, sweet girl, what are you doing here? I didn't think you'd come" she sobs "I prayed for this moment" she continues, still hugging me and it's like she doesn't want to let me go, It's clear that she blames herself for what has happened to my father, she seems to be on edge, I can tell because she keeps looking over at him as if checking on him.

"It's good to see y'all too," I say as I hold her at arm's length and I follow her gaze and look over to my father in the hospital bed, slowly making my way to him, I notice it's roasting in this hospital, I'm surprised he hasn't moaned about that, I cuddle him as much and as gentle as I can. As I do, he wakes up and I realised that tears have now escaped and are now rolling down my face, I wipe them away with the back of my hand.

"How ya doing Pops?"

"Beatrice, are you really here?" he asks me in a daze as if trying to clear his vision

"Really me Pop, how y'all doing?"

"Ohh you know me, tough as old boots me, tough as old boots" he repeats as if trying to convince not only himself but everyone else in the room.

I give him my best fake smile and sit on the end of the bed, listening as they explain to me what happened in more detail. He looks so small sat there in that bed, his grey hair now on the longish side and he's grown his beard longer than I remember it, his blue eyes look so tired, I notice his skin is slightly grey in colour but he's still the cuddly built man he's always been.

It turns out that my father had been out in the stables at home, with the horses mucking out, and got terrible chest pains and weird achy pains in his arms. Luckily for us and him, Dawson had been there yesterday helping out, He was busy talking to Pops when he stopped answering him and giving him witty remarks, he then found Pops laying on the stable floor and called for an ambulance.

"So how long do you have to stay in here for Pops?" I ask knowing it's a rather sore subject for everyone and I can hear the tuts and moans from my brothers that are now dotted around the room.

"Well, they're telling me about two/three weeks and then six months with no hard work at the moment, you know no lifting, carrying, or doing any manual work, but you know me I'll be out and back to it before then"

"Hey, Pop's you know what the doctors have said, you need to take it easy," Spencer tells him with a stern look

"Doctor Schmockter" he winks at me "Everyone's different you know" he snaps and Spencer rolls his eyes.

"Jefferson you know what they've said and it's for your own good you know," Mama tells him in a stern tone

He sits there and smiles at her "Okay, okay" then goes quiet and rolls his eyes so only I can see and as if to silently say I know what she's like and I better do as I'm told, Mama can be scary when she's angry.

After catching up with everyone, me telling them about my life in Chicago, how I work for the best people, I tell them about Willow and the girls I work with, about my apartment and studying to become a publisher at the University of Chicago -Grahams school, they all seem really proud and pleased that I'm happy and I've got to admit its really nice to hear. They tell me about their lives here in franklin and how not much has really changed over the last seven years. although I find out a few interesting things, Dawson still works at the ranch, looking after the horses, harvesting, and generally running the place, he's still living there too but has recently got engaged to a local girl named Ruth Carlyon, she went to my high school, I just remember her always having her head in a book and being really clever but all the same, I'm really pleased for him, after all, he was the one that we all thought would never leave home or get a girlfriend.

"She's a real nice gal, real down to earth and Oh and she can bake," Mama tells me as if baking is a really impressive thing to her, and then I realize I can't remember the last time I actually baked something.

Looking at Dawson I see he is a nice shade of beetroot in colour. My brother Spencer on the other hand…….

"Ohh Spence what am I going to do with you?" I tell him after hearing the news. Finding out that my eldest brother was the local man whore was just hilarious, Spencer was never really interested in girls, he always use to be a man's man. We always thought he would actually turn out gay, so to find out he's a real lady's man was a real shock and to be honest, made my year. I just stood there grinning, I had to hold in the laughter that was ready to burst out of me.

"That's it laugh it up," Spencer tells me "I'm also an officer of the Law at the local station, and that right there is why the ladies love me"

The whole room erupts into laughter, even Mama and Pops laugh

"Yep sure" Clay says with an eye roll as we continue to laugh

"So, any ladies at the moment Spence?" I smile looking at Clay and Dawson who continue to laugh and sit on the edge of their seats as I know they're dying for him to answer the question so they can rip into him.

"Ohh there's always loads of ladies" Dawson jokes playfully, "I think half the town has seen his pee-pee, but not one of them can hold him down apparently"

"Hey, it takes a special woman or three to hold all this down" Spencer jokes waving his hand down the length of his body, with a cheeky smile "But you know bros before hoes and all that"

"Yes, and all that," Clay says as he rolls his eyes again "Real ladies man you are" and with that we all laugh

"Boys," my mother says as though she's totally disgusted, but she's used to us all talking trash and I can see the smirk playing on her lips, I sit there and can't quite believe my brother has become a serial dater, being thirty-four years old you would think by now that he would be ready to settle down by now but oh how wrong I was.

"Thank god he's not still living under my roof" my mother finally says

Clay is the quieter, shyer one out of the three of them, he tells me he's currently working in security and working on a new security software; however, he keeps it brief in describing it. I think he's designing it for a top, a big-money company, he tells us works globally, and he tells me he gets flown all around the world for work too. He still lives with Pops and Mama at the ranch as well, well when he's not a way that is. I think he's saving for something special though a house of his own maybe, Clay always did hold his cards close to his chest. But he also tells me his boss has recently gifted him a new Mercedes for all his hard work.

"When I'm not flying around or out of town, I'm working on the ranch with Dawson too," Clay tells me

"No lady friends for you then Clay?"

And it's like he's taken back and slightly embarrassed by my question "Oh…..No, no" he tells me brushing off my question quickly "I'm far too busy for that" I can see his cheeks are now burning red and he can't look at me. When he leaves the room, Mama informs me that he has a crush on one of the ladies in our local grocery store, but he's really shy about it.

With that, a nurse comes in and tells us that visiting hours are over and that we need to leave to let Pops rest. Mama hasn't left the hospital since Pop's arrived here two days ago, but she gives me her keys to their house and tells me to go make myself comfortable and that she will be staying the night here, again. I tell her I'll bring her some clean clothes and toiletries tomorrow.

Walking to the exit with my brothers I inform them that I'll follow them back to the house in my truck.

"I'll come with you Bea," Dawson says as he jumps in the passenger's side beside me, we sit there for a few minutes, and I take a deep breath as we watch Clay and Spencer jump into the police cruiser and disappear. He turns to me "So how are you holding up?" he asks

"I'm okay, what about you? And thanks for getting me to come home, I know you're the one that made Spencer call me. I know y'all tried to get hold of me, I'm just so sorry I wasn't there when it happened, I kinda feel like I've let y'all down"

"I'm doing okay" he hesitates "listen I know it's a big thing for you to come back here, none of us would have blamed you if you didn't, we know how you feel about being here, we understand all the shit you've been through, but we thought you had a right to know and thought you would want to be here for Pops, You haven't let us down at all. We're all very proud of the women you've become, I mean look at you all grown up and it really seems like you've got your life together"

"I know but I had to put my big girl pants on Daw, my family needs me"

He goes quiet and says nothing for a moment and then says "They miss you, you know, we all do, it was really hard when you left"

"I'm really sorry Dawson, I didn't mean to upset anyone by leaving and I had planned to come back sooner than this, but the longer I left it the harder it became, and I just couldn't stay not after what happened, it was just too much. You were right, I needed that fresh start, I never planned to stay there in Chicago, I just thought it would be a stop-gap for a short while"

We both sit in silence, and I start the truck, which roars to life.

"So, tell me about Ruth and when I can meet her" I ask as we leave the parking lot

He smiles at me "In about twenty minutes. Ruth's a really great gal Bea I think you'll like her; Mama and Pop's love her too"

"So, how did y'all meet?"

"Well at the Hideaway one night about eighteen months ago. I was standing at the bar after a long day at the ranch, I decided to drag Clay out for one, and she just came up to me asking me what she had to do to get a cowboys number. of course, I laughed obviously at her being so forward, I bought her a drink, we played a few games of pool, and I took her number and we just got to know each other a bit more over the course of a few weeks, she's really great Bea" he tells me enthusiastically "A couple of weeks later she came to Pops and Mamas place, and she hasn't really left since, I think you'll get on like a house on fire, she reminds me of you in some ways, funny like you and stubborn. I recently asked her to marry me on a horse ride down by the creek and she said yes….of course, it's funny you know I never even noticed her before or looked at her in that way and BAM here we are inseparable, were hoping to buy the old Jewson farmhouse just outside of town but we don't want to leave while Pops is so poorly, so, for the time being, we're just staying here to help out and support where we can. Hey at least you'll have some female company now your home" he tells me, and I can hear the fondness in his voice.

After a short while and when we stop talking, I realise we've reached the entrance to the ranch, it hasn't changed much and the sun's just setting over the hill, the sky is all different shades of pink, and it really is beautiful. I've missed this place and its beauty. I drive through the entrance and up the hill on the dusty old path, the trees on either side in the field are still as they once were but slightly more overgrown than they use to be and the white fence has been replaced with new wooden ones, at the top of the dirt track we pull up outside the front porch and I park the truck beside a baby blue BMW Mini, who's I can only assume is Ruth's, a white pickup truck which I know is Pops, Clays Mercedes and the police cruiser that I can only assume is Casanovas.

Getting out, I look around, I can still see the large wooden barn behind the house, the stables are to the right of the house, but it seems to have grown in size since I was last here. There are a few trees missing by the stables and paddock, I assumed they were all cut down for the wood that would have been used for the wood burner, Mamas potted plants had finally made it out the front porch like she'd always talked about, and the house had been painted white instead of the dull cream colour that it used to be but apart from that, it was pretty much the same as I remember it. smiling I grab my bag from the footwell of the truck and follow Dawson inside to the place that I once called home.

Chapter Four

The Ranch

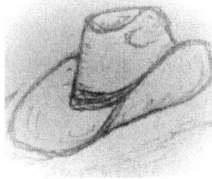

We walk into the kitchen and I take off my dolly shoes and the slate flooring feels cool beneath my feet, we're suddenly greeted by a bouncy girl who I can only assume is Ruth, she wraps Dawson into a warm long cuddle.

"Hey, sugar how you doing? How's Pops doin?" she asks looking at him and then notices me behind him, she pushes him aside and also wraps me in a big embrace then holds me at arm's length as to if checking me over then finally she says "And you must be Beatrice, I've been hoping to meet you, I'm sorry it's just on such rubbish terms"

"Please call me Bea everyone else does but it's nice to meet ya all the same" I smile at her

She offers me an apologetic smile and I can't tell if she's sorry to hear about my Pops or if she knows why I left. She then wraps me into another cuddle (something I'm not used to with strangers), but I'm almost taken back by her kindness, it's as if they've made her aware of what happened and why I don't come back here. She's beautiful with her long dark wavy hair, dark, chestnut eyes, tanned skin, and she's tiny not only in height but petite in size too, (she hasn't changed much, from the young girl I remember from high school) she's wearing light blue jeans, a white strappy top and cowgirl boots and seems like a very kind-hearted and down to earth gal, just like my mother had said, Dawson takes her hand, and they head off into the living room.

I take a deep breath and a moment to take everything in, looking around the kitchen that I once knew so well, placing my shoes next to the wooden stable door, I notice the large wooden bench is where it's always been, in the middle of the room, this is where we would usually have family meetings and meals for every occasion. I remember it best at Christmas and thanksgiving. I notice what's on the oak kitchen worktops and it looks like Mama was cooking before she set off to leave with Pops. I make a mental note to clean and clear it for her tomorrow, just so she doesn't have a mess to come home to, knowing my brothers won't do it, it looks like she was making the cheesecakes before she left. The kitchen cabinets have been painted cream where they use to be oak wooden cabinets and they've been extended all the way around the kitchen right up to where the staircase is, whereas when I lived here they were only down one side of the kitchen. It's not huge but it's a fair size, I notice they've put up plenty of wall cabinets where they didn't have them before, the flooring is grey slate and I've really missed the coolness under my feet, it basically looks like a standard cosy country kitchen. I head on through into the large cosy living room, its stone walls still the same colour of cream, and the log burner is in full swing in the fireplace with a wooden piece within the chimney and a slate hearth beneath it, the flooring is a lovely, thick, soft beige carpet and family photos are hanging on the walls all around the room just as they always have, Clay is sitting in the tanned soft armchair, that I know is known as Pops seat and Spencer is lounging on the matching couch both sat with a Budweiser in hand. Dawson sits in the other armchair in the far corner by the small window with Ruth sat on his lap, They look so happy and it's so nice to see him this way, he always used to be the annoying brother that would get me into trouble and take the mick out of me and now he's all loved up, I've got to be honest it's nice to see him this happy.

"It's nice to see some things never change," I say smiling and nodding to the Budweiser looking at Clay and Spencer

"In the fridge," Spencer tells me looking up from his cell "You guys took your time leaving the hospital"

"Lots of catching up to do" Dawson comes to my rescue before I can answer the question or become questioned myself, I give him a subtle nod as a thanks

"I think your rooms the same as it has always been, the sheets will be clean and fresh Mama does them every few weeks along with the rest of ours" (I know she does this just in case I decided to come home or show up unannounced) he tells me looking up from his cell phone and then back down at it.

"Thank you for all y'all have done over the last few days and for getting me to come home but I really think I need to hit the hay," I tell them suddenly feeling exhausted after the long few days and, with that I head on through the kitchen and up the stairs. The landing is light and airy, upon the white walls I notice more photographs, as I reach them I notice they're mostly of Mama and Pops, their wedding day, us kids, school photos, ones of us all on the ranch and of course the standard embarrassing baby photographs. Walking down the landing, I come to a room at the end of the corridor on the left which used to be my old bedroom. I open the small wooden door and notice everything is still in its place. I walk around the room as if to inspect it, I open one of the draws and find there are new clothes in there as if they were once expecting me to return home, I choose a fluffy pair of red pyjamas that must have been put there as a just in case, pulling them on I'm delighted to find they're just my size. After looking around the room I notice the little trinkets, old dolls, stuffed animals and think to myself it's funny what you miss. It definitely feels like I've come home. I take to my bed, laying under the weight of the covers I take note of the way the bedding smells, it's a soft floral smell that now fills my nose and it's a smell that is crossed between my mother and fresh jasmine, the bedding is so soft that I barely want to move again. I think about the day's events and how grateful I am to be here with my family, all of them, and how without realizing it that I've missed this place.

It then dawns on me that I haven't checked my cell phone all day. When I check it, I have elven messages and four missed calls all from Willow.

"Hi Bea, I hope you're ok??"

"Hey Bea, I haven't heard from you all day, I just wanted to make sure all is okay??"

"Is your Pops okay?"

"You took off so quickly and you said you'd call"

"Call ME!!!....... Please!"

"Please reply to me just so I know you're okay please!!!!"

"Hey!"

"Are you alive?"

"Bea I've spoken to Carlos, and he's mentioned somethings wrong with your dad, call me"

"Hello!!"

"Beatrice Coleman! call me!!!

Shit I think to myself I totally forgot to call Willow, I pick up my phone and dial her number and she picks up on the second ring.

"Bea! Oh my god! Are you okay? where are you? Is everything ok? How's your dad? What's happened?" Her voice is full of urgency as she fires all these questions at me.

"I'm sorry, I haven't even looked at my cell till now, I'm at my parent's place in franklin, my Pops had to have open-heart surgery and its touch and go at the moment, he's in the hospital, they're telling us it's going to take a while for him to recover so I don't know when I'll be back, they're really going to need as much help as they can get here at the moment. I do have a slight problem I really need my work for the university, I didn't have time to collect anything before I left"

"Okay," she starts "Oh god Bea I'm so sorry, fingers crossed, I wish him a speedy recovery, don't worry about the university things that's not a problem. I'll pop to the university tomorrow morning, explain the situation, and see if they can email it across to you, I'm so sorry Bea is there anything I can do or is there anything else you need?" She asks

"Thank you that would be awesome if you could, I'll drop them an email now and give them a heads up on the situation and let them know your picking some bits up for me. I'll ask them to email me with anything else I might need, I don't think there's anything else apart from that though, thanks for your help Willow, I hope you don't mind but I really have to sleep, it's been a long few day's"

"That's fine Bea, you get some rest and I'll call you tomorrow once I've been to the university, night Bea"

"Night and thanks again Willow" with that I hang up, place the phone on the wooden bedside table, and fall into a deep peaceful sleep.

Over the next few weeks, I'm back and forth from the Williamson medical centre, bringing homemade meals for Mama and Pops. he's been doing much better but complaining about the lack of homemade food in there, so I've taken to bringing them homemade meals that Ruth and I have taken in turns to make for them both. Things like macaroni cheese, casserole, peach cobbler, cornbread, and of course Pop's favourite, apple pie. However, the nurses and doctors are incredibly pleased with his progress and have said it might be time for Pops to come home soon. The staff have been really supportive, and they have kept us up to date with his progress, telling us how we can help him when he comes home and what he is going to be limited to do, we know he's going to be terribly frustrated with all the changes.

I'm woken one morning with the sunshine beaming through the windows within my bedroom just like it use to seven years ago and suddenly there's a light knock on my bedroom door, it opens, and I see Dawson and Ruth standing there,

"How are you doing baby Bea?" Dawson says playfully using my childhood nickname, which was once given to me by a special lady.

"Ohhhhh god" I moan at him burying my head in the pillow "I haven't heard that for years"

He starts to laugh, and Ruth smiles beside him

"We bought you a coffee, Black one sugar yeah?" Ruth asks me as she places it on the bedside table as Dawson takes a seat on the end of my bed.

"Thanks," I say with a smile "Sooo what's the plan for today?" I ask as I sit up

"Well, we can't visit Pops till this afternoon" Dawson informs me

"I need to travel into town today to get some bits, your more than welcome to come with me if you like?" Ruth asks and I can see Dawson looking sceptical and slightly worried

I think about it for a few minutes, and I really need to pull up my big girl pants, people will know I'm home soon enough and maybe they've forgotten about what happened or maybe they haven't, we will see I guess.

"You know what that sounds like a perfect plan" I finally say "I need to get some new clothes anyway; I haven't really got much with me, and we need some groceries from the store, it's a bit empty down there isn't it"

"Are you sure about this Bea? You know what they're like around here"

"I've got nothing to hide Dawson, it wasn't me in the wrong" I state

"Okay, as long as you're sure you want to do this, you know they'll talk," he tells me

"Well let's give them something to talk about" Ruth pipes up beside him smiling

I smile at her "I like this one Daw, were keeping her"

"Of course," He laughs and then rolls his eyes

"Okay well, we will let you get changed and ready, meet you downstairs in half an hour?" Ruth asks me

"Yep, I'll be there soon and thanks for the coffee," I say to them both as they leave the room, leaving me to change and get ready, plus it will be nice to spend some time with Ruth and actually get to know the girl who's stolen my brother's heart.

I sit there and take a long sip of my coffee; it tastes sweet but strong, just how I like it. I then turn over to check my phone to see if Willow has contacted me, there's nothing there yet, I remind myself to contact her to see how she's getting on, it's been a few days since we last spoke now. I emailed my professor at the university to inform him about my current situation and that Willow would be coming to collect any paperwork that they couldn't email to me, I've almost finished my course and graduation is in a few months but there are just a few loose ends I need to tie and then all my hard work will have paid off and I honestly can't wait, I suddenly realise I don't have my laptop with me and that I left it back at my apartment, and I know I'm not going to be able to do all the work from my cell, I must ask if Willow can collect it at some point and send it out here.

Looking around my room I walk to the dresser and open it, sieving through clothes that haven't been worn in years, I pick out a few bits that I hope will fit and I make a mental note to go through these drawers and throw out the crap that I clearly haven't missed, it's a hot day so I decided on denim shorts, a strappy t-shirt, and a red flannel top. Searching the room, I find myself set on finding my cowgirl boots, I know I'd left them here as I wanted to be rid of everything that reminded me of home, I search the wardrobe and can't seem to find them and finally I find them hidden under the bed, all dusty, I pull them out and brush them off. Slipping them on I remember how comfortable they are, much better than the little dolly shoes I've been living in since I got here. I make the bed and head downstairs to the kitchen and start to clean up the mess my brothers have made over the last few days, I start by putting the wasted produce and rubbish that's lying around in the bin, then doing the washing up, and then finally putting it all away.

Ruth comes in "I'm sorry I didn't really know what to do with all that, I didn't want to step on toes"

"It's okay," I tell her "I know my brothers are messy house guests"

She smiles "You ready to go?"

"Yep, I just need my keys and purse"

Picking them up from my bag, we head out to the truck, spotting Dawson in the barn we give him a wave as we get in and head off into town, I can't help but notice the worried look on his face.

"He's really not sure about this" Ruth tells me "He's worried you'll leave again"

"No, I'm ready for this, I'm not the same scared girl I once was," I tell her but as we approach the town, I start to get nervous and feel slightly sick, the anxiety kicking in and taking over. We drive down through the small town and pull up in front of the grocery store.

"Ready?" Ruth turns to me

I hesitate for a moment as the fear washes over me, I take a deep breath and turn to look at Ruth

"Ready, let's do this like you said, let's give em something to talk about"

She smiles at me, I take a deep breath and we get out of the truck and head on in, we start walking around the store, Ruth has grabbed a shopping cart and starts picking up produce she needed to make dinner for the next few days. I forgot how little this grocery store was, but we pick up the ingredients we need, as well as plenty of fresh fruit, vegetables, and snacks that I know my brothers will like, I pick up a large bar of chocolate and tell Ruth that it's a pretty essential thing, we find ourselves walking down the fresh meat aisle, I reach down to pick up the steak and that's when I hear it.

"Well, well, well, Beatrice Coleman is that you?" the voice shrieks, I freeze, this is the moment I've been terribly worried about, slowly I turn around and come face to face with Melanie Bridges who's standing at the very end of the aisle, behind me. The local gossip, her blonde hair cut into a round bob and her stick-thin figure looking as it always has (like she's really in need of a good meal) and she must now be around 38 years of age with her freshly manicured nails and prim and proper look to her, she looks very out of place in our little town, almost like she belongs in a city or somewhere where they have lots of money and fashion shows. I turn and look to Ruth, and she rolls her eyes as Melanie makes her way towards us in her white dress suit and black high heels "Well, how are you dear? Where have you been hiding? We were all so worried when you left, thought you'd never show your pretty little face here again no, not after what that Nathan Parker did to you" she drones on in her high squeaky voice "Was such a scandal that was, having that all happen to you must have been terribly humiliating" she tells me as she scoffs' "We haven't seen him since, you know, sold up and moved on he did….. and that's got to be …umm…around six years ago now"

"Seven" I correct her, here we go I think to myself

"Well, I'm glad you thought you could show your face here after that all came out from the hiding, apparently you had a breakdown deary," she says eyeing me as if she knows it all "According to Nathan anyway, and you just took off and left him without a word"

I stand there looking at her dumbfound, Ruth is beside me about to open her mouth to say something that I know she would regret, and I just snap.

"For your information Melanie I wasn't hiding from anything or anyone, I needed to get away for a little while to clear my head after what that low-life, piece of shit did to me. I took off yes, but I didn't put him through anything, and I certainly did not have a breakdown, not that that's got anything to do with you or anyone else around here, before you start gossiping you might want to get your facts right, so you go ahead and think whatever you want and spread whatever vile gossip you think will make your lousy little life better and have a nice day" I say picking the steaks up and walking away with Ruth in tow.

As we make our way to the checkout that's when I realize it's suddenly all gone quiet around me and the only thing I can hear is the soft jazz music playing in the background, I think that most of the store probably heard my little outburst, paying at the checkout, I look over at Ruth and she is wearing the biggest smile I've ever seen and when I look at the cashier, I notice she can't stop grinning at me either. We grab our purchases, thank the cashier and head out to the truck, placing the shopping in Ruth turns to me.

"Well, that told her, remind me never to get on your cranky side okay" she smiles, and I let out a laugh, "If you weren't before now your definitely going to be the talk of the town for the next few days"

"Well, if they're talking about me there leaving someone else alone aren't they"

"Beatrice, you basically told her to fuck off in the kindest most southern way"

I let out a laugh "Yes… I guess I did" I say kind of proud

"Did you see the look on her face?" she continues to laugh "And Florence…I mean the cashier didn't even know where to look, but it looks like you made her day"

Walking down the street I can't hide my smile and it looks like Ruth's struggling to hide hers too. We come to a new clothing store that I've never seen before, called Stitch. The sign on the window is in frosted glass and the writing above the door on the awing is in baby blue.

"Shall we?" I ask Ruth, she nods, and we head on inside

It's a cute little store but very simple, looking around I notice we're are the only two people in the shop, not including the cashier. I find a little red dress that is knee-length and comes down over the arms, some jeans, a couple of strappy tops, the most beautiful cowboy boots I've ever seen, and an awesome Cowgirl hat. I try on the red dress and come out to show Ruth

"So, what do you think?" I ask

"You have to get it and then we're going out," she tells me

I help her pick out a couple of dresses to try on. She tries on three but the last grey one makes her look stunning, it's flowy and lacy and I try to convince her to get it.

"That's stunning Ruth, Dawson will love that"

"But it's so much money and I don't know if I can afford it at the moment," she tells me in a whisper

"That's fine, this one's on me" I wink at her

"No, no, no…. you can't"

"Well, I just have," I say taking the dress-up to the cashier and adding it to the things I've already selected and waiting to pay for. I hand her my credit card not asking the price and she hands me the bags and with that, we head back to the truck, bags in hand and cowboy hat on my head, suddenly I feel like I've come home.

We head back to the ranch, when getting there we find Dawson and Spencer standing outside on the porch chatting to one another, I notice the police cruiser as we come up the track and they watch us as we park, they make their way over to us both while we stay seated in the truck, Spencer taps on my window and points down for me to undo it, I do as he asks.

"So, somebody's the talk of the town," he says to me "Apparently you told Melanie bridges where to go"

I can't help but smile and Ruth beams beside me trying to hide her delight too "Might have done" I say looking at him

Ruth pipes up next to me "Honestly it was the best thing I've ever seen; she didn't know where to put herself" I start to laugh and Dawson smirks behind Spencer who's looking very unimpressed.

"Ohh…..C'mon the local gossip had it coming," I tell him

"Well, they certainly know your back now," Spencer tells me "I know it's hard but try and behave, Bea, I actually wanted to check to see that you're okay, but I can see that you're doing just fine," he says as he makes his way back to the police cruiser and drives off down the dusty track.

I get out of the truck, bags in hand. "I'm pretty proud of you, Spencer on the other hand….." Dawson tells me with a nudge as we watch Spencer drive down the track "Look at my baby sister, standing up for yourself and everythin, so what you got in there?" he asks pointing to the bags it's as if he's realised there a quiet a few.

"Well, we've got some groceries and I thought after my little outburst I would treat myself to some new clothes"

"And she treated me too," Ruth tells him excitedly

"Well, that's very nice of her Darlin" he smiles turning to her and pulling her into a hug "I was thinking we could all go out tonight if you fancy it, you know to kinda celebrate?"

"Celebrate?" I ask

"Well, you've come home, and they think Pops will be home next week"

"That's fantastic news," I tell him "I'm going to stay for a while to help out with Pops and things on the ranch" he pulls me into a tight hug and we all head inside.

That afternoon I spent the remainder of my day sorting through my room, I start with the wardrobe pulling out the clothes that I haven't seen in years, some of them I decide to keep, (just because they fit) and put back knowing I'll wear it again, others I throw into the bin bags and by the time I've finished I've filled five bin bags, my brothers Clay and Dawson help me take them out the back ready to burn along with the excess trees and twigs from around the ranch, Dawson comes over as I put the final bag down.

"So, all your belongings from the house are in the barn," he tells me "Would you like me to bring them up to your room so you can start to go through them, you know before we light the bonfire? Just thinking there might be a few things you'd like to burn in there"

I look at him and I'm unsure of what to do, can I go through those boxes now, reopening all the thoughts and memories that have haunted me for the last seven years, it will definitely be painful to do….. or will it, I finally answer him "Yes I think I can do that"

"Only if you're sure?" he asks

"As sure as I'll ever be Daw, it can't sit in there forever can it"

And with that, he starts to help me lift all thirty boxes up to my room. Realising that a lot of my past is in there, I start with the first box, a lot of them just contain old clothes, shoes, handbags, and household things, which I mostly just put back into the box and tell Clay and Dawson they can take them back down for the bonfire, I figured I haven't missed them all this time so why should I miss them now. I open my 26th box and what I find inside are photos of me and Nathan and our relationship, looking through them brings back all the memories that aren't actually as painful as I thought they would be, there are pictures from our high school prom, growing up together, again us on holiday in France and London, him in his uniform and some of our engagement, those are just the most painful ones. I take all of them and put them in a box that's ready for the bonfire full of things that I no longer want or need. Just as I open another box there's a knock at the door.

"I just wanted to check in and see how you were doin?" Dawson says as he enters the room.

"Not too bad, there's a lot here but I think I'm almost finished," I say with my best fake smile trying to act like it doesn't hurt

"I was checking on you, not your belongings, I know how hard this must have been for you, going through all that" he points and then waves his hands around the room gesturing towards the boxes that are left

"Surprisingly it wasn't too bad, I haven't finished yet but look at these," I say pulling out two large photo albums and taking them over to him we both sit on the floor and open them up, inside are photos from our childhood, pictures of the four of us, climbing trees and hay bales, riding the horses, playing in the mud and stables, playing by the pond we use to have just in behind the house, being on the ranch and being down by the creek, and on the rope swing down there with the local kids and people we grew up with and a few of Pops and Mama when they were younger and their wedding.

"Look at their clothes," I say with a smile

"Forget what Mama and Pops are wearing, look at Spencer's trousers all tucked into his shirt, I don't think they could get much higher if they tried, looks like they would have fit him when he would have been eighteen years old instead of a ten-year-old boy, there huge" Dawson laughs

"Look at this one" I pull out a photo and can't contain my laughter, it's a picture of all three of my brothers after their bowl haircuts all lined up in the kitchen after Mama had attacked them with the kitchen scissors and clippers. "I vaguely remember this happening," I tell Dawson trying to contain my laughter

"Hey, I'll have you know that was very fashionable at the time, look a Spencer's cool curtained fringe," he tells me laughing to himself now "Seriously Bea you don't realise how lucky you were being a girl, no bowl haircuts for you" he points at the picture "look at our face's" we find a few more and he points out the kids we use to hang out with when we were younger, look there's Bow and Sienna Tanner and there's Johnathan and Billy Davies riding their bikes at the creek"

"Oh… look," I say as I pull out another photograph and it's of Dawson's best friends, grandparents

"Aww that's Nana Clara and Grandpa Bill," he tells me

"They were such lovely people; we were always welcome there," I say as we both sit and smile at the memories. "I forgot I had all these," I tell him

"Well, I'm glad you kept them, look there's another one of Nana Clara and Grandpa Bill," Dawson tells me pointing them out,

These people weren't actually anything to do with us, they weren't really our grandparents but as we didn't know our grandparents, that's what we called them and that's what they were known as around here and seeing this photo of them outside of their Manor house makes me smile. After we sit and go through a few more photographs finding more of friends and family and extended family. We're unsure of who some of the people in the photographs are, we sit and pick out people from the town, like Mrs Baker who used to own the old hairdressing salon where I had my first ever haircut at age thirteen (I wasn't allowed to have it done before my 13th birthday) and one of Mr Fram from the local candy shop (which is no longer there, we sit smiling looking at all the memories.

"I totally forgot about him, that's when you could get loads of candy for very little money," Dawson tells me "It's such a shame he died last year"

Suddenly my cell rings, looking at it I see it's Willow, I look over at Dawson and he gives me a nod as if to say I'll let you take this, and he gets up from beside me leaving the room.

"Hey Willow, how ya doing? How did it go with the university? All okay? I emailed them but haven't heard back yet"

"They need to get you to sign some paperwork, but it needs to be a hardcopy and can't be done electronically, plus I knew you didn't have your laptop with you, however they have said you can study at home and submit your final from there if you could get access to a laptop or computer that is" she adds

"I need to think what I'm going to do about the hardcopy because the way things are here at the moment, I just don't think I can come back yet, plus I need to do something about getting on to a tablet or laptop," I tell her

"Leave it with me, maybe there's an easier way to do this, maybe I could post them to you, and you just sign it and send it back to me and ill drop it back to your university, then we could just see about sending your laptop to you"

"Thanks, Willow that would be great if you could, I'll call John at number six and see if he can let you in, he's got my spare key, you know just in case I lock myself out again, let me know the cost to send it all please and I'll transfer you the money"

"Sure thing, just send me your parent's address and I'll get it to you, let me know what John says and when it's convenient and then I can go and pick up the laptop"

"Anything changed there? Carlos and family all okay?" I ask her

"No same old stuff here, they're all asking how you're doing and about your Pops, I've explained the situation, Carlos and Gabrielle send their love and old Albert keeps asking after you, I've told him that he'll have to put up with me for the time being and that you'll be back soon enough, he tells me that I never have his Guinness waiting and that it tastes different when I do it"

I laugh "Tell Albert that I'll be back soon, and Carlos and Gabrielle I miss them all, thank you for everything Willow you've been amazing"

Thanking her again we part ways.

Chapter Five

The Hideaway

The following day, I go back to the boxes that I've been avoiding and think to myself that it's almost over, only four more to go. I open the next one and pull out the stuff I know Nathan packed all those years ago. Suddenly the dread fills me, I pull out an old shoebox knowing this one's going to be more painful than the others, Opening it up I find letters we'd sent each other while he was away, movie tickets, random jewellery he'd bought me, my engagement ring box (the ring went in the ocean), souvenirs from every holiday we ever went on, some sentimental things we'd kept, a key from our first house and photos from throughout our entire relationship. You see me and Nathan had been together since high school and as I dug further into the larger box I noticed there was a lot in there, notes we'd sent each other in school, my old cheerleading outfit and pom-poms, his school jacket, photos from high school, a promise ring he'd once given me and our yearbook. I mean there was a time when we were inseparable, he was my everything and I was his but somewhere along the line, I guess we just fell apart and that's where Dawson had picked up the pieces more than once and even broke his nose a couple of times for the way he would speak to me sometimes. I guess I just wanted to make him happy, please him even and he wanted me to wait around for him, eventually, I just became his fallback, like I didn't really matter, kind of like he didn't really want me but didn't want anyone else to have me either and I guess it just spiralled out of control, then when we found out the terrible information after all the tests, then I guess he wanted it more than he had originally let on. Opening these boxes with all of that information in there was pretty painful. Without another look I throw it into another box which is full of stuff to be burnt on the bonfire, I open two other boxes and they are just full of clothes and shoes, I push them to one side to go on the bonfire too, I figured I haven't missed them all this time so I wouldn't miss them now plus I don't think I'd want to wear anything that he's touched. The final box I come to is the worst, I open it up and my stomach sinks, I feel sick and inside and realise I've found what was meant to be my wedding dress with a letter sitting neatly on top, I push the letter to one side and holding the dress up I remember how beautiful it is, the beadwork is exquisite and the lace is just beautiful, I remember how happy I was when I first purchased it, such a shame I think to myself just that I would never get to wear it but with that dress was horrible memories for me, I just feel sick to my stomach and I can't look at it anymore, I stuff it back into the box and decide it's going on the bonfire. I sit for a minute staring at the letter, I'm not sure if I want to know what's inside but if I don't open it I might regret it, and I guess I should give him a chance to explain, defend himself even, I slowly pull back the envelope and open it, bracing myself for what I'm about to read.

Saturday 29th November 2013

Beatrice,

I don't know why I'm writing to you or even if you'll ever get this, I figured this would be the only way I could contact you, seeing as you've blocked me on everything, but I wanted to tell you how sorry I am for everything I put you through. I was selfish and stupid, I wanted to tell you, I really did, but I didn't get a chance and by the time I was going to you'd already seen it for yourself.

I wasn't ready for a relationship, I was never there and that wasn't fair on you, and baby we were never really right for each other, you were meant for much greater things than me Beatrice and you needed much more than I could give you.

I admit that I fucked up and I'm really sorry for how I treated you but now I have to deal with the consequences of my actions. I want a family and after all the tests, I mean that was so hard on both of us and it clearly wasn't going to happen for us.

We weren't right for each other, all I can say is I'm sorry it's come to this, I will always love you and there will always be a special place in my heart for you but for obvious reasons I can't do this anymore.

I'm sorry doll but you need to move on with your life just as I am.

Good luck with everything in the future

Nathan x

Before I know it, tears are rolling down my face and I can't breathe, Spencer's at my side in an instant, I don't know when he got there, and I don't really care I'm just glad he's here, he pulls me into his arms.

"What's happened," he asks frantically his voice full of panic.

I can't talk, I just hand him the letter, he takes one look and shouts, "That SLY BASTARD!!"

Before I know it, Clay, Dawson, and Ruth are standing in my doorway. Holding me, pulling me tighter to him causing my cry's to be muted, Spencer hands them the letter, reading it no one is really sure what to do, Clay takes over from Spencer as he storms out the room.

"Where ya going?" Dawson yells after him

"To sort this" Spencer shouts back up the stairs and with that, we hear the slam of a door as he disappears out of the house, we're left with the sound of the cruiser leaving the ranch. I calm down wiping my face on the back of my sleeve.

"I need to get rid of this," I tell them waving my arms around at the boxes

"Okay…. what do you want to do with it?" Clay asks

"Burn it….. just burn it all," I tell them as the tears are rolling down my face

Clay places his hands on either side of my face and tells me "It's all over now, you're going to be okay Bea, we will deal with this the way we always do, as a family" the next thing I know, he walks over to the boxes and starts picking up a couple. Dawson follows his lead and goes to pick up a small one.

"No, not that one," I tell him "That's the family photos, but the rest of them can go, I need it all gone, but not that one please, just place it on my bed"

He nods and I can tell that Dawson feels guilty as sin, but I know it's not any way his fault. Ruth and I grab a box each and follow the boys downstairs to the bonfire, by the time we've finished it is getting dark and cold. Clay lights a match and sets it alight starting with what was going to be my wedding dress, Ruth to my surprise takes hold of my hand, she must sense I need a little support and then next thing we hear is the cruiser pulling up and we see Spencer heading over to us, carrying a six-pack of bud light which he starts to hand out to us all.

He comes and puts an arm around my shoulder "How y'all doing?" he asks looking down at me

"We're okay," Dawson says as I watch the fire burn

"I'm so sorry you had to relive that again Bea" he pauses "It won't happen again," he tells me taking a swig from the bottle he's holding

We all turn and look at him "What do you mean?" I ask

"Yes, Spencer what DO YOU mean" Dawson repeats

"I mean it won't happen again," he says looking into the fire and taking another swig from the bottle he's holding "I had a couple of buddies track him down and speak to him, just speak……...and maybe hit him a couple of times but all the same he won't be bothering you again Bea and were unable to know If he'll be able to have any more kids, not that we want that thing breeding"

Silence fills the air between us all when Dawson finally breaks it.

"You shouldn't have done that," Dawson tells him in a low tone "You're abusing your position"

"No one will ever know plus it's off the books"

I just pull and wrap my navy-blue blanket around me tighter, we're stood there for what seemed like hours, watching the bonfire burn and calm down. After a while, I tell them "I'm going inside" I kind of just want to be on my own at the moment. I go in and head for my bedroom, when I reach it I make my way to my bed and lay down looking up at the ceiling, feeling like I've been here before, about fifteen minutes have passed when Ruth comes bounding in wearing the dress I bought her.

I look over at her with a smile "Looks awesome" I tell her "But why are you wearing it now?"

"We're going out," she tells me with a weary smile on her face

"Ohh no…. no……. no, I can't, I don't really feel like going anywhere" I protest "I don't think I'm ready for that yet"

"Come on I saw the way you handled Melanie Bridges the other day, I think it's time we hit the town and get you out, you need this, come on you need to let your hair down"

She opens my bedroom door and I see all my brothers standing there holding a Budweiser in hand, shirts on, Clay in a green checked shirt, Spencer in a white slightly unbuttoned shirt and Dawson in a dark navy-blue shirt, all in jeans and cowboy boots and Spencer in his cream-coloured cowboy hat. Clay hands me a bud and I take it.

"And they think you're ready for this too, we've got to celebrate you coming home" she continues "Come on, up you get, we're leaving in half an hour" she grabs my arm and tries to pull me up from the bed.

"I don't think I can, I'm not happy about this…. I think I just need some time to be on my own"

"Come on Bea, your always on your own in Chicago and you need a bit of fun," Dawson tells me

"Where are we going?"

They all go quiet and then Spencer pipes up "It's a surprise, go get ready"

"Fine" I finally say knowing that I'm going to be forced into this so there's no point in arguing

They all smile, and Ruth kicks them out of my room "Right where's that red dress?"

"Okay, okay I'll get it" we spend what feels like ages getting me ready, I change into my red dress that's knee-length and has long sleeves, I take my hair out of the plat it was in and let the waves fall down past my shoulders, then

I apply a little makeup, and lastly, I dig out of the bag my brand-new tan cowboy boots that I purchased from stitch.

"So," I say to Ruth "Is this okay?"

"Damn girl," she says "If I was into women, I'd do you"

I start to laugh at her "Damn girl, really??, That's hilarious I wouldn't imagine those words coming out of your mouth if you hadn't just said them" I laugh

We both sit there laughing for a minute, "It's not really me is it" she states as we leave the room and I continue to laugh. Walking down the stairs she shouts for my brothers when we find all three of them in the kitchen, Spencer leaning against the cupboards near the back door on his cell, Clay sat at the kitchen table talking to Dawson who's sitting on the kitchen worktop, as we come down the stairs they all turn to look at me and Ruth.

"Damn, you've grown up baby Bea," Spencer says to my surprise

"Not baby Bea anymore" Clay jokes

"She'll always be baby Bea to us," Dawson says jumping down from the work top and placing an arm around Ruth

I roll my eyes at them, and I can feel my cheeks heat.

"Come on everyone in the truck," Ruth tells them as we leave the kitchen, and she jumps in the driver seat seeing as she's the only one who's not drinking. We all pile into Dawson's dark blue truck and head into town. Just like the old days when we were all wild and carefree. The radios on and they break into song around me, singing Luke Combs – Honky Tonk Highway, I sit and smile at them as I look around at my brothers and Ruth. They all seem so happy and clearly, in the party mood, Clay nudges me as he belts out the song and I start to laugh and join in. We head down the country roads and down into the town, Before I know it, the truck has stopped, and we're parked. We all start to pile out and that's when it hits me, I'm back here, they bought me back to the Hideaway bar, the place where it all happened. This was the last place I wanted to come, getting out of the truck I stand there frozen taking it in, when Dawson comes up beside me.

"Are you okay with this?" He askes

I turn to him "I'm not sure I can do this Daw"

"Sure, you can," Spencer tells me as he comes up beside me

"I'm sorry, I really don't think I can be here"

Clay comes beside me and takes my hand and tells me "Just one drink, it might surprise you, plus you said you were putting on your big girl pants"

"But I'll know everyone inside there," I say my anxiety suddenly taking over

"Just one drink Bea" I hear Dawson say beside me, He's always been my safety blanket, the one that's always looked out for me and fought my battles ever since I can remember "If your still not happy after one drink we will leave and go somewhere else but just one drink Bea, we've got you"

I take a deep breath and say "Okay just one drink then I'm out of here" but I suddenly feel way out of my depth.

"Okay," Dawson replies, As we walk into the Hideaway the memories all come flooding back.

This was the place that it happened on the night of the 23rd of November, it was a Saturday and I'd been convinced by my brothers to go for a couple of drinks, I had one drink but remained sober and I decided I would be the taxi for tonight. We had a good night, we laughed and joked with friends, we danced, played a few games of pool and they of course drank. We even ran into some people we hadn't seen in years, some old high school friends and friends of Mama and Pops, so safe to say the bar was heaving. We used to love coming to this place. everything was always so relaxed, and everyone was so friendly, we usually stayed until closing, but this night Clay had had too much too quickly so we decided to call it an early night. Walking outside and trying to get him in my truck was a bit of a challenge, it's as if the fresh air had hit him hard and he couldn't put one foot in front of another. I eventually got him into my truck with the help of a passer-by.

"I love you, Bea, I'm Sooo Sorry" he mumbles, and he flopped down into the passenger's seat and passed out, face squished up against the passenger window, it made me smile seeing him with his face squished against the glass.

locking the truck, I head back inside to find the other two, this was proving a bit of a challenge, I walked out of the back of the bar to the rear parking lot after searching high and low inside and that's when I heard Spencer's voice, it sounded strained like he was talking seriously with someone and like it was about to get heated, almost like he was trying to fight someone's battles or reason with them. I realised he was just down the side of the building, I could see him standing in the alleyway so I stood there listening…...

"What the hell are you doing here man? we thought you were overseas and who the fuck is that in the car?" That's when I saw him standing there looking guilty as sin and I realised I recognised the fancy silver, BMW X3 M sport that was parked and still running to my left. "Nathan man, listen don't do this to her now, think of all y'all have been through together" Spencer continued

Coming around the side of the building standing so that I'm in full view I ask "Do what?" as I stand there watching the scene unfold before me

Spencer ran his hands through his dark hair then ran his hands down over his face (something he always did when he was stressed) he obviously knew what was going on.

"Do what?" I asked again in a sterner tone

He just stood there looking at me, his blonde hair was cut into short, back and sides and his brown eyes just staring at me, wearing his oh shit, rabbit in the headlights expression followed by utter dread

"Come on! what's the secret?" I ask

"I'm….I'm so sorry baby I never meant to hurt you or for this to even happen," Nathan tells me as he walks closer to me and that's when I notice a ring on his left hand as he hands me a brown envelope.

"What the fuck is going on?" I shout at him "What the fuck is that? I ask pointing at his hand

"I'm so sorry Beatrice it………….it just happened"

"What the actual fuck, how can marrying someone just happen? What the hell is this?" I ask waving the large brown envelope at him that he had just handed me, Shaking, I open it as he watches me and I then pull out the handwritten letter. As I read it, I notice that a baby scan photo has fallen out and onto the floor, I bend down to pick it up. "Please tell me this is some sort of sick joke" There's silence and then the penny drops "Hang on…..This….This is yours?" I choke trying hard to swallow the lump that's formed in my throat, I feel like someone's smacked me hard in the face. I notice Dawson has appears behind me, I'm not sure when he got there but I'm grateful he is, Spencer walks to the other side of me, so I guess that Spencer went to fetch Dawson. I turn to look at them both. Dawson is looking absolutely furious and Spencer stands there not really knowing where to place himself because I know he already knows what's going on, I ask them to leave it and go get in the truck, they take a step back but won't leave me. I turn back to Nathan, he doesn't give me any answers and all he can do is stand there staring at me.

"What the fuck is this? What about me? What about our plans? Our future? Was it all just lies? did you just give up on this, forget to tell me and go off and get fucking married?" I say absolutely furious "We only spoke last week on the phone, you said you were being posted to Germany and that you loved me and couldn't wait to come home! What the hell is wrong with you!" I scream at him as a pace backwards and forwards.

"No Beatrice…… we just fell out of love with each other, and I guess people change, that's when I met her…." He tells me pointing to the car

"Fell out of love? Speak for yourself!" I realise I'm now shouting "Who the fuck is she? How long has this been going on? so Germany was just a lie then, you don't love me, and you clearly aren't coming home" I yell

"It's not like that and it…it doesn't matter how long," he tells me in a stern tone

"Well, it certainly looks like that! How fucking long Nathan?" I yell at him and he just stands there looking dumbfound "How fucking long?" I repeat

"A few months" he's silent for a moment and then says "After we had all the tests done and we realised we couldn't have children…. I…I guess it was my way of dealing with everything"

"Two fucking years!! Two fucking years Nathan!!!, are y'all for real! So let me get this right, so at our lowest point as a couple and you decide the answer is to jump into bed with someone else and get your dick wet, what the fuck is wrong with you!"

"I'm sorry Beatrice, I'm so sorry but everything's so easy with her," he says pointing in the direction of his car once more

That's when I realise, she's in there, she's in his fucking car, I storm over, Spencer tries to hold me back, but I overpower him, going up to the car I bang on the tinted window.

I ask her "Why me? Why him? How could they do this to me! I scream at her suddenly realising the tears are rolling down my face "Calling her a fucking whore and a tramp" banging on the window before I walk away, "Telling her I hope She's happy with disappointment because she won't be his last"

I hear her shout "I thought you said she was just a friend; I didn't know he was with you I swear it"

"His friend" I let out a sarcastic laugh and walk back to the window "Are y'all for real!" I shout back "Wow"

He tries to pull me back from the window, I let out another sarcastic laugh "You really are the most amazing amount of shit aren't you! get your fucking hands off me" I say full of anger, I don't know where it comes from, but I just turn around and punch him square in the face, Spencer grabs me to hold me back and prevent me from doing any more damage. I stand back and look at my handy work and see his nose is busted and that his eyes are already starting to look bruised, I suddenly feel lucky that I grew up with brothers who taught me well. I turn to walk away and shout "Have a nice fucking future arsehole"

"Ahhhh" That's when I hear another crunch, I stop in my tracks and look behind me and see Dawson has hit him hard in the stomach and is now walking after me. We left him there on the cold, wet floor and I got in the truck with Spencer and Dawson. Then I drove us all back to the ranch with tears in my eyes, trying to figure out how and what had just happened.

Walking back into the Hideaway I look around and realise that there isn't much that's changed, it's all wooden inside, kind of like being inside a wooden cabin. The bar itself is in the same place it's always been (immediately to your left as you walk in) and then there are about six small steps that lead down to the dance floor, there are wooden beams overhead, and six wooden pillars around the large circular dance floor that are from floor to ceiling and I assume there helping to hold it up, to the far side of the room there are a few little tables dotted around and booths to the back of the room with a few people sitting at them. Tommy the bar owner is in the same place he's always been, still serving drinks at the bar, that he's owned for at least the last twelve years, he's a bubbly guy, with a long beard and moustache that he clearly applies product to, to make the ends curl up, he looks like he should own a Harley Davidson, but I know that Tommy couldn't ride a bike if his life depended on it. The band is in full swing, doing a cover of Morgan Wallen's – Wasted on you and the atmosphere is friendly but there's a slight buzz in the air tonight. The pool table has moved slightly to the right and is on the opposite side to the tables and booths and the smell is just as I remember it, an old musky, boozy smell fills my nose, I see a few familiar faces who greet me with a smile.

Walking up to the bar I order a shot of whiskey to steady my nerves followed by a bud light.

"Good to see you back Darlin," Tommy tells me "That ones on me, welcome home" and it puts my nerves at ease

"Thanks, Tommy," I say, "You're looking really well, lost some weight?"

"Four stone," he tells me, and I can tell he's kinda smug about it "You owe me a very overdue dance later by the way"

"Good for you," I tell him "You look fantastic, very handsome and yes, of course, a dance would be great. How's Brett doing?"

"He's doing great thanks, Darlin," he tells me holding out his hand "got married last June"

"Aww that's fantastic, congratulations to you both," I tell him as he's called away to serve someone else

I turn and look around and I notice that Ruth has found a seat at one of the booths in the far corner, so I head over to her, the others find us and take a seat too, all but Spencer who has found himself a lady friend up at the bar. I start to laugh and shake my head as he's suddenly surrounded by four ladies

"Is it always like this?" I ask nodding in his direction

"It's a powerful force apparently or so he says," Clay tells me, and we all laugh harder.

Looking around I see that the place is really starting to fill up, I notice my brother Clay looking at the bar and that he's watching a dark-haired woman that I vaguely recognise. Ruth notices me looking.

"That's Florence Grey, she works at our local mini-mart where we were the other day, she probably saw our little show with Melanie Bridges" she adds

"That's the one my mother was talking about?" I whisper to her, "She told me that Clay has a thing for a young woman who worked in the local supermarket"

"That's the one and only….. oh, and she's British" she adds with a wink

I look at my brother, who can see that we're talking about the two of them and give him my best mischievous smile, He looks at me and tells me a straight "No" as he strokes his beard and he can clearly see what I'm about to do, I continue to smile and get up from my seat and make my way towards her, watching my brother squirm in his seat as I get closer to her, giving him and Ruth a thumbs up as I go. Clay looks mortified whereas Ruth looks like she's about to burst with excitement.

I approach her at the bar "Hey it's ahhh….Florence, right? Can I buy ya a drink?"

"Umm," she hesitates "I'm sorry…I….a …. I don't swing that way"

"Neither do I, honey, that's not why I'm here, let me get you a drink"

She laughs "Oh, yeah, okay thanks, I'm sorry I don't mean to be rude but do I know you?"

"Umm….. well, the little show in your shop, yep that was me, but I guess you don't really know me, but you might know my brother Clay, He's the strapping young hunk over there sat with my sister-in-law Ruth," I say pointing in there direction, Ruth gives us a wave as we both look in their direction and Clay lifts his head and gives us a little wave looking very embarrassed. "He thinks you're kind of hot," I say and it makes her smile as she looks over at him and then looks down

"I've seen him around" she admits

"So, fancy coming over to meet him properly?"

"I'm not really sure I should, I wouldn't want him to feel awkward"

"Well, here's the thing, he's too shy to approach you himself. So, I figured I'd help him out a little, I'm Bea by the way, his sister" I hold out my hand

She takes my hand and shakes it then hesitates before saying "Well Bea you know I think I'd like that" and she follows me over to where were sat. Clay suddenly looks so nervous like he's going to puke and becomes all fidgety, almost like a small child.

"Clay this is Florence, Florence, Clay" I introduce "He's got some awesome new dance moves," I tell her and wink at him. Clay rolls his eyes and then I hear Ruth and Dawson laugh

Florence smiles "My friends call me Flo" she corrects

Clay gets up and takes her hand as if to shake it but isn't sure what to do next, then he kind of pulls her into an awkward one-armed hug. I look to Ruth for help not wanting to make it more awkward than it already is.

"Anyone want to dance," she asks

A resounding "YES" comes from me and Dawson, and we get up from the table leaving them to get to know one another and head for the dance floor. We're there a good hour, I forgot how much I loved to dance and how much fun it is to be out with my brothers. I look over to check Clay and Flo every so often and they seem to be hitting it off, she's laughing beside him and he's smiling and waving his hands around as if he's trying to explain himself, I motion to Ruth that I'm going to the bar to get a drink, she nods. It's packed, everyone's fighting to get to the bar, people stand talking to each other and discussing their day to day lives, laughing and joking with one another. When people have moved, I finally reach the bar, I lean up against it waiting to be served, a voice beside me starts to talk.

"Hey there Darlin," the voice says in a slow tone, oh here we go I think to myself, another loser "Can I buy ya a drink?" I turn towards the voice coming from my left and now completely understand why Flo turned down my drink offer when I first approached her. I look him up and down and I can smell the alcohol on his breath, he's nothing to look at and is a very scrawny man with very light fluffy hair, dirt around his face with very few teeth and I can't help but notice he seems a little unsteady on his feet. I recognise him but only by his eyes, then I realise it's Noah Parkinson he was once head of the football team and boy he's changed, we went to school together and clearly, he doesn't remember who I am and maybe that's a good thing.

"God no, I can buy my own thanks"

"No, no, I'll get this" he slurs and tries to insist

"No thank you," I say sterner than I originally intended

"Sugar it's just one drink"

"But it's not just one drink is it, cowboy, it's one drink to start with and then I owe you something, then you think you have the right to eye me up and have a claim on me, possibly even touch me or take me home and guess what I'm not interested, thanks"

He opens his mouth and closes it again unsure of what to say "Geez chill out Darlin," he says before walking away defeated

"And I'm not your Darlin" I call after him

I hear a voice by me start to laugh "Well Beatrice Coleman you certainly know how to handle yourself" it says over the music and then I hear it make its way behind me.

"How in the world would…………..." I turn around and see a pair of piercing grey/ blue eyes staring straight at me

"Bow tanner is that you?!" I notice my voice getting higher in octaves more than I had intended

"Hey Bea, it's been a long time" he smiles as he pulls me into a hug

"It really has, it's got to be what nine years"

"Ten"

"Well, haven't you got a good memory," I say and he smiles

Tommy comes over "You're not causing trouble in my bar again Bea, are you?"

"Me, Noooooo, just telling people how it is Tommy, you know me"

He smiles at me "I'm kiddin Darlin, what can I get ya?"

I turn to Bow "Would you umm, like a drink?"

"God no I can buy my own drink thanks," he says quoting me after hearing my conversation and then winks "Actually this one's on me, but I want nothing in return" he jokes placing his hands up in defeat.

I laugh, "Thanks but it's just one drink Darlin" I joke and He smirks at me, "Tommy can I get two bud lights and two shots of tequila please," I ask, Bow looks at me and rolls his eyes with a smirk

"I see somethings never change," he says

The drinks arrive and we start with the tequila, notice he screws his face up just as much as I do.

"You can take the girl out of franklin, but you can't take franklin out of the girl" I joke taking a seat beside him at the bar with my Budweiser in hand then I turn to face him.

He laughs "So it would seem, how ya been Bea? I hope life has treated you well, I can't believe how crazy this is, I haven't seen you since we were in our teens, remember when we would mess around up at your parent's ranch with Dawson and your family and also when you would come up with us to Nana and Grandpa's Manor House"

"Yeah that seems like a lifetime ago doesn't it, Dawson's here somewhere," I say as I look around the room trying to spot him

"I'm sure he'll find us, he always does plus he told me he'd be around," He tells me as he picks up his beer and then says, "he always told me his little sister was off-limits you know" Bow teases and winks at me

"He did not say that to you, God I'm so embarrassed" I place my hands over my face and he laughs "He was always so protective but then again not that a lot has changed, he's here somewhere," I say looking around the room trying to spot him again

"So, what brings you home?" he asks me

"Well, that's a long story, So I won't bore you with the details"

"I've got time," he tells me

Me and my brothers grew up with Bow Tanner and his sister Sienna, He was and still is Dawson's oldest and most loyal friend, he used to come up to the ranch and we would all climb the trees together, play by the creek, he would occasionally help with the horses, bales of hay and general work on the Ranch, I thought he went to university and left town, but it turns out that he's also back home, I know Bow and Dawson kept in touch and still remain rather close, Dawson has also previously told me that they talk every so often.

"Well, I don't think you've got that much time," I say with a laugh "So what brings you back to town?"

"Well," he jokes "I heard you were home and couldn't miss my chance could I"

"Clearly" I joke back waving my hands up and down my myself "and the real reason?"

"Well, Grandpa passed away last year and left me his place, Sienna wants nothing to do with it as she was never there and feels it's not right for her to take anything from the house and has gifted her share to me, although I've told her we'd split the profits, she says it's too much work and doesn't want it or have time for it. I do think it's going to be a lot of work, maybe a full renovation but the gardens are beautiful. I'll do it in my own time and sell it. I think it's more of a family home, far too big for just me, plus my life's in New York City now" he tells me

"Bow, I'm so sorry to hear About Grandpa Bill, how is Sienna? Such a shame you're selling it though, it was always such a beautiful place" I say taking a swig from my beer bottle

"Sienna, well she's just Sienna, a businesswoman who a has her own real estate company, a very busy woman nowadays with a family of her own, she's engaged Liam young and had Benny who's seven and flic who's four and a half, we're not really as close as we once were but I check in from time to time" he sighs "Its fine grandad was very unwell, but hey if you find yourself bored anytime while you're home here I have a house that's in need of some work"

I laugh "Well I might just take you up on that, I always remember that house being so beautiful and full of fun and laughter, it's lovely that he's left it to you. Can't believe Sienna, sounds like she's done so well for herself. He nods "So, tell me what are you doing with yourself nowadays?"

"Sienna has done rather well for herself but like I say she's always busy, I'm very proud of the woman she's become but I don't get to see her as often as I'd like. Well at this moment in time I'm sitting here talking to you and having a drink"

 I raise my eyebrows while lifting my bottle to my lips

"Oh, you mean career?" He says, "I'm a lawyer, What about you?"

"Well back in Chicago I'm a waitress in a little Italian restaurant, I'm also at the University, where I'm studying to be a publisher, I want to give people something new and exciting to read and send them on adventures and get them to use their imagination, you never know when a book will change your life," I tell him

"Well, that's very inspiring"

The next thing I know Dawson as appeared beside me "Well I'll be damned if it isn't Bow Tanner, I heard you were back in town man, how ya been? You should have shot me a message or called" Bow gets up and grabs Dawson by the hand pulling him into a hug

"Dude, it's been a while," Bow tells him, they haven't seen each other in years but they act as though it was only yesterday.

"Yeah, I've been good man, I was just telling Bea here that I lost my Grandpa and he's left me the manor house, but all is good, I'm going to have to carry out a full renovation and sell it on…" he pauses and looks at Ruth as she comes up beside Dawson and takes hand.

"Bow this is my fiancée Ruth, Ruth this is Bow Tanner,"

She smiles "Ahh the famous Bow Tanner,"

Bow smiles at her "Well, it's nice to meet the lady who has finally managed to pin this one down, we always thought he might be into men – Funny superhero obsession" he adds as he motions to Dawson as he kisses Ruth on the cheek, and his superhero comment nearly makes me spit out my drink.

"Well, if you need a hand with the renovation just say the word, we're happy to help, you know two hands are better than one and all that," Dawson tells him

"Thanks, man, I'll probably take you up on that if that's okay?"

Dawson nods and shakes Bow's hand again and turns to me

"Listen Bea we're heading home" I look at the clock and realise it's 11.35 pm "Spencer has already headed out about an hour ago with a blonde on his arm and Clay's already in the truck, can't handle his drink again he whispers but we think he got her number," he says winking at me "Are you coming?"

I look to Bow not really wanting to leave now I've found a familiar face and am really enjoying myself and the great conversation

"I can drop you back if you want to stay?, I've only had this one" Bow tells me, he picks up the empty bottle and waves to Tommy for a Coca-Cola.

Chapter Six

The Creek

It's around 1.30 am by the time we leave the almost empty Hideaway, Bow only had the one Budweiser and tequila shot I bought him and then stuck to soft drinks all night, while I let myself go and drank pretty much whatever was being put in front of me. As we spend the night talking, the first thing I notice is he hasn't changed much, he's just got bigger, leaner, and fitter, his dark hair is still the same just with a few grey speckled hairs in there now and he has slightly more facial hair than he once had. I can remember Dawson always taking the mick out of him for not being able to grow much facial hair and I would say that Bow's grown to become a man who clearly looks after himself, I cannot help but notice that his eyes are the most stunning eyes I've ever seen, their grey in colour but with a slight blue tinge, but they're also the softest and kindest eyes I have ever seen. I watch him as we walk over to his truck, looking at the way his muscles move, particularly the way he moves his arms and the way that his bottom wiggles, when he walks, he's not huge but you can tell he definitely works out and looks after himself.

He suddenly opens the door to his black truck for me bringing me out of my thoughts, I curtsy and jump up and say "Why thank you, sir," as I grab hold of the side of the truck trying not to stumble as I pull myself into the cab, he grabs me to steady me and then helps me up in. Then closing the door, he makes his way round to the driver's side and when he's seated he helps me with my seatbelt, as he leans down to clip me in, he's so close that I can feel his hot breath on my skin and I can't help but notice the smell of his cologne and it smells amazing, almost musky, I had to stop myself from nestling my head there.

I suddenly realise I'm staring at him and look away when he asks "So, how long you here for?"

"Well, that's the question isn't it," I say flopping my head back against the seat "I guess until my Pops gets better, then it's straight back to Chicago for me," I tell him "What about you?"

"Just the month, then it's back to New York city for me"

"So, tell me what do you do there? Any Family?, a nice girlfriend perhaps? I ask him as the alcohol gives me the courage I need and I'm slightly fishing to see if there's anyone special in his life and what his current situation is

"Well, I own my own law company, Tanners Family Law," he tells me sounding rather proud of himself "And no, it's just Sienna, who lives in Texas and no, no girlfriend" he laughs as he's telling me

"Wow, well isn't that impressive, I always knew you would do great things and New York is supposed to be amazing, the city that never sleeps right?"

"That's what they say," he replies

"I've heard it's absolutely magnificent at Christmas time, very pretty and that the department stores all go to town with their window displays"

"It's definitely something special, very magical you could say and the displays I guess are pretty spectacular," he tells me

"Maybe I could come see it for myself one day"

"You know I think I'd like that," he tells me with a boyish grin

We drive down the main street and head up the country road not far from the entrance to my parent's ranch. I get the giggles, "Oh god do you remember when you and Dawson were play fighting over Maggie Pearce down by the creek and you pushed him, and he ended up in the water" I pause to try and contain my laughter "We ended up having to walk back with him to my parent's ranch and his cowboy boots were so full of water and he was soaked from head to toe"

"God he was pissed for weeks" he laughs along with me "Do you remember how much he moaned all the way back, god he was mad at me for weeks and refused to go anywhere near the creek for ages, I use to make squelching noises just to annoy him for weeks after that happened"

I laugh "I haven't been up to the creek in years," I tell him

"Well let's go then"

"When?"

"Now"

"Now? Na......we can't"

"Yea we can, come on live a little" and I can see a smile stretch across his face as the moonlight hits it

And the next thing I know we're driving right past the road to my parent's ranch, and we're headed down the next turning on the right, although it's dark I already recognise where I am. The trees cover overhead, the hedges are higher than they once were and more overgrown. We stop the truck in the stony clearing, and I recognise my surroundings instantly. I sit in the truck and Bow comes around and opens my door for me. He starts to help me down, the ground is spongy under my feet and the smell of damp moss fills my nose, this is the smell of home.

Looking around I can see a few trees which are lit up by the moonlight, it's a dry, warm night and the stars twinkle up in the sky. There are a few bushes surrounding us and then I see two to the right-hand side where there is a small gap, I then notice what used to be the uneven path that we all knew so well. Bow puts an arm around me to steady me, I laugh because I don't really need his help but I'm definitely going to take it, I mean this guy is gorgeous and I would be a fool not to accept his help.

We walk down the small, dusty, stone, uneven path that we once did when we were kids, it's a little overgrown with brambles, weeds and shrubs coming out in every direction but we're able to flatten it down by walking on top of them.

"Well, this is looking a little more overgrown than it once was," Bow tells me as we head down the path and the next thing I know he's picked me up into a fireman's lift and is climbing over all the overgrowth. I squeal because it's so unexpected, which I then follow with a nervous giggle

"We can't have you scratching those pretty legs of yours now can we"

I laugh again at the fact that he's called me pretty and it makes me blush, thank god it's dark and he can't see me properly. Walking down the path in silence or rather him carrying me, even though I'm upside down I notice how uneven the ground has become and a couple of times Bow slips but manages to steady himself each time. Finally, we come into another clearing, and I can see the big tree we use to climb, it hasn't changed one bit, it's covered in many rubbery green leaves and moss even though in this light they appear dark, I know how beautifully light they are in the daylight, I briefly wonder if I can climb it like I used to. To my right is the creek we use to play in and swim in during the summer seasons, it seems to have gotten bigger in size, this is the same lake Bow threw Dawson in and that thought makes me smile again, I can see the tire rope swing hanging from the tree over the creek, it's been there for years, and I can remember when we dared Spencer to climb the tree to tie it for us. When Bow places me down, I am face to face with him. he looks at me smiling and pushes my hair gently from my face, I smile back at him and look at the floor, god it's intimidating how good looking he is, I look back up at him that's when a wide grin spreads across my face before I say "I bet I can get higher up in that tire than you"

He laughs "I don't think that's a very wise idea, Bea, it's been there for a long time, and you've had a few tonight"

"Pft, I'll be fine," I say as I run over to it (so unsteady on my feet that I nearly stumble and fall in the water) when I reach it I jump up and sit on it "It's just like I remember," I tell him "C'mon give me a push"

He walks over wearing his best smile and starts to push me, I swing out over the creek, back and forth and it feels amazing, I feel free like I'm 10 years old again. Bow just stands there watching me with a massive grin across his face and he shakes his head, I can only just see him visible in the moonlight, I return his smile, it's the best feeling, I sit there for a few moments enjoying the view, looking up I notice it's a clear night and the stars are clearly visible. "I wonder what it's like to be up there so high" I shout to Bow "You've got to try this, it's amazing!!" and suddenly I hear a loud crack and the next thing I know I'm plummeting into the water, it's cold and takes my breath away, I come up to the surface and Bow is next to me in an instant pulling me to the side of the creek. We both sit on a grassy area and we're absolutely soaking wet trying to catch our breaths.

"Are you okay?" Bow asks me as he sits down beside me trying to catch his breath

I take one look at him "Your soaked" and I start to laugh; I pull my t-shirt down and realise that I'm absolutely drenched myself.

"Well, I had to go in after ya didn't I…………. didn't know if you would come back up after all that alcohol you drank" he laughs a hearty laugh and I take a guess that it's because I'm also laughing

"Of course, I would, I learnt to swim after that day Dawson pushed me in……. remember? I tell him taking a deep breath while still laughing

"I remember, yes, I gave him hell that day"

We're both sit on the mossy damp ground, and I can feel the cold now.

Bow gets up and tells me "He'll be back in a minute" and he's back within what feels like seconds with two fleecy blankets in hand, catching his breath he wraps one around me and then the other one around himself and then sits down beside me and wraps an arm around me once again and I don't hate it.

"Lucky it's a warm evening and that I keep these in the back of the truck...... you know just in case, some crazy girl I grew up with decides to fall in a lake," he says smiling as he lays back on the grass and I do the same

"Very lucky, we could have been in trouble if it was cold, thanks for the blanket, it's very warm and cosy...but just for the record I didn't fall"

A smile stretches across his face "What would you call that then?"

"Falling with style" I say laughing

"he laughs too and then there's a long moment before either of us says anything. We just sit there taking in our surroundings and the silence isn't uncomfortable.

"Soooooo this renovation......big job huh?" I say breaking the silence

"Yeah, it's going to need a lot of work, but it'll be worth it in the end"

I pause "Can I see it?"

"The house?"

"Please? I always loved being at Grandpa Bill's and Nana Clara's house, it always had such charm and character, I use to love going down there to run around their gardens and play in that attic room that they had, I use to love looking out of that big round window up there. you would always be able to see all around their beautiful garden and see who was coming up the driveway from that room. I remember your Grandpa Bill loved tending to his vegetable garden and your Nana Clara loved her roses that were dotted around outside the house, I loved to watch them together they were always such fun and always seemed so happy with each other, I used to think they were such amazing people and that their house was like a castle"

Everything is silent for a moment and then he says "I've got to empty the whole house out soon" he tells me in a glum sort of tone

"Why do you have to empty it?"

"Well, I've only got a month here and I really need to sell it and clear it for new owners and a lot of it's got to go so I can make a start with the renovation, obviously I'll keep the sentimental things but most of it will go, it will be weird going back into the house, I haven't been back there in years, it's like it's been frozen in time, like a time capsule and I'll probably find a few things that were my folks"

"You could always refurbish some of the furniture and sell it with the house, might help with the house sale, everyone loves an original piece of furniture, and it might make you a little extra money too"

"Hmm, that might be worth doing, you offering?"

"Of course," I smile

"I've got to be honest I'm a little bit worried about finding things that were my parents and old things that were mine and Sienna's when we were kids, I think the attic room is still as we left it from when we used to play around up there as kids," he tells me

There was a short pause and I say "I bet you miss them…….. you know, I'd love to see that room just one more time"

"Every day, nothing worse than losing a parent, but losing my grandparents was pretty horrific too"

"I'm so sorry they were amazing people; I will miss Grandpa Bill. He was real funny he always told us the best jokes that weren't really that funny at all, and I miss your Nana Clara's hugs, she was so gentle and kind, what I'd class as a proper Nan…………and her brownies, god I miss them too"

"They really were amazing people weren't they" he smiles "listen Bea I'm really sorry about what happened between you and Nathan Parker, I speak to Dawson every now and then, he keeps me up to date about everything that's going on, so he updated me about you coming home, I know he was devastated when you left, they all were, but Dawson took it the hardest, I know how close y'all are"

I fidget "I know they were, but I didn't mean to cause upset I just needed a fresh start and to find out who I was……. you know to just break away and forget everything that happened, that caused me to break"

He holds his hands up as if in surrender "I know, me of all people would understand that"

I turn on my side to face him "Do you ever miss this place?"

"Sometimes," he says looking up at the sky then he turns to face me "But not much to stay, for now, I use to visit a couple of times a month, but there's nothing to keep me here now"

"Well, maybe we can keep each other company, while we're both home," I tell him "And you can keep me entertained by doing the house until Pops needs me at home, you know then I need to help out there a bit, that IS why I came home" I laugh

"I'll help him where I can too, I think we're in this together," he tells me with a wink and then he sits up. We sit in silence, I don't know how long for, but I know it's a while. The only sound I hear is the sound of the gentle water passing down the creek, the crickets and an owl hooting in the distance.

"Come on Sweetheart, let's get you home"

I don't really want to go but I know it's getting late or early depending on which way you look at it, taking my hand he pulls me up to stand on my feet, I've started to sober up a bit now and we head back down to the truck with the blankets wrapped around us.

Driving back down the beaten track Bow turns to me.

"Pops isn't home tomorrow, is he?"

"Not for two days, Tuesday I believe," I say

"I'll pick you up at 10 am sharp tomorrow morning okay? And you can come to the house with me?

I'm not sure if he's asking me or telling me but I just say, "That would be nice" and the next thing I know he's pulled up to the entrance of the ranch.

Chapter Seven

Dawnwood Manor

The following morning I'm greeted by a very bouncy Ruth sits on the end of my bed, I take one look at her and pull the white teddy duvet back up over my head with a groan.

"Soooooo…….. how was YOUR night?" she asks as she nudges me, and I can hear the smile playing on her lips

"Ooh, why are you in my room, Ruth?" I grumble from under the covers

"How was Bow?" she continues talking like I haven't even spoken

"Bow was fine, it was good to catch up"

"Ohh, catch up hey, yeah, yeah sure it was"

"We're just old friends," I tell her, my head feels all fuzzy and I can feel the hangover starting to kick in, in all honesty, I just want her to go away and let me sleep it off.

"It was a late one… with just a friend" she teases making an emphasis on the word friend, and I can hear the smile in her voice

Late I think to myself "Hang on, Ruth what time is it?" I say pulling the covers back and sitting bolt upright

"It's 9.47 am sugar" she smiles

"Ohh shit, shit, shit," I say running around my bedroom "I'm going to be so late" I go to the shopping bag in the far corner of the room, which is full of the clothes that I haven't yet managed to put away and I pull out the jeans I bought, the white strappy top and the red checked shirt.

Ruth laughs as I run around the room frantically getting changed into them, I stumble and fall a couple of times.

"What's so funny?"

"Well, I've never seen you flap so much"

"I'm going to be late," I tell her when I'm finally dressed, I stand and check my face in the mirror rubbing the mascara off my face, first with the back of my hand and being unsuccessful and then grabbing a face wipe.

Ruth just sits there smirking at me and then after a few minutes she says "Would it help if I told you Bow's already downstairs and has been down there talking to Dawson for the last thirty minutes"

"WHAT," I say to her "Why didn't you tell me!?" I say in a whisper "shit, shit, shit" and she laughs

Quickly I start to put my face on and decide that mascara is all that's needed today because I don't have time due to the fact that my so-called sister-in-law didn't wake me before now. I spray on some deodorant followed by a little bit of perfume because know-one wants to spend time with stinky Pete.

"Why didn't you wake me sooner?"

"Well, you looked so peaceful and snug, plus Bow told me not to and that he's not in any rush to go anywhere anyway"

I smile thinking that's actually pretty sweet of him "I'll get you back you know"

"I know you will" she smirks as she hands me my sunglasses as I start to look for my boots

"Thanks," I tell her

I find one of my boots down by the bed and when I open the door I find the other one out on the landing, pulling them on, I pause at the top of the stairs and compose myself pulling my top straight trying to look at least a little bit presentable, Ruth gives me a thumbs up and I head down the stairs and into the kitchen. As I enter Bow and Dawson both turn to look at me.

"Morning boozy" Dawson teases "Did you enjoy your swim?"

Bow lets out a little laugh "Looking dryer this morning Bea" and it brings me back to when we were kids and when they use to tease and gang up on me.

"Just a little…hey I'm really sorry about that" I smile, feeling slightly embarrassed and then I feel the heat in my cheeks "Clearly drunk me thought it was a good idea," I tell them as I adjust my sunglasses just to be certain they can't see the bags that have formed under my eyes.

"Don't worry about it, I think I needed a cooling off, like I said it was lucky it was a warm night and I think it helped sober you up" Bow tells me with a smile playing on his lips

I return his smile and then say "Shall we go"

I'm suddenly desperate to leave the conversation there with everyone in the kitchen, I notice out the corner of my eye Dawson is standing there grinning

"Can we pop to Roses on the way, please? I really need a coffee" I say as we make our way out of the stable door and head towards his black truck.

"Sure thing," he tells me

When I reach the black truck, I look at myself in the truck window and notice my hair looks like I've been playing with an electric fence, I try to smooth it down as much as possible and when he looks at me, I pretend to not notice that there's a problem and stop what I'm doing, and also that this is a perfectly normal way for me to look, I look up at my bedroom window and see Ruth with a massive grin across her face, getting in the truck I pull out my cell phone and text her.

"Could have mentioned the bush on my head!!!"

I write and press send then I can see her laughing from the top window then she places her head against it. Which makes me smile and with that Bow hugs and says goodbye to Dawson and jumps in the driver's seat beside me. We pull away from the house and we head down the driveway.

Pulling up the track to Dawnwood Manor the memories of my childhood come flooding back and I start to smile.

It's breathtakingly beautiful "It's just how I remember," I tell him

Bow is quiet beside me as we go down the track, the overgrown trees above us form almost like a tunnel, the wildflowers are out in bloom, pinks, whites, and yellows and when finally, the manor house comes into view on the hillside, it's still as charming and is just as beautiful as I remember. It's sat in about twenty acres; however, it does look a little tired. The building itself is rather large, the house is a tarnished white colour with a wooden porch that stretches all around the front of the house, it's made of wooden panels and the windows are single glazed and has what used to be tiny blue shutters at the sides of each window, I notice some are slightly hanging off and are a very faded blue colour. We then pull up outside the wooden faded red garage door and I notice that it's padlocked. We both get out of the truck and stand upon the grey gravel that is definitely in need of weeding and some attention. Looking up at the house I'm speechless at its beauty.

"Shall we take a look around?" Bow asks me as we walk around to the front of his truck and head up to the front door

"How long has it been empty?" I ask

"Around nine years….I think. I know Grandpa Bill was in Brookdale Nursing home for roughly eight years because he could no longer look after himself properly. A few years after Nana Clara's passing he became very forgetful, we just had people in to tend to the gardens every so often and when grandpa was diagnosed with Alzheimer's, Sienna and I decided there was no point in keeping it up anymore, I haven't been back here since"

"Oh, I thought you would have come back to check it out before now but I'm glad you're not doing this alone………. my goodness, I'm so sorry, I didn't realise Bill had Alzheimer's," I tell him "I know he was all you had left and how close ya both were"

"No, it's fine these things happen I guess, Nana Clara and Grandpa Bill practically bought me up ever since I was small. I visited him every few months. The last time I visited was around seven months before he passed away and he didn't even know who I was. I couldn't put myself through it anymore so I would call him every week on a Wednesday, but it got to the point where he would call me by my Father's name and even that was tough, then eventually he stopped talking altogether when he answered the phone he just mumbled instead, so I would just sit and read to him down the phone, he enjoyed that though it seemed to just calm him down. I tried to keep everything as normal as possible"

"That must have been terrible for you, really hard actually"

"It was heart-breaking, but he just deteriorated from there" then Bow goes quiet "To be honest, I was really shocked when I got a call from Sienna saying she'd spoken to Grandpa Bill's attorney actually, I thought he had sold this place years ago, and I never thought they'd leave it to me and Sienna, but apparently that was Nana Clara's wishes"

"Wow, what a lovely man and lady, what a gift," I say looking up at the house "He always had one of the biggest hearts, I can remember me, you and Dawson being in trouble with Mama and Pops and your Nana Clara and Grandpa Bill would always put us up for the night, and feed us or be able to talk us around and/ or send us home, we were always welcome here"

He smiled "He did that, they were the best people and so in love with each other, If I could find and have a relationship like theirs, I will die a happy man. They were always laughing and joking with each other, never took life too seriously but they were oh so loving. anyway, enough of the soppy stuff, shall we go on in and have a look around? He asks as he moves forward and unlocking the large wooden front door with the old bronze fancy key and then starts to make his way inside.

I stand there in the large hallway looking around, it's incredibly dusty and the sun is beaming through the windows, but not a lot has changed since I was last here, it's a little draughty and the beige wallpapers faded with some of it peeling off the walls in places, the wooden floors are all oak, I think, and just need to be cleaned and polished. The staircase is breathtakingly beautiful, it's very ornate, all made of wood, it goes up and then parts to the left and the right too, I notice it leads all the way around the large landing. Before going upstairs, we head into the door on the right and go into a massive lounge, the ceilings are high, and the two bay windows are as big as I remember them. The fireplace is made of mahogany with a marble inner part and slate hearth. The room has the same oak floors as the hallway and a huge red dirty rug is in the centre of the room with two armchairs on either side of the fireplace and a long red sofa has been pushed a little further back almost in the centre of the room. The walls were a deep red colour with a dado rail a little way down from the ceiling and faded red curtains are hung around the large bay windows.

I turn to Bow "I remember the huge Christmas tree they use to display in that window and the fireplace being lit throughout the winter months with the stockings hung just there and being allowed to roast marshmallows up against the lit fire, we always felt like we were so lucky to be able to do that, It was such a treat, Mama and Pops would never allow us to do that at home"

"There are so many memories here isn't there," he tells me

Walking around the house I notice that all the rooms are huge but something else I noticed is that their belongings are very much still where they were left, it was kept like a time capsule, books were left face down on the wooden coffee table, As if they were coming back to read them, large ornate paintings hang around the rooms and fancy cups and saucers that you would see in the 1800s were sat upon the chair-side table, the type that I would imagine would have come out of Alice in wonderland.

Within the dining room the ceiling has partly fallen down, and the table is set as if a family would be coming to take their seats at any moment with two candelabra's in the centre of the large table and an antique dresser that sits down the far end of the table containing plates and cutlery, that we know would never have been used unless it was a special occasion. When we walk into the kitchen, the first thing I notice is that it's very dusty but clean at the same, you can tell these were people who were very house-proud, a single plate sits in the sink that's covered in thick dust, that it's gathered there over the years and the cupboards are full of pots, pans, plates, and some food that had obviously gone out of date a long time ago, the cupboards are an old wooden style and look like they've all been hand made to fit, there's a large cupboard that sits in the left-hand corner of the room too, its full of cobwebs and is kind of like a pantry.

Bow also shows me the large family room just down the hall which was always known as the parlour. This room has the most beautiful white marble fireplace, the walls were once a baby blue in colour but is now looking dusty and tired and the furniture in here is all very ornate and French-looking, it makes me excited to upcycle it. we walk out and into the next room, the study and it's a darker room with darker furniture, with a desks that sits just beneath the large window, there are bits of dark wooden furniture dotted around in here, things like a funny shaped liquor cabinet which I know that used to hold alcohol like whiskey and wine (where Bow, Dawson and I once discovered, getting drunk for the first time and the hangovers were dreadful) there are also a couple of bookcases that hold some large files and lots of different paperwork, we never really knew what grandpa Bill did for a job but it must have been important because he has so much paperwork in here. We finally find ourselves upstairs. there are lots of rooms up here, which are also left untouched and a huge library that has loads of wooden shelves all around the room all containing hundreds of books and it takes my breath away, we pass two bathrooms one peach in colour, the other sage green, Bow's mother and fathers' bedroom very much left untouched, it's a very pale lilac colour, the master bed was a white metal and there were little things like mugs and a newspaper that were left on the bedside tables, just as if they were coming back at any moment to read it. Bow's grandparent's bedroom was a dark cream colour and was full of very old-fashioned furniture, as well as five additional bedrooms and a well-used nursery. The main bathroom was a lovely peach colour with a vintage shower over the top of it, it would have been top of the range when it was first fitted, with halfway up the wall around the bathroom being part tiled with peach-coloured tiles. Looking around I know this is going to take a lot of work, but it will be a lovely family home for someone when it's done.

Finally, we head into what used to be Bow's old bedroom and it's exactly how I'd imagine this teenage boy would have lived. (We were never allowed in here), The mental bed is to the right of the room, the carpet is an old deep, green colour and one of the walls is a deep blue with the three other walls white. Standing in the doorway I watch as he walks around looking at the items on the shelves picking them up and placing them back down, looking at marvel and beano comics on his old bookshelves and then opening the chest of drawers that are directly opposite the doorway, placed under the little window, his clothes are still in there, years old. he pulls out a white t-shirt and stands there holding it up.

"Well, there's no way these will fit me now," he says with a laugh looking at it, I can see that the shirt would have fit him when he was about twelve or thirteen years old and he was much skinnier back then, now he wouldn't even get an arm in there.

I laugh too "Oh I'm not sure I think you could squeeze an arm in there or get your head in the hole, I reckon you should try" I smile

"Well, I don't know it might fit," he tells me trying to squeeze an arm in one of the tiny holes

I laugh "Do you wanna start in this room then? We could start by clearing things out and boxing them up?"

"I think so, it would probably be the easiest to do, I guess we should make a start on this today, I know time is short, we could move all the furniture into the garage to sell or do up and put some out back in the garden so we can burn it because I know some of this is rotten," he says as he touches bedside table, snapping the corner off and it just crumbles in his hand. "There should be some empty boxes in the back of my truck, we can store the sentimental stuff in the dining room for now"

"Are you sure you're okay to do this? it's a huge thing and I know it will be hard for you, we don't have to start today if you're not comfortable, remember you don't have to do this if you don't want to"

"I think so Bea, I don't think I'll ever do it if we don't start today and thank you for being there for me and doing this with me, it's nice to have some support and not have to do it on my own, to be honest, I'm not sure what I'll find here"

I just nod and then head down to the truck to grab the plastic boxes we need, picking five of them up I head back up the staircase and that's when I hear muted sobs; I follow the sound to his grandparents' old bedroom where I find Bow sitting on the edge of their bed.

"What's happened? Have you found something? Aww, geez Bow please don't cry" I tell him, and I don't really know what to do

"No, there's just a lot of memories here, I'm sorry Bea"

I look down and see he's holding a photograph of Clara and Bill on their wedding day and a pendant that I can only assume was Nana Clara's,

"It's just a lot…. I think I'm just very overwhelmed" Bow tells me

"Hey, don't ever be sorry, we can do this together. it's going to be okay; you don't have to do this alone; I know it's going to be tough" I bend down so I'm up on my knees facing him and pull him into a tight cuddle.

He lets me go and then wipes his face on the back of his hand "I'm so sorry" he tells me "I don't know where that came from, there's just a lot of memories here, some good, some not so good"

"It's okay I completely understand, I know this is going to be hard on you" I hug him again longer this time, I pull back and look him in the eyes "I'm here for you, whatever you need I'm here to help"

I see his grey/blue eyes staring into my green and with that, I suddenly feel his warm, soft lips on mine, he kisses me slowly and passionately. After a short, while he pulls back "I'm sorry, I shouldn't have done that, it was wrong of me, I've overstepped the mark"

I look at him, his grey eyes are simply stunning, I lean forward and kiss him again, I feel as though fireworks have exploded inside me and the more I kiss him the less I want to stop, when I open my eyes, he's smiling back at me "Right, where were we" I say, "Where did I put those boxes?" I go to get up and he pulls me back

"Well, that was very unexpected," he tells me

I look away shyly "I see you're not complaining though," I tell him, as I get up and head out onto the landing to grab a box, looking back I watch him staring at me and notice he's wearing the same smile as I am.

We start in his old bedroom. A few hours have passed, and we have his room all packed up, his metal bed is dismantled and ready to be placed in the truck and taken to the recycle centre as it's very old and starting to rust in places. There are five bags of old toys for charity, two boxes of keepsakes that we place in the dining room and all that is left are the two big pieces of furniture the chest of drawers and the wardrobe, which we decide needs to go into the garage and the bedside table to our burn pile out the back of the garden with a couple of trash bags because a lot of things are falling apart. We head down the staircase with the chest of drawers, I can't help but giggle because it's utterly ridiculous, this chest of drawers is huge, and I must look like a small child, and he laughs too because I'm lost behind them.

"All I can see is two big, green eyes looking at me" he laughs

"That's it laugh it up" I giggle

When we finally make it to the garage, we place the chest of drawers on the floor, Bow walks over and unlocks the padlock then pulls open the garage door, it is absolutely jam-packed with the tiniest walkway to the left of the garage, there are things covered with sheets and cardboard boxes placed everywhere, little bikes suitable for children not to mention a couple of motorbikes and various other things.

"You have got to be kidding me," I say when I see that's there's not much room for the chest of drawers. .

"I thought he sold this" Bow gasps

Lifting off the cover he reveals the 1952 baby blue vintage Cadillac, I walk up close and see the interior is cream leather and she seems intact after all these years.

"She's a real beauty," I tell him

"That she is" he turns the key that's been left in the engine and it just clicks

"Sounds like she's going to need a new battery and maybe a little work," I tell him

"Since when do you know about cars?" he asks me

"Since I had to rely on myself to fix my truck," I tell him "I'm not just a pretty face you know" I follow with a wink

"Clearly not" he smiles at me "So I'm thinking we'll make a start in here then," he tells me gesturing towards the things in the garage

"I think that's a grand idea, we're going to need somewhere to put all the furniture" leaving the chest of drawers outside the garage, we make a start on everything within it.

We find some treasures within the garage, the Cadillac is just the tip of the iceberg, we also find not one but two vintage motorcycles which we decide we can sell on, old tools, some of which are terribly rusty which we can't save, old toys he had when he was a small child most of which are broken and needed to go to the recycle centre, old photographs of him but also some of people that he didn't know and some odd bits and pieces, wood, nails, screws which we decide could come in handy, so we leave them in various pots on the workbench at the back of the garage and a couple of boxes of old China ornaments. We start by loading up the truck with things that can go to the recycle centre so that it starts to clear some space. After a morning's hard work, we can finally put the chest of drawers in the garage and have made room for other pieces of furniture. Once it's cleared a little, the garage actually seems pretty large even with the Cadillac and the bikes in there. By the end of the day, we have cleared not only Bow's childhood bedroom of furniture and belongings, but we have made a start on the dining room, placing the old fancy plates and tea sets into boxes, and putting them to one side, he's decided he'd like to keep them. We move the vintage dresser, large mahogany table, and beautiful ornate chairs into the garage so that there out of the way, for now, I pick up the photos that we found earlier from the garage and place them in the front room on the vintage coffee table, I don't think he'd want to lose those.

"We really should get that ceiling down in the dining room," Bow tells me "Then we can take all that stuff that's in the back of the truck to the recycle centre, then I'm thinking we could stop at Rose's café for some lunch"

I turn to Bow "Yeah, Roses sounds great! I'm starving and that will be a blast from the past"

"I'll be back two secs," he tells me and the next thing I know he's gone to the garage and left me standing there in the dining room, he's back within seconds carrying a tall wooden foldable ladder and a crowbar "Stand back" he warns

I slide the keepsake boxes down to the other end of the dining room so that there out of the way and stand in the doorway. I watch as he makes his way up the ladder, he can only just touch the ceiling because of its height, first, he pulls the insulation that's hanging down and then takes the crowbar into the hole and pulls, he does this several times on various parts of the ceiling and it all comes tumbling down onto the deep green rug below revealing the thick wooden beams within the ceiling.

"Well, that's that done," he tells me as he starts to pick up the larger pieces of plasterboard placing them into rubble bags and then we roll the rug, I help him take it all to his truck, after locking up the house, we jump in and head to the recycle centre.

Chapter Eight

Home Coming

We pull up outside Roses café and it's just as charming as I remember, as we walk towards the wooden door, Bow walks slightly ahead and holds the door open for me and I don't hate it, he then takes my hand leading me inside, Walking in the first thing I notice is nothing has changed, it's still as quirky as it once was. We walk up to the counter and that's when I hear her.

"Well call my name and kick me sideways, if it isn't Beatrice Coleman" she shrieks, I spot Rose as she walks around the counter arms open wide "Darlin how have you been? It's been far too long"

"Hi Rose," I say returning her hug "I've been really well thanks"

She holds me at arm's length as if inspecting me and then says, " Ohh, that's good, I heard about Jefferson dear, how's he doing?"

"Much better now thanks Rose, he comes home tomorrow"

"Ohh that's a relief, I heard he's coming home, don't you worry I'll be there," she says with a wink and placing her hand on her chest if as if she hasn't noticed Bow stood slightly behind me "So what brings you here? Lookin to take up your old position again dear?" she jokes "Could always do with an extra pair of helping hands"

And it's like my mother has mentioned to her once or twice, that if I should come home, to mention it to me and see if I wanted my old position back "No, no Rose just here for lunch and to catch up with an old friend" I say motioning towards Bow

She takes a step backwards "Well, well………. if it isn't ……….Bow Tanner" she gasps "what a surprise this is, goodness haven't you changed all grown up, I'm so sorry to hear about old Bill, such a shame, such a shame, but you, look at you, such a strapping young man" she says giving me a wink

"Hello Rose, I hope life is treating you well," he tells her as I watch his cheeks fill with colour.

She gets all giddy and a tad excited, "Well table for two is it?"

"Please" Bow replies

Rose leads us to the back of the café and seats us at a wooden ornate table with two funky chairs on either side, one bottle green and the other a plum red. we sit, and she lights the candle in the centre.

"What can I get ya to drink?"

Bow looks to me

"I'll have an espresso coffee; one sugar please Rose," I tell her

"And a latte please"

"Comin right up," she tells us in a southern drawl as she walks away but occasionally looks back at us smiling, leaving us to enjoy each other's company

"Old friend huh? Ouch, not going to lie, that one hurt" he jokes

"Well……what would you call this?" I say not knowing where to place myself and feeling slightly embarrassed and uncomfortable, I look at him with a beaming smile. "I've missed this place," I tell Bow looking around and trying to change the subject

He winks at me "It is rather quirky isn't it"

"I bet there's nothing like this in New York"

He laughs "There really isn't, people are always so crazy busy in New York and don't really have the time to stop, so this is a real change of pace for me……plus I always get my lunch delivered to the office, time is money I guess"

Rose walks across the café with a spring in her step and is back beside us with our drinks and a menu in no time, she hands them to us. We both look it over as she waits, wearing a beaming smile, we both decide on the house special burgers and fries because they always were and still are the best I've ever had.

"So, Dawson mentioned this morning, you're having a home-coming party for Pops"

"Yeah, we are, in the barn, I think a few people from the town are coming along …...it would be nice if you could come too, I know Mama and Pops would love to see you"

"You know I think I'd like that," he tells me "Dawson already sent me a message and asked me, but I thought it was best I checked with you too, I wouldn't want to intrude"

"Intrude, you know you are always welcome there so yes, please do come, We'd love to have you there"

When our food arrives, it looks just as good as I remember, the burgers are huge and the fries are just delicious and covered in a special seasoning, I just can't wait to tuck in. We continue our conversation over our lunch, and I find out what Bow has been doing with himself these past few years and what life in New York is like, he seems very trustworthy, honest (like he's always been) and like he's done really well for himself. he shows me the company he owns through the website on his cell and tells me about what him and his employees do, and who they all are, I've got to be honest its all really quite interesting, he really seems like he's got his life together, with his fancy apartment, nice truck and easy life style. He makes me feel really safe and wanted in his presents, it's a really nice feeling, I've never had that before, it's like he really wants to get to know me, you know the real me and is actually interested in me as I am him and not only thinking about what he can get from me. After we've finished we order two hot drinks to go, he insists on paying the entire bill, even though I put up a fight and then we head back up to Dawnwood Manor.

We spend the next few days up at Dawnwood Manor. First, we organise for a large dumpster to be delivered outside the front of the house, then we spend most of the day clearing, and ripping out the old dated wooden kitchen, (We've decided to go room by room), We find pots, pans, enough dinner sets to feed at least 60 people, little trinkets and other bits and bobs in there, that we mostly just throw in the trash or on the burn pile. We're nearly finished emptying the room and to my surprise, it hasn't taken long to rip everything out.

"There should only be that small end unit by the back door left to empty and that big storage cupboard over there" Bow points to the small one within the kitchen units then the large one that's built in the left-hand corner of the room.

I start with the small one first knowing that after I've emptied it out, he can finish ripping the units and worktop out of the kitchen and place them on the pile outside ready for burning, then it would leave the room completely empty, well everything apart from the sink that is. I walk over the dusty large kitchen floor, making my way to the small end cupboard and open the door I see lots of old brown cookery books. That have all been crammed in there, Nana Clara loved to cook, she was always in here making something for us all.

"Bow, what shall I do with these?"

"Put them with the trash, I don't think anyone will want them" he calls as he pulls down another wall unit from the wall.

I sit cross-legged on the dusty wooden flooring, it's cold under my bottom and I start to pull them out one by one, carefully opening them to see what's written inside, I find inside that they are all cookery books and there are hundreds of recipes within them.

"It's such a shame to get rid of them though," I tell him

"Well, if you want em, take em" he replies

"Oh no, I couldn't….. oh Bow come and look at this you can't possibly get rid of this"

He walks over to me and kneels down beside me. I hand him a book that has obviously been handwritten by Nana Clara.

"Look at these, you can't just throw them away, there her old family recipes and it would be so wrong for me to take them"

He takes the book and flicks through the pages and comes across a brownie recipe; I look over at him watching as he turns the pages and comes across her other recipes, all handwritten.

"Those brownies were always the best," I tell him

He smiles "I'd kill to have one of those brownies just one more time" he says continuing to flick through the book.

"Me too, I think you need to keep this, it would be such a shame to get rid of such lovely recipes and possibly old family recipes"

"I don't know Bea I don't really cook, I don't have the time, honestly if you want to take em, there yours" and with that, he kisses the top of my head and gets up, then walks back to the kitchen unit he was ripping apart and I watch him carry it out to the burn pile. I sit there holding the brownie recipe, unsure of what to do, a few moments later I've decided it's what she would have wanted.

"I hope I do you proud Nana Clara," I say in hope that somehow, she might hear me and that when I make them, they taste just as good as hers once tasted, I scoop them up, place them into a small brown box and walk out to the truck placing them on the passenger's seat and then head back into the house to make a start on the large cupboard in the corner.

I grab a black sack and open up the door, it smells very musky, and I can also smell the copper pipes hidden at the back, this cupboard is huge almost like a small bedroom. The first thing I notice is all the old cans and bags of food sat on the shelf. I start by picking them up and placing them into the black bag I'm holding. When I get to the bottom shelf, I notice there's a very large metal trunk hidden in it, I pull it out slightly but it's really heavy and I've barely moved it.

"Bow" I yell "BOW!!" I yell again just to make sure he heard me

He comes running in "Everything okay?" he asks

"Yes, perfectly fine" I smile at him "But look at what I've just found," I tell him pointing in its direction

We both pull it out of the cupboard by the handles and drag it across the kitchen floor

"It's incredibly heavy, isn't it, any idea what's in here?" I ask

"None," he says as he looks around the box then finding a label attached to one of the handles "Well it says August 7th, 1990"

"Does that date mean anything to you?"

He's silent for a moment as though it's just dawned on him. "That's the day we lost my Mother and Father…..I'm sorry Bea, I….. I think …I just need to place this in the dining room for now and maybe go through all that's in there another time"

"Okay," I say not wanting to question him "You grab that end, and we'll take it through"

He nods at me "Thanks Bea" and I can tell he's grateful that I've not questioned him any further on what the box might contain

As we set it down, I hear the grandfather clock from the front room chime, I walk and stand in the doorway checking it and I notice it's now 4 pm.

"Gosh look at the time, I guess time really fly's when you're having fun"

"It really does, doesn't it, thank you for all your help today Bea," he says taking a step closer to me

"Your, umm your welcome" I stutter as he's standing close enough for me to feel his hot breath on my face

"So, I better get you back then, the homecomings at 7 o'clock tonight right?"

"Yep, that's right, I suppose we better go get cleaned up then," I say looking down and realising how dusty we both are

       He looks down at me and I move myself closer placing my head on his chest, he wraps his arms around me tight and place's his head on top of mine, it's as if he needed this just as much as I did, I look up at him and once again his lips are on mine, and I feel as though I never want it to end. He eventually pulls away looking down at me

"Right sweetheart, we better get back so you can prepare for this homecoming"

"You're still coming, right?"

"Of course, I can't miss seeing you again can I"

I blush, and with that, we head for the truck, and he drives me back to my parent's ranch.

I find myself walking around my room, pulling every item of clothing I own out of the drawers and wardrobe. it's been an hour and a half since Bow dropped me home and I still can't decide on what to wear. I sit down on the end of the bed, frustrated, I place my head in my hands facing out the window, I can't seem to get Bow out of my head. When suddenly there's a knock on my door.

"Ruth, I'm so glad you're here I need…." but as I turn around to my surprise its Dawson stood there "Oh sorry Daw I thought you were Ruth

"Just thought I'd check-in, you doing okay?"

"Yeah, all good thanks, I had a good day with Bow up at Dawnwood today"

He walks into my room and then says "You seem to be spending a lot of time with Bow Tanner lately"

"Yes, well, I like him, he's a nice guy"

Dawsons silent for a minute before saying "Listen, Bea, I know he is but I'm just a little worried that you're getting too close and that you'll end up hurt"

"What do you mean? does Bow have some sort of reputation that I don't know about, I just really like spending time with him Dawson, I don't think that's anything to worry about"

"No, he doesn't but I'm just scared that you'll end up like you were all those years ago and we don't want to lose you like that again"

"I doubt that Bow would ever hurt me like Nathan did Daw"

"But tell me what happens when he goes back to New York, and you have to go back to Chicago?"

"I……. I don't know Daw……… I guess we'll figure it out when it happens"

He's silent for a moment, "Okay Bea, just….just be careful, yeah, I don't want to see you hurt again" he gets up and heads for the door "Oh and Mama and Pops will be here at 7.30 pm tonight, we will see you downstairs when you're ready"

I sit back down on the end of the bed again, I place my head back into my hands. Almost instantly the door opens again, I look up at it thinking it's Dawson again.

"Need some help?"

"Would you mind?"

"No of course not" Ruth smiles at me and she's looking stunning in the grey dress I bought her.

"Wow, just look at you," I tell her

"So, what we wearing tonight?" she asks

"I'm really not sure, I have nothing to wear," I say running my hands through my hair

"I can tell," she tells me with a smile as she looks around the room "So where's that beautiful red dress you wore last weekend?"

"But I've already worn it" I moan

"I thought you'd say that," she says making her way back to the door, she opens it and pulls in a brown paper bag she'd hidden on the other side "This is just a little something from me to you" I see her smile as she hands me the bag

"Oh, Ruth you shouldn't have"

"It wasn't just me, Dawson helped me pick it, go ahead and have a look"

I open up the bag and pull out a baby blue dress covered in white lace, it's buttoned up to a collar and is knee-length, it's really pretty and so me

"Wow thank you it's stunning, you both know me so well"

"Your welcome we thought you could wear it with those boots you love so much, come on, get it on and then we can sort out your hair and makeup because Dawson's just mentioned that you look like you've been out sleeping with the horses"

I laugh "Yeah I don't want my hair to be like it was the other morning thanks"

We both sit laughing "Yeah should have warned ya about that shouldn't I" she laughs "So, Dawson said he came to talk to you about Bow"

"Yeah, he did"

"He's only worried about you, you know, and he knows what y'all went through last time and that Bow's heading back to New York in a little under a months' time, Dawson messaged Bow to see what was going on between the two of you and to make sure he doesn't mess you around"

"Oh god How embarrassing," I say placing my head in my hands "Bow's really not like that, he wouldn't hurt me, I think we're just seeing what happens and where life takes us," I say finally buttoning my dress up feeling a little frustrated that Dawson's sticking his nose in.

"Okay Bea sit down here" she gestures for me to sit at the dressing table, and she starts curling my hair "Well, we're here if you should ever need us, you know that right? We wouldn't let you down and will never let you fall"

"Thanks, Ruth please tell Dawson he doesn't have to worry though," I say as I start to do my makeup "Bow's a good guy"

"I'll try but we both know he can't help but worry"

"So, tell me have I missed much today?"

"No not really, it looks really good down in the barn tonight, the fairy lights and the bunting are all up and the tables are all out with the hay bale seats. I think Clays got the music all sorted now, I know earlier he had some trouble with the speakers but it's all okay now and I think everyone that's coming is bringing a dish to eat and there's mountains of drink down there too"

After about ten minutes we're all finished, I stand up and look in the full-length mirror and hardly recognise the girl looking back at me, my hair falls in loose curls down past my shoulders and my makeup is subtle, but I actually think I look slightly pretty and happier than I have done in years.

"Wow Ruth you're in the wrong job," I tell her placing my cream cowgirl hat on my head

"Well, I am a hairdresser you know, but look at you," she tells me with a wink "Your glowing"

"I don't think I've ever looked or felt this good in a long, long time, thank you," I say giving her a big hug

"Your welcome, I'm glad you feel as good as you look, oh and just be happy Bea….. oh and before I forget a little happy news me and Dawson spoke and we've set a date for our wedding on March the 12th this year and I was wondering, well hoping really that you would like to be my maid of honour? You see I don't have many friends or girls I consider myself close to, so I thought you'd fit perfectly, We're going to speak to Mama and Pops about it hopefully tonight, we'd like it to be here, in the barn and we're hoping they will give us their permission"

"Aww Ruth thank you so much, I'd love to, such fantastic news, I'm sure they'll be fine about it"

We hug again and both head down the stairs to the kitchen, where we find Spencer and Dawson sitting at the kitchen table playing a game of poker.

"Anyone know what that amazing smell is?" Dawson asks me

"Well wouldn't you like to know," I tell them

"I would actually that's why I asked" he jokes

I open up the oven door and pull out the tray revealing the one thing I'd been so desperate to make……. Nana Clara's chocolate brownies

"They smell incredible," Dawson tells me as he leans over to grab a slice as I've started to cut it into small pieces, I swat his hand away.

"Hey! hang on those aren't Nana Clara's brownies, are they?" He asks

"Yes, they are and there not for you. We found the recipe up at the manor today" I tell him

"There for me aren't they," Spencer asks jokingly

"Nope, not you either"

"Aww you know how much we loved them; she use to make them for us all the time! Hang on….. then who are they for?" Spencer says sounding slightly annoyed

"Stupid question Buddy" Dawson answers

"Bow" Dawson and I say in unison

"Bow Tanner?? I didn't know he was back in town"

"Yep, The old Dawnwood Manors been left to him and he's renovating it, I was there today, we've been hanging out a lot recently, ripping it all out and we found Nana Clara's old brownie recipe and he let me keep it, so I wanted to make it for him"

"Ahh we always miss out on the cakes" Ruth Jokes as she winks at me

I place six slices into a small cardboard cake box "You guys can have the rest" I say placing them in the centre of their poker match and there like wolves as they all go to grab a slice, I take two pieces with me as I head out to the barn with Ruth and handing her one but just as we leave the kitchen all I can hear behind me in the distance is.

"Bow Tanner, well I never thought that he'd come back to town or that they'd even hit it off," Spencer tells Dawson "Well as long as she's happy that's all that matters, Right Dawson?"

"That's right, but if he hurts her, I'll make shit rain on him"

It's 7.30 pm in the barn and all is quiet as we're waiting for Mama and Pops to arrive. Bow arrived about half an hour ago and is casually talking to Dawson about the San Francisco Giants and his business in New York City with one arm casually draped around my waist.

"Yeah, business is good thanks man, I have a lot of good people working for me and hey the next time your free we will definitely see the San Francisco Giants play, I think there's a game next month if you fancy it? but how're things here it doesn't seem like much has changed?"

"I'd like that…… Well, you know this place same old really nothing really ever changes does it, we're hoping to get married on March 12th this year, you'll have to come back for that"

"I wouldn't miss it for the world man," he says turning to me and kissing me on the top of the head

I turn to Bow "I'll let you ladies talk, I'm just going to grab a drink before Mama and Pops arrive" I look down at my watch they should be here any minute "Anyone else?" they all shake their heads

Bow releases me from under his arm and I head to the makeshift bar grabbing drink's for myself, Bow, Dawson, and Ruth, just as I've reached the bar Mama and Pops appear at the doorway of the barn, they are greeted by cheers from everyone within it, they whale and holla and pop off their party poppers that Spencer had insisted on having.

"Well, isn't this a surprise," Mama says aloud which is followed by a lot of chatter, more hollaing and cheers.

Leaving our drinks on the bar I walk up to her and Pops giving them both my biggest hug and smile "How we doing now Pops? I ask

"Much better for being back here pumpkin"

The next thing I know Mr Selton who owns the butchers and Peggy the nearest neighbour has appeared beside me welcoming them both home. I notice the music is now a little louder than it was before they arrived, I also notice how full the barn is looking; it looks like everyone in town has turned up to welcome Pops home. I give them both a polite nod and head back over to Dawson, Ruth and of course Bow.

Dawson nods and tells Bow "Don't let me down, yeah?" and then walks off with Ruth beside him as they head for the stage to make the speech he'd been planning and taken hours to write.

"What was that about?"

"Oh, nothing important, I was just clearing a few things up with Dawson"

"God how embarrassing," I tell him as my cheeks glow red "Well I've got something that will make you smile"

"Oh, you mean more than you?"

"Way more than me," I say as I walk to the bar and then back, I hold out the brown cardboard box full of Nana Clara's brownies

He takes the box from me, wearing a massive grin "What's this then?"

"Open it"

He opens the box to reveal the brownies

"Are these what I think they are?"

"Yep, I made them as soon as you dropped me home, I just hope there as good as your Nana Clara's"

"Thank you" he beams "They certainly smell just as good" then he pulls me into a tight hug and gently kisses the top of my head "You didn't have to do that sweetheart, I'm going to go and pop them in the truck, you can share them with me later"

With that, he leaves my side and is back beside me within seconds. We find an empty table and sit with our drinks as we start to listen to Dawson drone on about our family.

"Excuse me, everyone, hey excuse me, can I have your attention please?" he's being ignored, and it's as if no one seems to know he's there.

"HEY QUIET" Ruth shouts down the microphone and silence falls over the barn I sit there smiling followed by a small laugh and I can see Bow smiling too as Dawson pulls out his piece of paper

"She definitely knows how to handle herself doesn't she," he tells me grinning

"She does that" I laugh

Dawson starts to speak "We just want to take the time to thank y'all for being here with us tonight, we are so lucky to have so many good, supportive family members and friends. We want to thank y'all for your kindness and help from within the community, We are so grateful for each and every one of you, I know that myself and my family – Pops and Mama mainly are overwhelmed by the support that's been given, even things like the shortest phone call to Pops and/or to Mama, to us it has just meant the world and kept him going" there's a cheer from everyone within the barn "We have been incredibly lucky to have our Pops back here with us today, we know how scary it was when you became so poorly and we all wish you a speedy recovery, if not for his sake but Mamas, but another thing that the gods graced us with is that they bought us back our beloved little sister Beatrice who is back from her fresh start, so here's to old friends and new beginnings" he turns and looks to me and Bow. Everyone raises their glasses and takes a drink "Now let's get this party started" he looks to Clay who cranks up the music once more.

A few hours pass and it's just got dark outside, everyone here is having the time of their lives, Pops looks like a totally different man and Mama looks like she's finally had the rest she needed – almost like a weight has been lifted from her shoulders. A new song comes on, cover me up by Morgan Wallen, it's slow and one of my all-time favourites and Bow turns to me "Beatrice would you dance with me?"

"I think I'd like that very much," I say taking his hand as he leads me to the dance floor. We're there for about a minute and my mother and father come up beside us.

"It's good to see you back Bow"

"Good to be back Mr Coleman"

"Please call me Jefferson"

Bow nods

"May I cut in?" my Pops says looking to Bow

We swap and my mother goes off to dance with Bow as my father takes my hand.

"So, how are we doing Pops?"

"Much better now Darlin, how you finding being home?"

"It's good to be back, I'm really enjoying being here, it's funny how some people can change the way you look at the world in such a short space of time isn't it" I look in the direction of Bow who is dancing and now laughing with my Mama

Pops follows my gaze "It is indeed, so what are your plans?"

"Well, I will be here for you and the family for the time being and then I guess when things get better, I'll need to head back to Chicago"

"Hmm, well please don't feel you have to stay because of me or have to go if you don't want to"

"No, no Pops I want to," I say catching Bow's eye

"Oh, I see maybe another reason you want to stay or go so soon?"

"There might be yes" I can feel myself turning a nice shade of red

"You know he's not staying don't you"

"Yes Pops, it's been mentioned once or twice"

"Okay well, as long as you know and we're here if it doesn't work out okay?"

"Thanks, Pops," I say wrapping him into a hug "But that's not going to happen"

The rest of the night goes smoothly, Mama and Pops seem to have enjoyed themselves and the company of people other than each other and the hospital staff. Looking around I notice there's lots of alcohol dotted around, that Pops couldn't have and was under strict instructions from not only the doctor but Mama too, they have told them that alcohol is a big no, so much so every time he was given a drink by someone, Mama wasn't too far away ready to swat it from his hands. It was pretty funny to watch. Standing at the bar and looking around the room I notice Clay has found Florence, I watch them make their way from the bar to the dance floor, it looks as though he's trying to teach her one of the local country dances and they seem to be getting on so well. Dawson and Ruth have found Mama and Pops and are now sitting on some hay bales, it looks like they're having a very in-depth conversation, must be about their wedding I briefly think. Spencer once again is surrounded by women of all ages as he's sat at a table, there of all shapes, sizes and ages and all laughing at his undoubtedly unfunny jokes however each one clearly hanging on his every word and dying to take him home, I wish the commitment-phobe would find the right girl and stop messing around and perhaps settle down and have a family of his own.

There's a certain buzz in the air tonight and everyone seems to be having a great time, Mrs jones approaches me and starts up a conversation about how good it is to have me home, with that Bow who had been talking to Clay's boss, spots me and makes his way towards me.

"Excuse me," he says turning to her "May I borrow Beatrice for a moment please?" she nods

"Bea so I was wondering if you fancy taking a walk?" he asks

"A walk? Oh no you don't want to go to the creek again do you"

He lets out a little laugh "No just a chat if that's okay?"

"Yes, of course, everything okay though?"

"More than ok, c'mon," he says as he places a hand at the small of my back and guides me outside the barn. We start to walk down the bank and into the field away from the crowds

"So, what's going on?"

"Well, I was just talking to Dawson, and I've spoken to your Mama and Pops tonight and I was wondering whether you would let me take you out on a date?"

"A date?"

"Yes, a date"

"You want to go on a real date with me?"

"Yes"

I'm speechless and ask "But why?.... I'm so annoying" I say, and I can just see the smile on his face

"You are a little bit, yes, but yes I'd like to take you out"

There's silence between us as I start to think about the thing that's worrying me the most and before I can stop myself I've said it

"But what happens when you go back to New York and me Chicago?" I ask

"Well, I'm not sure but why don't we just see what happens and take it a day at a time? I don't think we can make any promises can we"

"And Dawson's okay with this?"

"Yes, I made sure I asked him before I asked you" he takes a moment to turn and face me "so will you go out on a date with me?"

Chapter Nine

The Discoveries

Over the following weeks, I juggle helping out Pops at the ranch and helping Bow up at Dawnwood Manor. Todays a Monday morning and the sun is shining, and it's around 27 degrees. I always feel like everyone is happier when the sun is out, I know I am. The house is quiet this morning as I walk across the landing and fly down the stairs

"Morning Pops," I say in a jolly tone

"Morning Darlin," he says in a southern drawl

"Need any help today?" I say as I go to grab a slice of toast from the table

"Nope I think I'm okay and Dawson seems to have it all in hand"

"Hmm" I nod taking a bite from my toast and make my way across the kitchen to the coffee machine filling up my travel mug

"Any plans today Darlin?"

"Well, if you don't need me, I thought I'd go up and help out Bow up at the manor, we've nearly cleared out the whole house, just the attic to do now," I tell him rather proudly

"Well, you better get going then, Darlin"

I nod "Thanks Pops" I smile and with that I leave the house making my way to my truck

I just sit down and buckle myself in the seat, when my cell phone rings, I pull it out of my pocket and look down to see that it's Willow calling me.

"Hi Willow, how you doin?"

"Beatrice! I've got such a surprise for you" she tells me her voice sounding so enthusiastic and excitable

I smile "Okay Willow I thought we were done with the whole surprises thang"

"No, we agreed we were done with me finding you Mr Right"

"Well, that's good because I think I might have found him but okay go on, what's the surprise?" then it dawns on me "Hang on should I be worried or excited?" I ask her

"Ooo check you out, you have to tell me all about him, umm and Excited I think. Ahhh balls" I can hear her fumbling around, almost like she's dropped something

"I will I promise, well tell me then… I need to know what this surprise is," I say now laughing

"Well, I'm on my way to you, I've got your laptop – John from number six gave me your key and I got your paperwork from the university that you need to sign,

Carlos said I needed to take some time off so I chose a week with you as my breakaway, plus I picked you up some clothes from your apartment – I hope you don't mind, and I figured that you could do with a friend and a break so I'm on my way to you, Oh shit…..I dropped my coffee"

I smile trying to stop myself laughing "When?"

"Right now, I'm calling from my car"

"Oh, Willow this is fantastic! I can't wait to see you and show you around"

"I've noticed there aren't any big hotels in your town so I'm staying in a motel, umm….a place called…… The Red fox, The GPS is reading five hours, but I'll stop over in another motel that's on the way to you for tonight" she tells me excitedly "I'll call you tomorrow when it tells me I'm near"

"Oh, Willow I can't wait for you to meet everyone!"

"Me either," she tells me "Well Bea gotta go, speak soon"

"Speak soon Willow, travel safe"

I hang up and start the engine feeling excited, a little surprised and grateful by her unexpected visit then I head on over to Dawnwood manor, when I arrive, I find Bow already outside, I jump out of my truck and walk towards him.

"Well, Sweetheart, I didn't expect to see you today," he tells me

"Well, I thought I'd surprise you"

He walks up to me and wraps me into a big hug "You know those brownies were divine, thank you they were exactly how I remembered, you must have the right touch please don't ever stop making them"

I giggle "I'm glad you enjoyed them, are there any left?"

"Yep, I left you one, it's on the passenger's seat in the box"

"Aww thank you, just one," I say looking at him giving him my cheekiest smile. "I love that you thought of me, So only the attic room left?" I ask as I walk to his truck to grab the brownie he saved me and place it in my mouth "Mmm, this is just like Clara's, Mmm…. so good"

He laughs "Well they were pretty good. And yes, It would seem so, just the attic left to tackle" We had managed to make our way around the whole house finding treasures that Bow didn't even know existed, really old jewellery, books, photographs and vintage trinkets and other belongings and we've placed all the furniture into the dining room as the garage now contains most of the things that we need to work on.

"Need a hand?"

"Please"

        He leads me inside the house and it's looking very different. he starts by showing me around and all the things that have changed over the last few weeks. The hallway is bare, the walls have been stripped, walking into the living room I notice all the furnishings have all been removed and moved into the garage and dining room (which is now pretty full). The walls again have been stripped of its paper and the old rug has been rolled up and placed in the corner of the room ready to be cleaned and put back where it once was, all the trinkets have been placed into boxes and are now in the dining room with the rest if the personal belongings.

Walking into the kitchen all that he's left is the kitchen sink, and it looks incredibly bare.

"You've taken the tiles off the walls"

"Yes, hard work that was"

"Did you find out what was in the basement?" we had both been too scared to go down there because it was pretty dark, and we couldn't find the light switch.

"Oh, nothing special, once I found the light switch at the very bottom of the stairs, I just found there were just lots of old Christmas decorations and old appliances, a spinner dryer I think it's called, there wasn't really much down there to my surprise, a box of newspapers too and a few old books"

"That's surprising" I smile and so does he

"The study was a lot too empty there were books everywhere, I've kept them all and boxed them up so once it's all painted and cleaned they can go back on the shelves and be sold with the house. The three rooms downstairs that were just used as storage one including a study, were kind of a nightmare to empty, but I've done it, most of that just went on the burn pile because there was loads of it and it was mainly junk and really old furniture that was just falling apart whenever I touched it" he sighs and then gets excited and jumps up "Ohh, I almost forgot, I found a weird thing in the floor of the parlour, come see"

I follow him down the corridor and into the parlour, it's almost empty, he pulls back the large light blue rug from the floor and reveals what seems like a small door

"What is it?" I ask

"I don't know, I didn't want to open it without you," he tells me with an excited grin, and he leans down and pulls the handle which has been carefully carved into the wood, I would imagine so that you would never know it was here. opening it up we find a small, extremely dusty wooden box, which has very beautiful carvings into it.

"What is that?" I ask

"I'm not sure," he tells me as he pulls the box out of the hole in the floor and we notice that its padlocked "Stay here," he tells me as he leaves the room and re-emerges moments later with a bolt cutter "This should do the trick"

I hold out the rusty old padlock so it's away from the box and he cuts, it takes several attempts, but it doesn't want to cut through. "Hold it tight Bea" I do as I'm told, and he squeezes the bolt cutters, after 30 minutes of trying he finally cuts through it, he removes the broken rusty padlock and carefully lifts the lid on the box. I sit down beside him, Inside we find that the box is full of a small amount of paperwork, and then what looks like a bundle, Bow pulls it out and he starts to read.

"What does it say?" I ask

"It's the original deeds to Dawnwood Manor" dated back to the 1800s

"Wow, that's pretty incredible, May I?" I ask as he continues to read

"Please do" he gestures into the box

      I reach in and pull out two books and notice there are more below – all classics, one is Lewis Carroll's Alice in Wonderland, and the other is Tess of the d'Urbervilles by Thomas Hardy "These are really old Bow, look at them" I hand him Alice in wonderland, and he opens it, I also sit and open the book by Thomas Hardy that I'm now dying to read. But when I open it up and start to look through the pages I'm shocked at what I've found, the first few pages look perfectly normal and when I turn about twenty pages in I notice the middle of the book has been cut out and there are thousands of dollars all folded neatly within it, "Bow look!" I say handing him the book "look at this!" he takes it from me, and his eyes light up.

"Wow, I can't believe this, this will really help with the renovation, what's in this one I wonder" he starts to open all the books within this box all containing thousands of dollars, there are about twenty-one books in total, he gets to the last book and opens it up and to our surprise this time it doesn't contain any money but a letter and a small box.

9th October 1807

Dear Lord or Lady Tanner,

I hope this letter finds you well, if you are reading this you have already discovered our treasured secret, We have no use for it and have decided to place money in this box every year so that there is money to fall back on, should we need it or that you our ancestors, can have a better life, use it well.

You will also find the original deeds to our family home Dawnwood Manor, by the time you find this we will have been and gone to join our loved ones. we hope that this will have been in our family for centuries and that our only request is that you keep Dawnwood Manor within your family/ our family.

My darling wife, Daphne has also concealed her engagement ring in hope that it will bring you as much happiness and laughter as it has us.

Greatest wishes

Daphne and Philip Tanner

1807

"Wow…. this is incredible, what an amazing find and a wonderful thing to do," I tell him excitedly

He's silent for a moment "I don't know what to say, there are so many small treasures here" he looks back into the box and he pulls out a picture of who I can only assume are Philip and Daphne, they are the most beautiful couple and look like they were very well respected. Daphne is wearing a floor-length dress and it looks to be light in colour with a darker edge to it with the matching headpiece, her hair is dark and pinned to the top of her head and she has a very kind and gentle face, and Philip looks very smart in his dark, buttoned-up tails jacket, top hat with light-coloured trousers, he also has dark hair and a moustache that curls a little towards the ends, he looks like a very strong assertive man but with very kind eyes, kind of like Bow's. We also find newspapers at the very bottom which has every detail of life at this period in time and it's all very interesting.

"What a beautiful couple and this is all so interesting Bow, in their letter they are asking that you keep Dawnwood Manor in the family, what are you going to do?"

He closes and picks up the box and then places it back in the floor where we found it "I know all that money should go to the bank, but I don't really feel it's right that it leaves the house, I really don't know what I should do now finding out all that information, I didn't realise the house has been in the family for so long. I just thought Grandpa Bill and Nana Clara had bought it all those years ago, you know when they married"

"I know I get that, but I guess it's never really something you ask is it," I tell him

"No but I don't think we should mention this to anyone," he says gesturing to the box

"Agreed," I tell him "You can't trust anyone around here, some people can just be out for themselves in this little town"

A little while later, we carry on with Bow showing me around the house. We walk up the beautifully carved wooden staircase this is the only thing that hasn't changed, but I notice he's pulled the dirty brown carpet up off the stairs and it now creaks as we walk up it. Getting to the landing he gets very excited as we stand outside the bathroom door.

"Look at this," he says as he opens the door, I notice all of the peach bathroom suites have gone, all the tiles, the bath, matching toilet, and sink, and that the carpet has been lifted from the floor revealing the solid oak wood flooring. It's the same in the second bathroom, which was once a sage green.

"Wow look how hard you've worked in here; I feel like I've missed out on all the fun"

"You have, it was fun chipping all the tiles off," he tells me

We then make our way around each bedroom I think he must have worked really hard, the wallpaper in each room has been removed all apart from the deep blue colour which has been left in Bow's bedroom because it's been painted on the brick walls, we will have to paint over that soon and by looking at it, it's going to take several coats of paint to cover.

"Well, I guess all that is left is to put everything back and redecorate and then we just need to tackle the outside and the garden am I right?"

"No there's the attic room and then all that"

"I almost forgot about that, it's my favourite room in the whole house"

"It hasn't been touched for years and I haven't even been up there yet"

"C'mon then let's go," I say

"Not yet"

"Why not?"

"You can only go up there if you go out on that date with me this weekend" he smiled a cheeky grin

"Hey……That's bribery"

"Will you go out on a date with me this weekend?"

"Will you let me go into the attic room please, I really want to see it"

"Oh, c'mon Bea! It's one date, you know…… it's only a few hours of your time"

"I want to see the attic" I reply with a smile

"Saturday night, me, you and a date"

"Okay, fine, yes" I smile "can we go now?"

"Yes?"

"Yes" I laugh

"YES" he shouts "Okay let's go then" he takes my hand and in one swift motion, he drags me up the small, single spiral staircase that is found within the library, to the back of the room on the right. This staircase is also very ornate just like the big one downstairs and we giggle as we make our way up it.

When we reach the top I turn and look at Bow "You nearly pulled my arm out of its socket" I laugh

"Well, I wanted to share this moment with you"

We stand there looking around speechless, The attic is larger than I remember but also as full as I remember, there are cardboard boxes everywhere and lots of household belongings, free-standing lamps, old furniture, a cradle, and lots of old suitcases that I think must contain treasures, Bow starts by opening a box.

"I think that we should take all these down into the living room then we can make a start and go through them, then the things I want or need to keep can be placed into the dining room with the rest of it"

"Okay good idea," I say as I walk over to the huge, round, ornate window, and call Bow over to show him what I'd found "Wow, Bow come look at this"

He walks over beside me "Oh lord"

"They never changed it, or put it all away"

"No obviously not," he says, and I know he's just as shocked as I am

In front of us, in a small area in front of the huge window, kind of like a circle has been made out of boxes, there are toys like trains, books, old dolls, old China cups and saucers, books, old small metal cars and teddy bears, as well as fake beds we'd made as children and a tepee in the left-hand corner, but also a rocking chair to the right of the large window, I could just imagine Nana Clara sitting there enjoying the view while sewing or reading a novel.

We both stand and smile at the sight, I thought they would have got rid of all of this he smiles. "I need to get an empty box to box it all up and then I can put it in the dining room, it's such a shame to get rid of it all"

"Okay well let's make a start on all this first then we can find an empty box," I say motioning around the room.

We spend the morning taking all the boxes down into the living room, its hard work but we both can't wait to see what's in each box, by 2 pm that afternoon we have brought the final box down

"I make that forty-two, you?" Bow asks me

"Yep, me too, forty-two is a lot of boxes"

Bow starts with box number one; he opens it up to find inside clothes that were once his Nana Clara's, all of which were from different periods in her lifetime.

"Bea, can you go empty this on the bonfire, please? I don't think theres anything in here I want to keep, plus a lot of this has got a little damp and marked, Then we can use the box for the little bits and pieces that are in front of the window up in the attic"

I nod and take the box and do as he asks, coming back into the room holding the empty box, I watch as he starts to open the other boxes, he finds lots of old clothes. Men and women's, I notice on the side that the box reads Grace and Simon, I realise that the ones he's going through are in fact his parents. He carries on going through the next seven boxes that are full of their clothes and I realise it's suddenly becoming all too much for him.

"Bea could you……." And then it's like he can't speak.

"Of course," I say as I start to pick up the boxes and take them out to the bonfire that we're due to light tonight. On my way there I take out two sweaters that once belonged to his parents and on the way back I head to his truck and carefully place them under the passenger's seat, I'll do something with those later, I think to myself. I then walk back into the lounge.

"Bow, are you okay?" I ask him

"Yes, I just need these gone, it's just clothes," he tells me but I'm not sure if he's trying to reassure me or himself

"Okay let's get these gone," I say doing as I'm told; I take box after box out to the bonfire. I carefully search through Grandpa Bill's and Nana Clara's clothes to find two more sweater's. When I find them I also place them into his truck along with his parent's ones, I plan to make them into cushions in memory of them so that he will always have a part of them with him.

A short while later I have taken all of twenty-two boxes out to the bonfire all containing his mother and fathers clothes, as well as his grandparent's clothes too. They must have been put there when his parents had died in that tterrible car accident when we were kids, and then when Clara died too I know it broke him, they were eve so close, she kind of took over from his parents when they passed away, I know Bow once mentioned that Grandpa Bill would keep his winter clothes up in the loft so that he could swap them over with the summer ones throughout the year and I'm starting to wish he hadn't. The rest of the boxes that have been left unopened he decides to keep and that they are too painful to go through at the moment, so we place them all in the dining room, nearest the door so that we know we still needed to go through them. We decide to head up to the attic and box the toys up using the empty boxes.

"What do you want to do with these?" I ask as I start placing it all into the box

"Well, I'll keep them for the moment," he tells me

I stop and stand there looking out the window, Bow comes to stand beside me and then placing his arms around my waist he pulls me into a tight hug.

"I hate that you only have two weeks left here," I tell him as I snuggle into his chest

"I know, it sucks doesn't it, but I'll be back, and you have my number, plus now I need to come back to figure out what to do with this place don't I"

"But I might have gone back to Chicago by then," I tell him

"It won't be that bad I promise, we can video call, speak on the phone and text all the time, you'd probably use your phone more than you do now" he jokes

I smile looking up to him "I know I'm terrible at using it aren't I, kinda repel technology" I tell him, and he bends down to kiss me, that's when I see it up in the beams of the roof.

"What's that?"

"What's what?" he asks

"Up there" I step away from him and try to reach it

Bow beats me to it, he reaches up, grabs, and pulls down what seems to be letters bound together with string "What is this?" he asks out loud

"It looks like some sort of letter," I tell him

"But from who"

"Maybe it's more from Philip and Daphne, quick open it up"

We sit on the floor both of us cross-legged once again and open them, I take the first one and read it aloud:

Wednesday 9th December 1936

My Darlin Clara,

I miss you terribly, I am counting the days until we're back together, I know my trip was only supposed to only last 2 weeks but unfortunately, it has been extended and shall be a little longer, I can't give you an idea as to when, but I can tell you that I will think of you every single day, Morning, Noon and Night.

I can't wait to come home and make a start on our future my darling wife. I can't wait to hold you, worship you and make you happy every day for the rest of our lives.

With you, I become a better person, thank you from the bottom of my heart. I am and always will be totally devoted to you.

I love you with all my heart

Your William x

After I've finished reading, I turn to Bow "These are your grandparent's letters that they must have sent to each other in the past. I guess your Nana Clara kept them after all this time, I bet she would sit here in the window then reread them, occasionally looking out to check if he were walking up the driveway, gosh this house is definitely full of surprises isn't it"

"It is that, but that would explain the rocking chair that was up here," he tells me

"We have to put these somewhere safe," I tell him

"I know just the place," he tells me as he reaches up and places them back on the beams "They've been safe here all this time"

"But what happens if you decide to sell the house"

"I'll cross that bridge when I come to it," he tells me "plus it's growing on me"

Chapter Ten

Willow

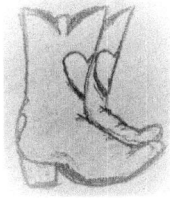

It's Saturday, the morning of my date with Bow. I have to go into town and meet Willow, also to collect my laptop, and to read through and sign the paperwork she needs me to sign for the university then I can submit my final and then I thought we'd do lunch at the same time, perhaps at Rose's, which I felt might give Willow a real southern experience.

I leave the house and get into my truck, before setting off to drive I send out a text message firstly to Willow.

"I'm on my way, see you in 5 minutes"

Okay, I'm by a large sign called Stitch???"

"Okay, Yep, I know where you are!! See you soon"

And the next one I send out is to Bow

"I can't wait to see you later"

"Me either, wear something nice, we're going out of town"

I smile a wide-tooth grin at his reply, I'm so excited that I can't hardly contain it, but firstly I must see Willow and then find something nice to wear. I start the engine and make my way down into the town. I drive through taking in all the little shops and that's when I see her standing outside Stitch, looking very lost and even more out of place than normal and it makes me smile.

I pull up, parking in front of her and stop the engine, getting out I give her my biggest hug, I've really missed her

"Strange little place this isn't it," she tells me when she lets me go taking a step back.

I laugh "Well it's certainly different from Chicago"

"I know right people even talk to me in the street here" she jokes

I laugh again "Well it's good to have you here"

"It's good to be here, Oh while I remember you better take all this," she says handing me a bag containing my clothes and another one containing the paperwork that needs signing and my laptop too, I decide to place my clothes in the truck and take the other bag containing the paperwork and my laptop with us.

"Thanks, Willow,", I tell her, "I thought we'd get some lunch where I use to work and then You could come back and meet my family"

"Well, a girls gotta eat" she jokes as we walk down the street "So tell me any nice cowboys around here?" She says looking around the street

"Willow you've been here like five minutes" I laugh

"Well got to give me something to look at" she laughs and winks at me

"There's not much around here to look at," I say trying to hold back my laughter as we walk into Rose's

"Well, isn't this a funny looking place," Willow tells me as she stands in the doorway looking around

I shh her and smile, rolling my eyes "Hi Rose, could I have a table for two, please?

"Right over there Sweetie," she tells me pointing to the spare ornate table and purple and orange armchairs over by the window, I look around and notice how busy it is and think, yeah she's right she could definitely do with some more staff, it's so busy in here today almost like it used to be.. When we're seated, I take out the paperwork Willow has bought with her and start to read through it, Rose is with us in an instant.

"What can I get ya?" she asks as she sighs, and I notice she seems stressed

"It's busy in here today isn't it Rose" she just nods looking exhausted "I'll just have a latte please, Willow?"

"Ooo I'll have the same please and one of those yummy looking blueberry muffins over there, ooo and one of those club sandwiches too please," she says pointing to the counter. This girl is as skinny as a rake, but boy does she love her food.

Rose nods and goes back to the counter to fetch our order as I continue to read through the paperwork.

"I think you just need to sign the back page, or that's what they told me anyway" she informs me

I nod as I continue to read on, I always read everything thoroughly before signing anything, you never really know what you could be signing up for. When I finally get to the back page I sign my signature and date it, Willow sits there looking around the café, as if lost.

"It certainly is different here isn't it," she tells me again and it makes me laugh because I know this is definitely a bit different to what she's been used to, not only back in Chicago but California too. "Everything's so relaxed and chilled isn't it"

"Yes I guess you could say that," I tell her "people here are so chilled and not a lot bothers them"

Rose comes over with our drinks and then a voice appears behind me

"Here again?"

"Haven't you finished stalking me, Spence?" I say not even bothering to look at him as I continue to read

"That's my job I'm an officer of the law," he says looking at Willow who perks up and looks directly at him with those bedroom eyes.

I speak to her not bothering to look up from the paperwork, "Don't waste your time honey, this one's got commitment issues" I feel Spencer roll his eyes and Willow laughs

"Not from around here Sweetheart?"

Willow shakes her head "Nope, originally California and I moved to Chicago about three years ago where I met this southern belle" she tells him nodding her head in my direction "The names Willow" she says as she holds out her hand for him to shake.

"Well, it's nice to meet you, Darlin," he says taking her hand and then tipping his cowboy hat forward

"Leave her alone, she's not for you Spence, I'm serious get back to work or I'm calling the station"

"Like that will make any difference, I'm in charge" he scoffs

"Then I'll call Mama," I tell him

"Okay, Okay no need to be like that," he tells me, his face now serious

And Willow laughs "I'm bringing her home later to meet everyone before my date with Bow, I thought she could hang out with Ruth and Mama tonight"

"I'd definitely like that," she tells me giving Spencer that look that I know too well

"Ahhh tonight's the night is it?" he teases "Well, I might catch you guys later then Darlin," he says tipping his hat again, then winking at her and finally leaving us

"Who was that?" Willow immediately turns to me and asks as she picks up her latte then looking after him

"My brother Spencer, Like I say don't waste your time, he's a total man whore"

"Hmm, Well he can arrest me anytime"

"Willow, eww that's disgusting," I say, and we both laugh

I finish signing and place the paperwork back in the bag, before handing it back to Willow, then making sure I've taken my laptop out

"So, tell me how's everyone back in Chicago?" I ask her as I watch her take a bite of her club sandwich

"Well, everything's the same really, the restaurant is really busy. Daisy handed in her notice last week so she's leaving; she wants to pursue her career as an exotic dancer"

"Ohhhhh…Aww, that's a shame I really liked her but I'm glad it's so busy, Carlos and the family doing okay?"

"Yeah, they're fine, but I do really need to tell you something?" she tells me suddenly very serious

"Okay, what is it?"

"Bea…… It's Albert"

I smile when I hear his name "I bet he's been keeping you guys on your toes and missing me"

"Well, he did, Bea I'm really sorry to have to tell you this but he passed away"

"What? When?"

"Last Wednesday"

My Stomach drops and the tears start to come, and I don't know what to say

"Bea I'm so sorry," she says as she takes my hand "It was a real shock for all of us, he didn't turn up for his reservation on Wednesday night, Caroline finished early and knocked on his door on the way home because it's so unlike him, I mean he's never missed a reservation in the last five years. No one answered and the neighbours hadn't seen him all morning but when Caroline looked through the window, she could see him slumped in his armchair, I'm so sorry Bea I know you too got on so well"

I take a long sip of my latte, tears still rolling down my face "Thanks for letting me know Willow, it's just a bit of a shock…. He was such a lovely man"

"It's okay it's bound to be, I didn't really want to tell you over the phone, I didn't feel it was right" she gets up and hugs me "but at least he's with Josie now and he missed her so much," she tells me as she takes my hand

There's silence between us.

"So anything you want to do today?" she asks me as she takes another bite into her club sandwich.

I grab a napkin, blow my nose and wipe my face on the back of my hand "Well" I say taking a deep breath "I need to go to Stitch, the clothing store just down the street and to get something to wear for my date tonight"

"Okay well let's do that then, and you have to tell me all about this guy"

We finish our lattes and Willow takes her muffin with her; gathering our things. Willow picks up the paperwork and I pick up my laptop, We head to the truck first so we can put them in their safe and then head over to Stitch, I tell her all about Bow Tanner and how wonderful he is and about how I'm helping him renovate Dawnwood Manor

When we get there, we look through the racks and I can't find anything that I really like.

"What about this one?" Willow says pointing at a yellow flowy one

"I don't think yellow really suits me"

Willow picks out a few more and I just shake my head, I look to the shop assistant, "Do you have any others?" I ask feeling deflated

"We've just had a delivery of new styles this morning, there all out the back, would you like to take a look?"

"Yes, please that would be great"

She gets up and heads to the back of the store "What size are you?" she asks

"I'm a U.S size 6"

She disappears and is back within minutes with five dresses in hand, she holds them up one is navy blue with a pink and yellow floral pattern, a purple bodycon wiggle dress (very simple but nice) and a very beautiful navy Bardot flowy dress also with a floral print, another fitted Bardot dress in an emerald, green colour, and a flowy black summer dress. I try them all on and decide it's between the emerald green one and the purple one, they both fit me perfectly.

I turn to Willow "What do you think of these?"

"Well, they're both stunning Bea"

"I knew you'd say that, but I can't decide between the two"

"So, get them both" Willow tells me with a mouth full of muffin

"I really shouldn't" but I stop and think for a moment, maybe I will, I turn to the shop assistant "Do you have a pair of heels and the matching bag that would go with both of these two?"

"They would both look lovely with these black lace ones and this matching black clutch bag or these silver, sparkly ones and this sparkly clutch bag," She tells me walking up to them and showing me them on the shelf which is all lit up with lights in behind. "Which would you prefer?

"Ummm...... the Black ones I think"

"What size shoes are you? She asks

"Size 38 please"

She picks them up and walks over handing them to me, for me to try on.

"Thanks," I say placing my feet in them and walking around the store, they're so comfortable, unlike most heels I've worn before. I take them off and make my way to the checkout, standing there I see that she has lip balm for sale and within the counter, I notice a pair of beautiful silver, sparkly earrings, "I'll take them too please" I say handing her my credit card.

When we're done we head to the truck, I turn to Willow looking at her and notice she has the remainder of her blueberry muffin around her lips, "Willow, just there" I say pointing to her lips and she lets out an embarrassed laugh. After I've paid we get in my truck. "Well let's take you to meet the family shall we," I say as we leave the town and head towards Pops and Mama's ranch and before we know it we're heading up the dusty track.

"This place is so beautiful, look at all the green fields" she says beside me.

"Nothing like Chicago, right?"

"No, it's much better than Chicago," she tells me "I'm never going to want to leave, it's just so green"

We pull up, grab the bags and as we get out of my truck, we're greeted by Mama

"Hello, my sweet girl," she says and then she notices Willow "Oh and you must be Willow, Welcome it's so nice to finally meet ya," she tells her as she pulls her into a hug, "Thank you for looking after our baby in Chicago"

"I think it's more like she looks after me, Mrs Coleman"

"We look after each other" I correct

"Come on in and meet everyone," Mama tells her as we follow her in through the kitchen "JEFFERSON!!" she yells "We have a visitor" she walks on into the living room and we follow her through to find my father sitting in his usual spot in his armchair by the fire, reading today's daily newspaper.

"Darlin," my Pop's says as he gets up and greets me kissing me on the cheek

"Pops this is my friend from Chicago, Willow Stedman"

"Well, Hello there Willow, Welcome to Franklin," he says with a welcoming smile "How are you finding it so far?"

"It's very pretty here Mr Coleman"

"Where are you staying dear?" Mama asks as she enters the room carrying a mug of Coffee for Pops and herself

"Just in a little motel down in the town….a placed called umm…the Red Fox, It's simple but rather cute," she tells them

"Oh no, no, no, we can't have you staying there honey, Can we Jefferson?" she turns to my father nudging him

"Oh no, it's not a very nice that part of town, you will stay here with us," He tells Willow as he takes a seat once more

"Oh no, I couldn't, I wouldn't want to impose," she tells them looking kind of embarrassed

"I'll set up the guest bedroom," my mother says as she places Pop's coffee on the coffee table in the centre of the room.

"Ohh, no, no, I couldn't possibly," Willow tells them again but my mother's out of the room before we know it and I assume she's headed for the guest bedroom, my father smiles at willow and I just look at her, as I place myself on the sofa with a smile on my face.

"Well, that's settled then, better go get your stuff, from that horrid place," my father tells her with a kind smile

I pat the seat and motion for her to sit down beside me on the couch

Clay and Dawson walk-in "Pops we've got that new foal arriving today, we're wondering where you want us to put her?"

"In the large one? Number four would do I think?"

"Yep, okay" and he turns to look at me and Willow who are now sitting on the sofa "umm, who's this?" Dawson says nodding in Willows direction

"Oh, hi, I'm Willow," she says standing and holding out her hand

"My friend from Chicago," I say

Dawson shakes her hand "She has friends??" he jokes with a cheeky smile, she then she shakes Clay's hand too, My mother pops her head back through the door, "Who's here for dinner?"

I briefly wonder how she has the ability of knowing that they have come into the house "I'm not, date night" I say feeling suddenly uncomfortable like all eyes are on me

"Me and Ruth will be when she finishes at the salon"

"And me," Clay says

"Willow?" my mother asks

And it's like she's taken by surprise "Ooo…umm yes please Mrs Coleman, that would be lovely thank you"

Mama nods and then says "Okay and dear but please call me Jennifer, Mrs Coleman was my mother-in-law," she tells her with a smile

---

A few hours pass and I spend most of the day showing Willow around the house (mainly showing her the rooms, so she has an idea of where everything is) and then I spend a couple of hours showing her around the ranch. I start by showing her the horses in the stables and the sheep's in the field, I take her down to the creek where we use to play when we were kids. When we get there we sit on the large rock, the sun is high in the sky and it's warm, I briefly think about the night me and Bow were here last.

"So, a date huh? tell me more about him" Willow asks

I nod "Well he's just someone I grew up with here, Dawson's best friend, and to be totally honest he's a really great guy, totally gorgeous, honest, caring, funny, he really gets me like know one ever has before and oh god when I look into his eyes, I literally just melt almost like I could lose myself in them…" she nods and we both say nothing for a few moments " But live in Chicago and…. And his life's in New York so I'm not really sure what will happen"

"Careful….You sound like you like him"

"I really do…. but like I say I'm not sure what will happen, but he's taking me out on a date tonight"

"Well, what are we waiting for? Let's go and find out" she says jumping up "Let's go get you ready"

"It's early and we need to go get your stuff from the Red Fox"

"Na that can wait, let's go," she says as she gets up and walks in what she thinks is the direction of the house leaving me sitting there on the rock.

"Willow it's this way," I say laughing at her, getting up and walking in the actual direction of the house, the next thing I hear are her footsteps running up beside me as I continue to laugh, she always was pretty headstrong and dippy.

"Yep, got it, this way," she says as she walks beside me

We finally make it to the house, walking on into the kitchen I find my mother cooking dinner at the oven and Spencer sitting at the kitchen table.

"Well, hello there Darlin, fancy seeing you here," he says in a southern drawl, I watch as Willow smiles, and I roll my eyes

"Give it a rest Spencer," my mother tells him "Beatrice can you just place the topper on the cherry pie on the side there please?"

"Mama… I really have to get ready for my date with Bow and then I've got to quickly go and get Willows belongings from the Red Fox"

"I'll do it," Spencer says "I'll go with her; probably best for an officer of the law to go with her down there anyway, you go get ready" he turns to Willow "Ya never know what could happen down at those motels"

I roll my eyes as she's hanging on to his every word "God no, I'm not leaving her with you"

"It's fine Beatrice, I'm happy here, plus you've got to get ready and it's only a little trip, then I can hang here with your family till your back, go n enjoy yourself "

"Okay…. only if you're sure…I just feel bad… I mean you've come all this way and…"

"It's fine" she repeats

"Hey you, Don't be silly, I'll look after her and keep her entertained, go get ready" Spencer tells me as Willow makes her way to the table to sit with him.

"Okay but I'm not sure about this," I say eyeing him as I put the topper on the pie then placing it in the oven and then with one final look at them both sat there, I start to make my way upstairs with my shopping bags in hand, making my way to my bedroom to start getting ready for my date with Bow Tanner

Chapter Eleven

Date Night

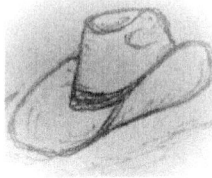

It's 6.25 pm and I stand looking in the mirror, the woman looking back at me looks so different, so much older, classy even. I've decided on the emerald green fitted Bardot dress with the black strappy heels, my hair falls in light curls down past my shoulders, but I have pinned it back so that it's off my face and I keep my makeup subtle, but you can tell I've definitely made an effort.

I walk down the stairs and into the kitchen, noticing it's goes quiet as I enter. my family and Willow all stop talking and freeze.

"Whoa" the first one to speak is Clay

"You look incredible," Willow tells me

Then there's silence

"Completely stunning if you ask me" a voice I instantly recognise tells me, I look to my right, behind the banister, in the doorway between the kitchen and the living room I see him standing there, leaning against the wooden door frame. He's wearing a grey 3-piece suit and tie; I suddenly feel like I've started to drool. I look at him with a huge smile and then at my family who suddenly starts talking again. Bow lets out a little laugh.

"Shall we?" he asks

I say goodbye to my family and Willow, then I nod to Bow, and we leave the house through the kitchen stable door. As we get to his truck he reaches into the back and hands me the biggest bouquet of red roses I've ever seen, they're absolutely beautiful and the kind gesture takes my breath away.

"Oh…… Wow thank you"

"Your carriage awaits my lady" Bow tells me opening the door

"Why thank you, kind sir," I say trying to hold back the laughter

I sit in the passenger's seat with the roses on my lap and they smell gorgeous and buckle myself in, I look back at the ranch and I can't help but notice the silowets of my family members in the window and I assume we're being watched. Bow has walked around to the driver last side of the truck and that's his seat next to me in no time.

"Thank you no one has ever bought me flowers before"

"No one?"

"Nope, no one"

"Wow you really must have dated some jurks"

"You could say that" I reply

there's a brief silence between us before he says

"Well, you deserve the best Beatrice Coleman, so you will get the very best,"

"Thank you," I say smiling at him "So where are we heading?"

"That would be telling and it's a surprise"

I giggle "A surprise huh, Am I overdressed?"

"God no Beatrice, your dress fits perfectly, and I mean wow, you look absolutely beautiful I guess is what I'm trying to say"

"Thank you, you don't look so bad yourself"

A wide smile spreads across his face. We drive down through the town, all the lights to the shops are off, all apart from Roses. I briefly wonder if we're going in there for our date and if we are, I'm way too overdressed, when he drives past, I can't help but feel slightly relieved.

"You didn't think I was taking you in there did you?"

"The thought did cross my mind"

"No Bea, I've got bigger plans for you," he tells me with a wink

We head for the freeway, and I briefly wonder if Bow goes on many dates. I wonder where we're headed, different places cross my mind, but I haven't taken this road in years, and it all looks so different. Bow leans over and puts on the radio, Josh Turner – your man, comes on and a massive smile stretches across my face.

"I absolutely love this song," I say to Bow "Kind of a guilty pleasure"

He looks at me and starts to sing

When the songs finished, I turn to Bow and can't help but smile "So how much further?"

"Roughly ten more minutes" he smiles

Before I know it we're in Nashville, I forgot how much I loved this place, there's never a dull moment here. As we drive through you can just hear music coming from the bars and the lights above them light up the sky. We pull up outside a hotel named "Ambitious" it's a tall building, very classy and it's all lit up, excitement fills me and I can't wait to go inside.

"We're having dinner here?" I ask, even I can hear the excitement in my voice

"Is that okay? I thought we could stay too, only if you wanted to that is?" he tells me with a weary smile on his face

"Stay here?.... together?"

"Well, I thought we could have dinner and maybe hit a few bars afterwards and then stay here the night, I've booked separate rooms just in case you wanted to stay, don't think I'm expecting anything like that Beatrice, I'm not that guy"

The valet comes over and take's our keys and Bow takes my hand wearing his biggest, goofy smile and leads me inside the revolving door. The floor inside is white marble as well as the matching pillars dotted around the foyer, and the grand staircase is right in front of us also made out of white marble. Looking at the banister I notice it's made out of a black and gold metal material, getting closer I notice it's been made to look like lots of golden leaves, The marble reception desk is to the left. Leaving me, Bow heads up to the receptionist and she points, I can only assume she's showing him the direction of the restaurant, and he motions for me to come over. I walk to him and look up to see the most beautiful Paris drop chandeliers and I notice there are around ten of them all dotted around the foyer, they take my breath away, this place is just stunning, and I don't think I'm ever going to want to leave.

"Are we staying sweetheart?"

I look up at him unsure of what to say "Umm" giving him my best smile and trying hard to contain my excitement "But no funny business" I say so only he can hear, and he nods

"So that's room numbers 203 and 204, your dinner reservation is ready when you are Mr Tanner, Mrs Tanner" she nods

"Ohhhhh no we're not…….."

"Thank you," Bow says cutting across me and he smiles and it's infectious.

We head down the hall and into the restaurant and head up to the waiter's booth.

"Mrs Tanner hey," I say so only he can hear, looking up at him and he just lets out a little laugh

"Do you have a reservation, sir?"

"Mr and Mrs Tanner," he says with a smile playing on his lips as I turn and look at him shocked again but also trying to stop the laughter escaping.

"This way Mr Tanner, Mrs Tanner," he tells us "May I take your coats?"

We hand them our coats and he leads us to a private enclosed table at the back of the restaurant away from all the other guests, Bow winks at me. We are seated at a well-presented table, the clean white tablecloth is pristine and neatly pressed, and the mahogany chairs are so comfortable, like the gentleman he is, Bow pulls my chair out for me to sit down, and it takes me by surprise, I've never been treated like this before.

"Thank you," I tell him as I sit, then he takes the seat opposite. I'm just about to address his little joke of Mr, and Mrs Tanner but the waiter is back in seconds with menu's and waits patiently beside our table ready to take our order

"Bea, Sweetheart what would you like to drink?"

"Could I have an elderflower gin and tonic please?"

"Ice, madam?"

"Please"

"And I'll have the house whiskey on the rocks"

He nods and disappears, We sit and read through the menu, it all looks very fancy and very expensive.

"Bow, this is pretty pricey"

"I know Sweetheart, it's fine I want you to have what you want, don't worry about the cost" he smiles

"Are you sure?"

"Definitely" he smiles at me just as the waiter returns with our drinks

"What can I get you both?"

I look up at the waiter and then back to Bow feeling a little nervous, Bow gives me a gentle nod as if to say go ahead order what you like. So, I turn to the waiter and say "I'd…..I'd love to start with the buffalo wings"

"Make that two" Bow tells him

"Then I think I'll have the BBQ ribs with the cob salad"

"And I'll have the steak"

"How would you like it, Sir?"

"Medium"

"Very good Sir and for dessert?"

"Ooo I'll have the cheesecake please"

"And the key lime pie"

The waiter nods and walks away, I look around and it's absolutely stunning here, I feel like I'm in a different world, not the one I'm used to anyway. Everything looks so classy, the wooden mahogany bar is to the back of the room with the bartender doing the fanciest cocktail's I have ever seen, he's throwing them around and catching them to mix them and it's all very impressive. The lights on the wall are very old fashioned and flicker like candles but it just adds to the charm of the room, six large chandeliers hang from the ceiling and the outside wall is made completely of glass which gives the impression that the room is larger than it is.

Bow follows my gaze "Do you fancy one? It's even more impressive when they catch the drinks on fire" he says as his eyes widen at the thought.

"I might do after I've finished this one," I tell him with a smile "I'm just curious to how they do it is all"

The staff are all dressed smartly in black and white and are very attentive, checking us for drinks and making sure we have everything we could possibly want or need; they just can't seem to do enough for us. The other customers all look so glamorous and high class. I briefly wonder where there from and if they are some sort of royalty, but as I look around the room, I notice that Bow has been watching me intently the whole time and it makes me blush.

"Thank you for bringing me here, it really is stunning, classy even"

"Your welcome, classy place for a classy young lady," he tells me taking a sip from his drink "And I kinda promised Dawson and your parents I would treat you right," he says as he takes another sip of his drink

I nod "But how can you treat me right if you're in New York?" the words are out before I'd even realised what I said

"Well, here's the thing sweetheart......... "he says picking up his drink and taking a further sip "We have something called email, video calls, text message and an occasional visit when we can"

"So, you mean long distance?"

"Well, yes for the time being and then I thought when you've qualified you could move from Chicago and come out to New York with me? I could help you find a job if you wanted to, I've got some really great connections"

"I don't really know if I can, my life's in Chicago Bow……. plus, what about Dawnwood, you can't sell that, not after we found Philip and Daphne's box"

"I don't think I will sell it; I've given this a lot of thought today and was thinking maybe I'll refurb it and use it as a holiday home. Listen, Bea, I know it's all very fast, but we have history and I really like you, maybe just think about New York yeah?" he tells me

I'm quiet for a moment and then reply "For the record…… I really like you too….. and I'm glad you're not going to sell the Dawnwood" I tell him, which makes me blush, it's all silent for a moment and then I finally say "I'll think about it"

"Good, I hope you do" he smiles at me

The next thing I know the waiter has appeared with our starter and places it in front of us "Wow, Bow this looks incredible"

"Can I get you anything else? Another drink perhaps?"

Bow looks to me and grins a wide-tooth grin something I learnt as a kid he would always do right before he would get up to mischief "Could we have some water please?…… and also, Mrs Tanner here would like to try one of your best cocktails?"

I roll my eyes but can't help but let out a little laugh at the fact that he's still referring to me as Mrs Tanner

"Will that be all Sir, Madam?"

We nod and we start to tuck into our starters they're just delicious the best buffalo wings I have ever tasted.

"These are so good"

"Aren't they, they just seem to melt in your mouth don't they"

"Mmm, soo good," I say with a mouthful

"So, tell me Bea what are your plans for the next five years"

"Well, that's a big question isn't it" and he nods "I guess I'd like to be successful as a publisher, own my own house in the middle of know where, have a nice family you know, a couple of kids, the dog, loving husband kinda like my parents did just without the ranch because that's way too much work, I want to a bit of a life and I guess I saw that my parents never stopped or have a break, still to this day they've never had a holiday abroad you know. What about you?"

When we've finished eating and the waiter is back to collect our plates with another waiter standing behind him carrying our main course, they swap the plates, and we look down at our main meals, my BBQ ribs look mouth-wateringly tasty, and Bow's steak looks just as good. The waiter leaves us and then brings over my cocktail that I'd forgotten all about.

"This one's on the house, terribly sorry for the wait Mrs Tanner.

"Oh, that's okay" I reply taking a sip and it's like the insides of my mouth explodes, its strong, how I like it, but also a hint of orange and strawberry in there and the coldness is very refreshing. "This is delicious, thank you," I tell him, and he smiles and walks away, I turn back to Bow who's also smiling "So you were about to tell me about your five-year plan?"

"Ahh yes, I was wasn't I, Well you know the usual, Become a multi-millionaire" he jokes "Na, I'm kiddin, in all honesty, I just want to be happy. I've got the dream job, the nice apartment, which can be sort of lonely sometimes, although I'd love the house in the middle of know where, the fancy car, the adorable family but I would settle for just being happy"

"Are you not happy now? I mean that's a nice thing to hear but are you not happy?"

"Kinda,Well, it's true I don't think you can buy happiness it just comes when you least expect it and sometimes from the places you would least expect, I am happy of course I am, I mean I'm here with you and spending time with you makes me happy, happier than I've ever been but I would like to continue with that happiness. Anyway, enough of that, let's eat"

We tuck into our main meals, and they are just incredible, possibly the best ribs I've ever tasted, I remind myself not to mention that to Pops, he'd certainly take that as an insult, he always thinks he's the king of the grill but these just melt in my mouth and fall off the bone, the cob salad is also just as good.

"Bow the food here is just……. I mean…. Just wow, it's got to be the best I've ever tasted, I mean I thought the food at Carlos's restaurant back in Chicago was good, but this is really something else"

"It really is very good isn't it"

By the time we've got to dessert I'm totally stuffed, The waiter comes over to take our plates, Bow gestures to him that we need a little while before we eat anymore.

"I'm' glad you said that god I'm so full, I think I'm going to burst" I tell him

"Pft me too," he tells me breathing out "So I've got a little surprise for you after dinner"

"Another one? as if this isn't enough" I pause "You know you don't have to do all these fancy things for me"

"No but I like to, plus I can"

"Hmm…. but you need to put that money towards the house renovations"

"Are you telling me you don't want to go?" he jokes with a wink

"No, I mean, of course, I want to, I mean it's nice that you would even consider doing something for me"

He smiles from across the table "So let's finish up here and go then" he signals for the waiter to bring our puddings, they also look incredible, the cheesecake is huge, and the key lime pie looks just as big. I take a small amount and place it into my mouth, and it just melts.

"You have to try this," I tell him, placing more on my fork and putting it by his mouth for him to try. He opens and tries it.

"That's real good, you always did love a cheesecake," he tells me "Try this sweetheart"

I try it and it's both tangy and sweet, but also creamy. "That's possibly the best key lime pie I've ever tasted!" I tell him

We finish our desserts, and the waiter is back in seconds "Mr and Mrs Tanner, did you enjoy your meal?"

"Very much so Kristoff, thank you," Bow tells him

"Your welcome Sir, can I get you anything else, perhaps a coffee?" he looks to both of us"

I'm about to answer with a yes when Bow beats me to it "No, we probably should get going" he says as he hands the waiter, Kristoff his card then he looks at me and I obviously don't hide the disappointment on my face very well, although we have been sat here for around two and half hours already. "You know we have that surprise to get to," he tells me

We get up and Bow takes my hand as we head for the exit, the waiter's hands Bow his card and receipt, and we head towards the cloakroom to retrieve our coats. Bow then leads me to the exit and through the revolving door and out onto the street. luckily, it's a warm night and he takes my hand as we cross the street, we come to a bridge, standing there in the centre of it, and I find myself wrapped in his arms looking out across the water of the Cumberland River.

"C'mon this way," he tells me wrapping an arm around me as we walk to the other side of the bridge when I look below, I see a beautiful boat with fairy lights all wrapped around the ropes and masts, we head on down and are greeted by a guy that I can only assume is the captain.

"Thanks for doing this Jerry" Bow says shaking his hand, we are then approached by one of the cabin crew who hands us both a glass of what I can only guess is champagne

"Wow Bow this is incredible"

He just smiles clearly unsure of what to say to me. "Shall we?" he asks as he gestures towards the back of the boat and then we head on through to the seating area. "I thought this would be a nice spot for us to spend some time together as we are both aware that both of our time here is short" As we sit, the cabin crew comes out and places another bottle of champagne in an ice bucket beside me and some nibbles on the table in front of us,

"This really is something special you know, I've never been out on a date quite like this Bow, thank you, it must have taken a lot of organising and the cost must have been out of this world"

"It's nothing really, I just want to see you happy, treat you how you deserve to be treated and be there for you"

For a moment I'm utterly speechless and all I can say is "I'd like that, you being there for me I mean, but I'm not used to this, this is all new to me, I don't get treated like this"

"I know you are, but you better get used to it Sweetheart" he says as he takes a sip of his drink "You know I've always had…..." and he suddenly stops himself

"No, go on," I say trying to encourage him with a smile playing on my lips

"No, it's embarrassing, forget I said anything"

"That's why you should say it," I say still smiling

"Ahh, god I don't know if I should"

I just look at him, smile and take a swig from my champagne glass, then sitting back against the seat I watch him, waiting for him to speak

"Okay, okay. Well, I've kinda always had a thing for you…you know I liked you, even when we were kids… I even asked Dawson if I could take you out once and he told me you were off-limits because you were his little sister"

"Why didn't you ever tell me?"

"Out of respect for your brother and I didn't think you'd ever go out with me, then Nathan was on the scene, and I thought I'd lost my chance" he pauses "Then when I heard you left… I was gutted and thought about calling but I didn't know how I could make it better"

"So, you coming home here wasn't a coincidence?"

"No that was definitely a coincidence, I honestly had absolutely no idea you would be here until Dawson told me what happened to Pops and that you might be coming home, but I was already in town and when I saw you in the Hideaway, I just knew I had to talk to you"

I blush "Well I'm glad you did," I say kissing him on the cheek

He smiles "You know you were always very carefree and caring towards everyone, I don't think you realise how special you are Bea and what differences you make in people's lives"

I just smile at him I'm unsure of what to say "You know you're a lot different to the guy I once remembered, the guy I remembered used to be very quiet and shy, and small and scrawny, and would gang up on me with Dawson, but you are…… I mean just look at you, you've finally grown facial hair" I laugh and so does he "you now have muscles and your definitely not shy and you're so, so caring and funny now" I laugh some more.

"Thanks, funny what puberty can do for you isn't it," he says laughing "But you, you haven't changed one-bit Sweetheart"

A member of the cabin crew comes over "Sir, are you ready to go?"

"Please Caitlyn"

She nods and leaves us, suddenly I hear the engine start up and notice the suns just starting to set

I stand up and lean over on the side of the boat "It really is beautiful here" I say looking around at the view "I never knew you could do this, thank you for bringing me"

"Your welcome, I'm hoping you'll let me take you out again"

"Maybe," I tell him with a wink "If your lucky" I smile

"Well, I consider myself to be a very lucky man," he tells me

We sail up and down the Cumberland River over the next couple of hours. Talking about old times and finding out about each other's lives, I find out that Bow has been on quite the adventure since he left all those years ago, he went to university when he finished high school, just like he had planned, then worked for a Law firm as an intern, where he was treated unfairly and he tells me that they did had a tendency to not do things by the book, so he decided to set up his own firm with the support of Grandpa Bill and some guy called Bruce that he trained with. he has also bought a fancy Modern apartment in the centre of New York City right near times square, which I find awesome, I know it's always busy there and full of people. Bow tells me that he'd been on a couple of dates but nothing like this before and the women he's dated haven't really been right for him, always wanting him for the wrong reasons or I guess you could say the wrong things. It seems I suddenly have so many questions for him, but I don't want to ruin the moment, I just stand there looking out at the sunset with his arms wrapped firmly around me and its nice to feel so safe and content, like nothing in the world matters but us two, I kinda feel I'm a way that no one else has ever made me feel before. I'm suddenly brought back from my thoughts when we hear a voice beside us that we recognise as Caitlyn's.

"Sir, Madam, more champagne?" she says as she hands us both another glass each

"Thank you," we both say

"A toast," I say "To new beginnings"

"To new beginnings"

I smile as we sit down on the white comfy padded seats, I snuggle in closer to Bow and the smell of his cologne fills my nose, I've noticed it's starting to get a bit chilly and it makes me shiver. "I'm going to miss you when you have to leave, I feel like I don't ever want to be apart from you"

"Your cold" he says pulling me closer, " And I know, but I will make sure that it will never be for long"

I smile lean up and kiss him, his lips are inviting and soft and kissing him just feels so right, everything about him is perfect, I snuggle a little further into his chest and it's warm and I love that I can hear his heartbeat. Before I know it, we've come to a stop, and we realise we're back where we started. Bow stands and holds out his hand for me to take, I take it in an instant. We head for the exit, and thank Jerry again as we leave the boat. We walk along the path arm in arm and head for the hotel "Ambitious", But little did we know we were being watched.

"That was just so lovely, thank you. Come to think of it the whole evening has just been like a dream and I'm waiting to wake up"

"It really has, but Bea you don't need to keep thanking me, I told you, you deserve the very best"

We get to the hotel and Bow walks me to my room, 203. He opens the door for me before handing me my room key.

"There are spare clothes in there for you for the morning, I had a member of staff here collect a spare set for you, I didn't think you'd want to do breakfast in that stunning dress of yours"

"I'm speechless Bow, that's really kind of you"

"It's nothing honestly"

I smile and he gently kisses my lips and then pulls me into a big cuddle, I just love being in his arms. He then kisses the top of my head before walking to his door directly opposite and saying "Good night sweetheart, I'll knock on your door in the morning for breakfast"

I just nod, I can't believe how he leaves me utterly speechless. I go into the beige walled room and slowly close the door behind me, making my way to sit on the queen-sized bed, I lay down on top of the freshly cleaned sheets and can't believe how respectful he is, he's just so different to the guys I've ever been out with, A wave of sadness flows over me, I don't want to be away from him, I don't want him to leave, and we've had the most magical evening. The feeling must be mutual because suddenly there's a knock on my door, I get up, quickly straighten my dress, and run my fingers through my hair trying to make myself look presentable and open it to see Bow standing there in front of me. He comes into the room pushes me up against the wall, his lips are quickly on mine, giving me the most passionate kiss I think I have ever had. He wants me I can tell by the way he's kissing me. He pulls away and looks into my eyes then says "I'm not expecting anything Beatrice, I'm sorry I shouldn't have done that...... I'll go now and see you in the morning sweetheart" he stands back and heads towards the door.

"No, I don't want you to go, please, stay with me and before you ask yes I'm sure"

He stops in his tracks, by the door, I then hear the click of the lock. He turns around picks me up and carries me to the bed and the next thing I know his gentle hands are on me.

Chapter Twelve

The Stranger

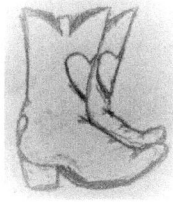

The following morning, I am woken by the sun beaming through the balcony windows, Bow is fast asleep beside me, and my head is on his chest and that's when I notice the tattoo of a lion on the left side of his chest. I can hear his soft breathing and his heart beating, it's calming, and he definitely feels like home. I lay there for what feels like the longest time, just watching him sleep, he looks so peaceful and content, I lean up and kiss him on the lips.

"Hmmm"

"Wakey, Wakey sleepy head" I playfully say

He opens his eyes and once again his lips are on mine. "Ohh, Good morning Sweetheart," he says in his southern drawl, and it just makes me melt

"Good morning," I say sitting up looking at him "Did you sleep okay?"

"Better than okay" he smiles pulling me down to him and trying to kiss me again

"No, no we don't have time for that, We'll be late for breakfast"

He sighs as I get up, wrapping myself in the white sheet and heading into the bathroom for a shower, stepping in, the water feels warm on my skin and within minutes Bow has appeared behind me wrapping his strong arms tightly around me and it's nice, he has a way about him that makes me feel so safe and loved.

"You are so Beautiful, Beatrice"

"Shh, you'll make me blush" instantly my cheeks flush and he places his hands on my naked behind "No that can't happen again. Stop it" I laugh trying to brush him off "Bow I don't want to miss breakfast when the food here tastes incredible"

He laughs "I'll make sure we won't miss it" he whispers in my ear "I just don't want our time to end so soon because as soon as we go down to eat then it's nearly time to go home and I want to enjoy the time we have left together"

"Hmm, that's true but I want to enjoy breakfast and plus you're here for another week"

He laughs "God what have I created, hang on a minute don't go anywhere" I watch him get out of the shower and walk out of the oversized grey tiled bathroom, he looks like he's been carved by the gods and then he's back in no time. He places his warm hands on either side of my waist and says "Now you won't have to miss it, room service will be here in an hour"

"An hours not very long, I thought you wanted to enjoy our time together" I joke with him

"Oh, and I will," he tells me as he wraps himself around me once more, kissing my neck and I can feel his smile against my skin.

We spend the morning in the hotel room "enjoying" each other, then around ten o'clock breakfast arrived, I have never seen so much food, there was fresh fruit, pancakes, waffles, French toast, cereal of all kinds, omelettes, muffins, doughnuts and of course there was coffee, Bow had also taken it upon himself to order four additional hit drinks including a latte, hot chocolate, peppermint tea and iced tea. We picked what we wanted, of course, went for a little bit of everything and then we spent the morning sitting out on our balcony, the view is beautiful, it looks out over the Cumberland River. We sit for a while, chatting and watching the boats go up and down the river and it's so peaceful, I kind of feel like I've stepped into one of the books I once read.

A little while later, When it's time to leave Bow takes our belongings and places them in a bag and we head downstairs to the exit to hand our room keys back. He then heads up to the valet to collect his truck and keys and as he does this, I'm left standing in the foyer, taking in its beauty. just then a stranger in a large dark long hooded coat approaches me, Their face is covered, and I can't tell if this person is male or female.

"Beatrice Coleman??"

"Yes"

"I thought it was you"

"I'm sorry, do I know you?"

"No, but I know you" and with that, they turn around and walk-off

"Hey, wait," I say but they keep on walking and as I try to look where they went, but the crowds are quickly around me and the stranger disappears.

"Bea, the trucks outside and ready sweetheart"

"Ohh okay" I paused turning to him then looking around again "Bow did you see that person in the large coat?"

"Large coat? Sweetheart, there are a lot of people here, C'mon let's get going"

I look around and the stranger has disappeared and is nowhere to be seen, I turn and take Bow's hand as we head to the truck, and then out of Nashville. On the way back we hardly talk we just sit chilling and listening to the music playing on the radio, it's a sunny, warm day with very few clouds in the sky and Bow is the happiest I've ever seen him., it kind of looks like he has that happy glow to him.

I'm the first to break the silence "Thank you for such a wonderful twenty-four hours, I just wish it could last longer"

"It could…...just in New York," he says with a cheeky smile

"Hmm maybe" I smile and turn to look at him and now it's starting to bother me who the stranger was back at the hotel "Bow did you really not see the person in the large coat?"

"No sweetheart, I actually thought you were trying to stall so we didn't have to go"

"No there really was someone in a large black hooded coat that spoke to me back at the hotel"

"Well, what did they say?"

"They told me my name and when I asked if I knew them, they know me and then they walked away"

"There are a lot of weirdos around Sweetheart, I don't think it's anything to worry about"

Nothing else is said on the matter after that, it's not important I think to myself maybe it was just some weirdo. We stop in at the Dawnwood Manor on the way to the ranch. when we get there, we notice the front door is wide open. I turn and look at Bow as panic fills me.

"Darn kids, they probably think it's empty and somewhere to play," Bow says

We both head in the house and take a look around, nothing has been moved, I mean what could they take or move, the house is empty, apart from the dining room, which we put a lock on that door the last time we were here, I know Bow has plans to start getting builders in next week while he's still here so he can overlook the work they do, and then he can start doing it back up and making it a home instead of it being the shell that it is now.

"Does everything seem okay to you?" he shouts down the stairs

"Yep, I don't think anything's missing, but you better lock the house and check the garage to make sure everything's there," I say as I walk out the front door, he meets me in the yard and walks over to the barn, the first thing he noticed is the lock

"Those BASTARDS!" he shouts, "They've cut the lock" and I can instantly see that panic fills him

He pulls back the door and inside we can visibly see that the Cadillac is still in there but some tools are missing and one of the vintage motorbikes, the blue one I think.

"For fuck sake, they've taken the blue Yamaha"

I'm totally speechless and can't believe what I'm seeing and if I'm honest I'm totally gutted for him

"Don't you find it a bit weird how it's been sat up in here for years and now that works being done on the house it suddenly goes missing" I finally say "I'll call Spencer and report it"

"Okay thanks, listen, Bea, you stay here, and I'll go get a new padlock, maybe we can deadbolt it from the inside and climb out the window out the back"

"Okay," I tell him "Pass me the keys I want to make sure everything's locked and secure in the house"

He throws me the keys to the house and then he's in the truck and speeding away. I head-on in the house and check every window and door to make sure they're closed and locked. I'm suddenly grateful that we put a yale lock on the dining-room door, the last time we were here. When I'm certain it's all locked, I stand outside the empty house and phone Spencer, he should be at the station by now, so I try there first. As the phone rings, I can't shift the feeling that I'm being watched.

"Good Morning, you reached Franklin police department, this is officer Daniels, What's your emergency?"

"Hey Jon, it's Beatrice Coleman, I'm up at the Dawnwood manor and we've had a break-in"

"Oh, hey Beatrice, how ya been?"

"Yeah good, but we've had a break-in"

"What? up at the ranch?"

"No Jon, Dawnwood manor" I roll my eyes as I repeat myself

"Oh, I always thought that place was empty"

"It is….was but now it's not, Bow Tanner has started renovations, he's had a break-in, and the house is fine because its empty, but a bike and a few tools have been stolen from the garage"

"Okay Beatrice, and what bike was it?"

"Umm, umm" I think hard trying to remember what it was "I'm really not sure….I think he said it was a Yamaha, I know it was blue and it didn't start because we tried that, so it would have had to have been pushed away or put in some sort of van or truck"

"Okay, Bea and what was the license plate?"

"Jon, no disrespect but I have absolutely no idea, it's been sat up in Grandpa Bill's garage for years, I'm not the owner but I just need to report it stolen, okay"

"Okay, Beatrice, if you should find any paperwork on it, you just let us know that would confirm the license plate, for now, we will just keep our eyes open for a blue Yamaha. I suggest you replace the lock and perhaps block the door somehow; it's probably kids Bea, but I'll keep you up to date if anything comes in, anyway, how's Spencer doing now?"

"He's umm" I pause and think for a minute and briefly wonder what he means "He's okay, why do you ask?"

"Oh, he called in sick early this morning, said he was really unwell in the night"

"Oh, that's right he said he wasn't feeling great after dinner last night, must have been a bad batch of seafood" I lie unsure if he's well or not

"Oh, yes that would definitely do it, Well got to go Bea nice talking to ya" and then he hangs up

I can see Bow driving fast up the long track, dust throwing up behind the tires, he parks the truck and gets out waving a large padlock at me and a new barrel key for the front door.

"I've spoken to officer Jon Daniels down at the station and he's said they will keep an eye out, but they need the licence plate, I've described the bike, but he's suggested we replace the lock and block the doorway.

"Okay but there's only one of us that will fit out the back window sweetheart and it's not me," he tells me as he gives me his cheekiest smile

"Ahhh," I say smiling back, his smile is infectious "It's fine, I'll do it; we start by placing the furniture by the garage door and blocking it up so someone would find it hard to move it all out of the way. Bow helps me climb over it all and then slides the door closed with me inside and I hear him place the padlock on, I push a few more things across the doorway and make my way to the bench at the back so that I can climb up and go through the little window, I pull the bench out so it's as far away from the window as possible but also close enough so that I can use it to push myself off of it to get through the window. As I do I can't help but laugh.

"Oh god, I didn't think it would be this small, I'm not exactly a skinny Minnie am I, I don't know if I can get through there" I shout to him and I can hear him laughing, I manage to pull myself through the window and Bow is there to catch me on the other side, "Hang on a minute it's stuck at my butt, I didn't realise it was that big" and he grabs my arms and laughs, finally he pulls me through and we both end up in a heap on the floor laughing.

It's nearly 3 pm by the time we pull up outside the ranch and we sit there for a moment, and I turn to him.

"Thank you for a lovely couple of days, even if some of it was unexpected" I laugh

"Your very welcome Bea, I was just thinking life would be so boring without you in it, this time next week's going to be tough on both of us"

"Yeah, but don't forget, we've got email, video call and text message" I quote his words to him, and he laughs as he hands me his business card which contains his email address and office number.

"If you can't get me on my personal number, here are the office one's," he tells me pointing to the card, "Louise my assistant will be under strict instructions to put you straight through"

"Oh, you really want a stalker don't you" I laugh

"You can stalk me anytime," he tells me with a wink. "Listen, Bea, can I see you tomorrow? I want to make the most of this week with you"

"I don't know, I'll have to send you an email to confirm" I wink at him

He smiles and kisses my cheek "I'm impressed that you know how to use email…Well, let me know"

"I might do," I say as I get out of the truck holding my huge bunch of roses and wave him goodbye

I head to the door and turn around watching him slowly drive back down the track, walking into the kitchen I notice how quiet it is, but my Mama is in her usual place, in the kitchen cooking over the stove.

"Hey Mama, that smells amazing, what ya cooking?"

"Oh, hey baby, I didn't realise you were home, oh its only meatloaf"

"Mmm smells good, Where is everyone?"

"Well Clay is away working, he left this mornin, Dawson and Ruth went out on the horses a few hours ago, your father is in his usual place, the living room and Spencer took Willow back to his place last night and I haven't seen either of them since"

"Oh, sweet baby Jesus! Mama, how could you let him take her back there?"

"She wanted to go and she's safe with him, you know he's an officer of the law and all"

I sigh "Hmm, that's not the point," I say running my hands down my face suddenly feeling like Willow has been a victim of Casanova, "Well I'm going to get my final finished and send it in to the university, I'll be out the front on the swing seat if anyone needs me," I say as I grab my laptop from the bag and head on out to the front porch. I sit there and it feels so warm sat in the sun and then I start to write. It's a couple of hours before I've finished and then I hit the send button to submit it to my professor. It's finally over I think to myself, just my graduation to go. I place the laptop down beside me and just sit taking in the view, it's stunning, the sun is beaming on the fields, and I know I'm going to miss this place when I have to go back to Chicago. I go to get up and head inside to get a drink, I just want to sit and enjoy the view while I still can, but just as I do I notice something on my truck that I hadn't noticed before, at first I think it's just the sun glaring on the windscreen, but as I slowly walk up to it, I realise it's an envelope. Bow must have put it there earlier I briefly think. I take it from under the wiper blades. suddenly getting all excited, how sweet is he I think to myself and when I open it, fear washes over me as I realise it's not from Bow and my face drops. The writing is all scribbled and in thick black ink.

Because of you, I never got the happiness I deserved, Karmas a bitch

Good luck getting around!!

I look around trying to see where or who could have put this on my truck. At first, I think it's a sad joke my brothers are playing on me but when I take a closer look, I notice all the tires on my truck have been slashed, looking beneath it, I notice the brake pipes have been cut and the headlights have been smashed too. Who in the world would do this I think to myself; my truck has been sat here for the last twenty-four hours. But also, how could my family not have noticed this. I pick up my phone and the first person I call is Bow.

It goes straight to voicemail "Bow, its Bea please call me as soon as you can, something weird has happened up here at the ranch, I think you need to check your truck and for heaven's sake please don't drive it"

The second person I call is Dawson, who picks up on the second ring.

"Hey, Bea, What's up?"

"Daw, have you been near my truck today?"

"No"

"Haven't played any tricks on me lately?"

"No," he says with a little laugh

"Haven't seen anyone around my truck?"

"No, Bea what's this about?"

"Daw, I've just got home, and all my tires have been slashed, the headlights have been smashed and the brake pipes have also been cut"

"WHAT?!, hang there Bea, were only down by the creek we'll be there in five minutes, you need to phone Spencer," he tells me and then he hangs up

The phone in my hand rings, I look down and see its Bow as I answer it I hear his cheeky tone, "You have an answer for me yet Sweetheart"

"Bow, Where are you?" I say my voice full of panic

"I'm nearly back at the motel," he tells me casually "You want to see me already, very cute that Baby"

"No, Listen Bow, I've just been out to my truck and the brakes have been cut, the lights have been smashed and the tires all slashed, are you driving?"

"I'm driving now sweetheart, yes" he voice drops sounding concerned

"Did you stop anywhere on your way to the motel?"

"Well, yes, I needed a few things, Bea what's this about?"

"Push your breaks"

"What?"

"Push your breaks on your truck," I tell him again

"Okay hang on" their silence for a few seconds and then he's back on the line "Bea, I don't think they're working"

"Ahhh, shit!" I say as I place my face in my hands

"Shit, What do I do?"

"Try and slow the truck down"

"It's not working," he tells me "Bea please know that I love you" And that's when I hear a loud bang and the phone goes dead.

"SHIT," I say as I start to cry

Dawson and Ruth come galloping up the field and jump off their horses.

"What's happened?" Dawson asks

"It's Bow, I think he's just had an accident in his truck, the phone went dead" I cry

"Okay, where is he?"

"On the way to his motel"

"Let's go, Ruth tell Mama and Pops what's happened" she does as she's told and runs in. Dawson pulls out his keys and we head for his blue truck.

"Wait," I say "We should check," I tell him gesturing towards it

He quickly takes a look around "All seems fine" he tells me as he jumps in the driver's seat, I get in beside him "You need to phone this through, and I'd phone Spencer as well"

I do as I'm told; I start first with the station and then Spencer. When I phone the station, Jon comes on the line again.

"Jon its Beatrice Coleman, there's been an accident involving Bow Tanner, he was on his way to the Turn-away motel just outside of town and his breaks have failed, I'm on my way there now with my brother Dawson but I think we're going to need an ambulance and you need to get down there"

"Okay Bea on our way," he says before he hangs up again

I then phone Spencer and it just keeps ringing and ringing, eventually, I just phone Willow because I know she'll answer, She picks up almost immediately.

"Bea I'm so sorry, I had no intentions of this happening

I cut her off, "Willow is Spencer there? I just need to speak to Spencer" my voice full of panic

"Listen Bea I know you're mad…..."

"I'm not mad I just need to speak with my brother" I shout as the tears run down my face

The next voice I hear is Spencer's "Bea I think you're overreacting just a little…..."

"Will you just shut up and listen," I say "Bow's in trouble, our brakes were cut on both our trucks and he's had a really bad accident"

"Where?"

"On the way to the Turn-away Motel, I was talking to him and told him to check his brakes and, and….." I can't finish the sentence

It's like Spencer already knows and then says "Okay, give me five, I'll see you there" he tells me, then he hangs up and the line goes dead

I sit there in absolute bits, the tears come, and I don't know what to do with myself "Can't you go any faster Daw? These are the only words I can master

"I'm trying," he says "But everyone seems to be driving really slow" he then pulls out onto oncoming traffic to overtake, putting his foot to the floor and heading towards the Turn-away Motel.

Chapter Thirteen

The Accident

We pull down the road and that's when we see the truck, he's driven off the corner and into the forest on the edge of town, it looks like it's rolled a couple of times, and like a crushed tin can. We get out of Dawson's truck, and we can instantly smell the gasoline. We both break into a run-up to what's left of Bow's truck, Please be okay is all I can think. The ground around his truck is all dug up from where the truck has slid on the moss and mud and the truck itself that was once a lovely black colour is now all covered in mud, bent and battered, as we get closer I notice that the windscreen is all smashed, every panel has major dents in it and there are scrapes and scratches everywhere. When we get to him, he's unconscious, it looks like he's in a really bad way. Suddenly I spot him there in the drivers seat, he's slumped down and his face is all cut up, it looks like he's broken an arm and from what I can see it looks like he's bumped his head pretty bad, his legs are trapped under the dash too. I frantically try to pull open the driver's door.

"It won't open," I tell Dawson my voice full of panic

"Out the way," Dawson tells me in a panicked tone as he tries to open it himself "It won't budge, its stuck Bea," he tells me as he runs around to the other side and after a lot of trying, he manages to open the passenger door, he swiftly unbuckles Bow and tries to pull him out of the wreckage, that was once Bow's prized truck. "We need to lift the dash; he's trapped under there" I jump up in the truck and try to lift up the dash but it's too heavy for me. "I'll push the dash up; you pull him out," Dawson says to me in a hurried tone

"Okay," I say as I lock my arms under Bow's and Dawson lifts the dash up and we manage to pull him out. Dawson grabs his feet, and we carry him back out of the way to Dawson's truck, putting the tailgate down and placing him in the back to wait for the ambulance and just like that the Bow's truck suddenly explodes.

"Oh shit, that was lucky," Dawson tells me trying to catch his breath. he bends down to check Bow's airways "He's still breathing" and he leans over and checks his pulse "He's definitely alive, he just needs to wake up, c'mon man, don't be so overdramatic, talk to me" he jokes but I can always rely on Dawson to try and lift the mood, even if he is worried sick.

"Bow, it's Bea can you hear me? if you can I'd really like it if you just opened them beautiful grey eyes…if you just open those eyes I promise I'll go out with you again… please" I sob as I try to be strong, but I can't hold it together anymore and I can't help but think that this is all my fault "Dawson I can't lose him, I love him" I take his hand giving it a gentle squeeze as I sit there with the uncontrollable tears rolling down my face. Dawson puts an arm around me and pulls me into a gentle hug, and that's when I notice he's also crying, In an instant, the ambulance arrives, followed by Spencer and several other police cruisers.

Spencer gets out of the cruiser followed by Willow "What the fuck happened here; We need some medical assistance over here" he shouts as he walks towards us.

The ambulance crew are with us in seconds, they carefully place him on a stretcher and are saying things I don't really understand then they place him in the back of the ambulance, and I follow with Dawson but suddenly Spencer stops us

"We're going to need statements from you two," Spencer says pointing to me and Dawson

"Let her go, Spence, she needs to be with him, you can take my statement now and get Bea's later" he tells in in a firm tone

He nods and I follow Bow into the ambulance, the next thing I know the lights and sirens are going and we're on our way to the hospital. The ambulance staff are very helpful and explain everything they're doing, they give him an IV and keep checking his pulse, When we finally make it to Williamson medical centre, they rush Bow inside and take him down to the theatre. I'm shown to the family room and inside I'm met by Mama and Pops, Ruth, Dawson, Spencer and of course Willow. Seeing them all stood there I just break. Dawson is the first person to come forward and hug me, when I finally pull away, I look up at him and realise he's also in bits and is all red-eyed. I can tell he's terrified of losing his oldest and dearest friend.

For a long time, we all sit there and say nothing, when finally, the doctor comes in.

"Are you the family of Bow Tanner?"

"We're his in-laws... kinda....... And old family friends too" my Pop's tells him "Can you tell us how he's doing doctor?"

"Well sir, it's not good, he was in a bit of a way, he's just come out of surgery. he's got a broken arm so he's in a cast, a head injury, and a punctured lung which we've managed to stabilise, but we've just got to wait for him to wake up I'm afraid, we're not sure if the head injury will have any lasting problems but at the moment it's just a waiting game, I'm afraid sir"

I'm shocked and terrified for him, I can't stop the tears from coming and I look to Dawson who I notice also can't control his emotions either "Can we see him?" I ask

"Not just yet he needs some rest, and we need to get him settled, plus Miss Coleman I have a couple of officers here that would like to speak with you"

I look to Spencer, "I'll come with you" We walk out of the family room and are shown to an empty private room on the ward. I sit on the bed and two officers come in

"Miss Coleman, Officer Coleman" they nod "We'd like to ask you a few questions about today's events Miss Coleman, where were you at the time of Mr Tanner's accident?"

"I was at my folk's ranch........I noticed there was a note on my car and then I noticed the brakes had been tampered with amongst other things, I phoned Bow......I mean Mr Tanner immediately to make sure he was safe, he told me he had stopped in town and was heading for his motel"

"Where was he staying?"

"the Turn-away Motel…then he realised his brakes weren't working……… I heard a bang and then the phone went dead"

"Okay Miss Coleman, so you believe he could have lost control of the truck?" Jon asks me as he scribbles everything down as I'm telling him, "and do you have that note to hand?"

"Umm, yes somewhere, hang on" I reply "yes here," I say pulling it from the back pocket of my jeans and handing him the note "and no Bow is a very sensible driver, I don't think he would purposely lose control of the truck or drive too fast, he's always a very safe, careful driver"

"Thank you," he says taking it and placing it into an evidence bag "do you know anyone that would have any reason to harm either of you?"

"Well, that's a stupid question isn't it Jon," Spencer tells him shooting him a dirty look as if to say don't be so stupid "they don't live around here and if they knew who done this, they would obviously tell us"

"Spence it's fine, no, no I don't"

Jon shoots Spencer an apologetic look.

"And was there anything else that you thought was strange that happened?"

I think for a moment "No, I don't think so"

"Okay that will be all for now" he nods but just as he's about to leave the room I stop him.

"Wait," I say and then I remember the stranger. "Bow had just taken me away for the night, as a surprise and this morning when we were leaving the hotel, someone approached me and asked my name" I suddenly feel Spencer's eyes on me as if to say you never mentioned anything and that I was in trouble. "They said I didn't know who they were but said that I would… when I turned to look for Bow and when I turned back to them, they had disappeared…oh and also there was a break-in at Dawnwood Manor but I'm not sure that's related with all this"

"And was this person was it a man or a woman?"

"I……. I don't really know they were in a really long, hooded black coat, I didn't see their face"

"Okay, Bea and what hotel?"

"Ambitious, I think it was called……. It's definitely in Nashville"

"We're on it"

"Thanks, Christine, Jon, Keep me in the loop yeah," Spencer tells them

"Yes, Sir," says Christine "Feeling better now boss?"

"Much, thanks," he tells her not quite meeting her gaze

Jon smiles at Spencer as he and Christine leave the room and it's as if he knows why Spencer called in sick, they have left us both standing there and Spencer is now glaring at me.

"Have I taught you nothing? Don't talk to strangers and you never give them your name" he starts then pauses and then there's silence between us "Do you really have no idea who that person was?"

"I would tell you if I did, I honestly have no idea Spencer; Do you really think I wanted this to happen?"

"No of course not…you don't have any enemies? or anyone would have any reason to hurt you? You don't owe anyone money or anything like that?"

"No of course I don't" I snap

"Okay well my bet is they saw an interest in you and followed you both home," he tells me calmly

"Why would they be interested in us? and why only do things to my truck and Bow's, it makes no sense. There are lots of other vehicles up at the ranch and none of them were touch apart from mine"

"No, I suppose that doesn't make sense, but people can be really weird, you know the worlds full of psycho's. But There's one thing you need to do now, or someone needs to do…" he tells me slowly

I look at him with a confused expression and I'm really unsure of what he's about to say

"Someone's got to phone Sienna, she's going to need to know about this"

A little while later I'm allowed to go in and see Bow. I pause at the door unsure of what I will find. When I walk in the first thing I notice is the room is dreadfully warm, it's a small white and blue room with a single hospital bed to the left of the room and the door wall is made out of frosted glass, beside the bed to the left is a small bedside unit and on the right is a monitor. Looking at Bow I can't help but notice his face is all cut up and he's covered from head to toe in bruises, with his arm in a sling and his head is all bandaged where he must have bumped it in the truck. There are tubes and wires everywhere and the monitor beside him is beeping consistently, with another making a noise which I can only assume is his oxygen. I'm almost afraid to touch him, I carefully sit down beside him gently taking his hand, I'm not sure if he'll know I'm here or if I should say anything but the tears now start to escape and are rolling down my cheeks.

"I'm so sorry Bow......I don't know how this has happened" I whisper as I wipe my face on the back of my sleeve "Who could do something like this to you"

A few hours pass, its dark out and my brother Spencer comes in and sits beside me.

"Still no change?" He asks

I shake my head.

"We're going to head home; I don't think there's a lot we can do at the moment. Why don't you come with us too? The staff here are brilliant, he'll have the best care and you could really do with some rest, they've said they'll call if there's any change.

I shake my head once more

"C'mon, just for tonight, plus you look terrible, you're covered in blood and mud and to be honest with you Bea you look like shit"

"I'm not leaving him Spencer; this is all my fault"

"This is not your fault, you've done nothing wrong Bea, I've got my team looking over your truck and what's left of Bow's, also we've asked for security footage from the Ambitious hotel so hopefully that will give us an idea of who this person is. I need to let you know Bea that we've also contacted Sienna, she has a right to know what's happened"

I nod "How was she?"

"Well, she took the news pretty well and told me that she would try and get down here over the next few days"

"Okay, Thank you"

"Okay" he replies "I'll keep you updated with what we find," he tells me as he heads for the door

"Thank you," I say as I watch him walk to the door and turn back to look at Bow "Oh, Spencer will you do me a favour? will you check up at Dawnwood?"

"Of course, but why?"

"We had a break-in up there while we were away, didn't Jon tell you?"

"No, he must have forgotten to mention it, I'll check it out"

"I don't think it's related but you know just in case"

He nods and gives me a hug, then leaves the room. I spend the next few days at Bow's bedside, almost afraid to move, not wanting to leave him. I just want to be here when he wakes up and I just sit watching the doctors and nurses come in and out of the room, they do what they need to do then leave again. It's around lunchtime and I have my head rested on the bed, beside Bow's hand that I'm holding. A few more days pass and still, there's no change and I feel exhausted. My family and Willow have visited every few days bringing me spare clothes and snacks, and Ruth has taken to texting me every day just to check in but it's been weeks and yet we still haven't seen or heard from Bow's sister, However, Dawson comes to check on him every day around dinner time. Days have passed and they eventually turn into weeks, three to be exact. The staff have been amazing allowing me to use the showers when Dawson comes in to keep Bow company and providing me with hot meals too, I don't want Bow to be left on his own, you know just in case there's any change.

It was a sunny morning and I have taken to reading to Bow every day in hope that the sound of my voice might wake him, sometimes I read him the local news other days it's a couple of chapters from a book. Today is a Wednesday and Dawson had visited at lunchtime and we had lunch together, my mother had prepared us both a brown bag lunch just like she used to when we were children. Finally, today's the day that Bow has been taken off oxygen, so he's able to breathe on his own. When Dawson left, I felt exhausted, I just lay my head on the side of the bed by Bow's hand, and I must have drifted off. A little while later, I think it must be mid-afternoon/ early evening, I hear the sound of a lady's high heels tapping as she walks across the floor, that's when I notice a very well-dressed lady has entered his room, I think she must either be another part of the police force that Spencer forgot to introduce me to or maybe she's a hospital official, I lift my head and blink, trying to focus my eyes.

"Beatrice Coleman," she says pausing "Ahh honey, how you doing, How…. Ya……Doing," she says slower the second time

"I've been better," I say through exhausted eyes "I'm really sorry I don't mean to be rude….. but who are you? If you're a lawyer or a reporter, then no comment" I tell her

"No Beatrice, I'm not a reporter or a lawyer I'm afraid, I'm ahh… just a friend of the person who put him in here," she tells me as she nods towards the bed "You don't remember me do you"

I suddenly sit bolt upright in the chair and stare at this woman, terrified, who is she? I vaguely recognise her face, but I'm so exhausted and dazed that I can't place it.

"What did you just say?" I'm silent, I don't know what to say to her "YOU put him in here?" I say my voice getting louder

She nods "No need to shout or scream Beatrice, you need to hear me out first and I don't want to have to hurt you," she tells me as she flashes a gun beneath her black suit jacket.

I'm in total shock and start to panic "Who do you think you are! Get out, now!" I slowly reach down on the seat I'm sitting on, making it look like I'm just fidgeting, reach for my cell and dial Spencer's number.

"Oh, you don't recognise me at all. Well, it has been a long time, but you're going to want to hear what I've got to say, plus this is much bigger than you"

"I don't have to listen to this" I hiss at her as I go to stand

"You don't want to do that Beatrice, sit back down," she tells me in an intimating tone

I do as I'm told and slide my phone under Bow's blanket out of sight "How do you know my name?"

"Well, you told me, at the Ambitious hotel back in Nashville a few weeks ago but I guess that's not important now but what is important is for you to know that you once messed things up for me, so what's going to happen now is I'm going to return the favour. The police are on their way, They're going to arrest you, you see they seem to think you did all this, they had a tip-off" she says gesturing around the room and winking at me as she says the words "tip-off"

"What! But I would never hurt him"

"Oh, you know that, and I know that, but Bow might not remember and then you'll get what you deserve"

"Why are you doing this?"

"Because you destroyed me, you took away my one chance of happiness and now I'm going to return the favour and he," she says pointing to the bed "And as it turns out this is very valuable to me"

"Valuable? What do you mean valuable? I don't even know what I've done! What we've done! I don't even know who you are" I suddenly find my voice getting louder

She holds up a hand as if to motion for me to be silent like I'm a small child "Goodbye Beatrice" she says as she makes her way across the room and leaves

I wait a couple of minutes to make sure she's gone then I rush to find my phone, when I pick it up I'm shaking "Did you get all that Spence?"

"I did, but she's right Bea, it's just been radioed through, they're on their way to you," he tells me

"What do I do?" I ask my voice full of panic

"You need to stay calm and let them bring you in for an interview, I'll meet you at the station "

"Okay," I say my voice full of panic "I didn't do it, I swear it, Spencer, I love him"

"I know Bea and I know you didn't, calm down and say nothing, I'll see you soon"

As he hangs up, I can see them coming past the window to the room, a nurse shows them in, Jon and Christine come in and start to read me my rights.

"Beatrice Alice Lily Coleman, You have the right to remain silent, If you do say anything, it can be used against you in a court of law. You have the right to have a lawyer present during any questioning. If you cannot afford a lawyer, one will be appointed for you if you so desire" Christine says to me as she roughly cuffs me, I have a feeling she's never really liked me and is enjoying this more than she really should.

Jon gently grabs me by the elbow "I'm so sorry about this Beatrice, we've just got to follow protocol"

The tears are now rolling down my face as we leave the room, I nod unable to speak then I just say "I know Jon, please do me a favour and make sure someone is sat in here with Bow at all times, It has to be a member of the force, someone who can protect him, please promise me that, I think he's in danger" he looks at me and nods. When we get to the cruiser, he radios through that someone needs to be sat with Bow at all times in the hospital, as a precaution and the person on the other side agrees. "They're sending two officers out to him now"

"Thank you," I tell him, and we head to the station. As promised Spencer is there to greet me. They take me through to a small room, sit me down and leave me. The room is cold, dark and very unwelcoming, but I guess that's how they would want you to feel.

Spencer casually walks in with two coffee's in his hands and sits down opposite me. "How you holding up?"

"Not so good Spence to be honest with you but I'm glad you answered the phone, I'm surprised you're allowed in here with me, to be honest, wouldn't it come under conflict of interest?"

"I'm just waiting for something, coffee?" he says handing me a coffee cup and it's as if he's as cool as a cucumber

"Thanks," I say as I take it from him

"I need you to tell me about this woman, I obviously heard what she was saying but what did she look like? Do you have any idea who she was?"

"No, no idea," I tell him taking a sip of my coffee "she was slim built, tall but not overly tall, Red hair that was scraped back into a high bun, and she was very well dressed, office like, you know black trousers and white top tucked in with a black suit jacket"

"She'd stick out here then, anything else Bea?"

"She had blue eyes I think, and her red fingernails were one of the things I first noticed"

"Was she wearing heels or flats?"

"Heels, they were tapping on the floor, I thought she was hospital staff, but I think we know her, but I can't think from where"

"Anything else I need to know?"

"She's armed and flashed a gun at me that was kept under her jacket"

"Right, Okay," he tells me as he continues to scribble down what I'm saying

There's a knock at the door and Jon comes in "Spence, its done, and I'm so sorry Beatrice, you know about all that earlier"

"it's okay Jon I know you have a job to do"

He nods and leaves the room, "Your free to go, Bea, I was able to record our phone call, so they heard everything she said to you" Spencer tells me as he gathers his paperwork and we start to leave the room "I'll drop you up to the ranch, I'm heading out for lunch today, with Willow"

I smile "Thanks for looking after her Spence, I feel like I've hardly seen her or spent time with her while she's been here, I cant help but feel like it's all been really unfair on her"

"Hey, it's nothing, I've actually enjoyed it, she's a really great, fun gal. We need to speak to you about something actually, Listen, you could always come with us to lunch with us today l, only if you fancy it, you know actually eat a decent meal? Talk about it there but I totally understand if you want to head back to Bow" he tells me as we leave the room and head for the cruiser.

"I'm sorry Spence I just want to get back to Bow, just in case there's any change, I wanna be there when he wakes up, but we can talk soon yeah? Is it important?"

"Well…. kind of but it can wait"

"Or you could just tell me now?"

He gives me a worried smile, very unlike him "Well, me and Willow have become really close over these last few weeks and don't be mad I know it's quick, but I've asked her to stay and move in with me"

"Wow, Spence, that's fantastic news, I couldn't think of a better person for you, she'll keep you on your toes, I take it she said yes?" I say hugging him

"Yep," he tells me, and I can hear the smugness in his voice "She goes back to Chicago tonight to collect her stuff and to speak to Carlos….. that's his name, isn't it? Then she'll be here as a kind of permanent thing"

"I'm really pleased for you both but sad that I'm losing my Chicago buddy"

"It's not really losing her though is it, she's joining the family, I think she's the one Bea," he tells me, and I can hear the excitement in his voice

"Finally, your old ass is settling down" I smile and playfully punch him in the arm, and he knows I'm joking "Spencer I just want to thank you for all your help and support lately, I don't think I would have been able to do this without you" he nods and there's an awkward silence between us "just so I know Spencer, there will be officers on Bow's door now right?"

"Yes, until we've caught who this is," he tells me, as we drive through the town and head up to the ranch "Did Sienna ever show?" he asks

"Not yet, but I think she's called the hospital a few times, thanks for having my back today as well Spencer"

When we pull up at Mama and Pop's ranch they all come outside and greet me, as if checking that I'm okay. Dawson hands me my keys to the truck and informs me that he's fixed the brakes, had all the tires changed and that he's replaced the headlights, he has also taken it for a test drive so that we know it's safe and thoroughly cleaned it. He tells me that he will pop in at the hospital later today to check on Bow. Mama hands me a brown paper bag containing meals and snacks and Ruth who has messaged me constantly every single day to check on me, gives me a hug and hands me another spare change of clothes "Two lots of knickers, you know just in case" she smiles. Clay hands me a book to read, one of my favourites he must have taken it from my room, The Tale of Peter Rabbit by Beatrix Potter, I remember my love of reading this book it's one of my all-time favourites one of the ones that made me want to become a publisher, I smile and thank him. Willow also wraps me in a warm hug, have you checked your email Bea? They've accepted your final, you've just got the graduation to go now, I called them because I sent your forms in the mail and I wanted to make sure they received them okay"

"That's incredible thank, you, Willow!" I say hugging her back. I then make my way to my truck, getting in and giving them a little wave. I can smell that Dawson has cleaned it. It now smells of citrus. I head down the uneven track and when I look in my mirror, I see them all standing there and disperse in different directions as they carry on with their daily lives.

As I drive down through the town, I notice a black Ford F650 Dominator truck pull out of a parking space and is now behind me, I haven't been here long, but I don't remember seeing one like that and I would definitely notice a truck like that. I decide to put that at the back of my mind and think of Bow as I continue on to the hospital. I head out of the town and carry on my journey to the hospital, to Bow.

When I look in my rear-view mirror, I notice that the truck that was in the town is now a little way behind me, it gradually gets closer so that it isn't that far away from me. I turn right down a side street, and it follows me, I then go around the back of several buildings and come back on the main strip of the town, and it follows, maybe there just lost I think. When I get to the end of the town I can either turn left or right, the left turning leads me to the hospital and the right is a small country road which then leads me eventually onto the freeway, just to make sure that it's not all in my head I turn right and the black ford follows, I carefully dial Spencer's number while watching the road and he answers.

"Spence, I think I'm being followed, it's a black Ford F650 dominator I think, (thank god I know my cars)"

"What's the registration?"

"I can't see one, I don't think it has one"

Suddenly, it comes up behind me fast, ramming my truck, everything in the truck comes shooting forward, even my cell which flies out of my hand and under the seat. I try to reach it, but my fingertips only brush the edge and it's just out of my reach. The ford comes up beside me and rams into the side of me, I struggle to control my truck, due to the impact, I can see her there sitting in the truck with a determined smile on her face and I brace myself for another blow, but it doesn't come, I break, and I don't know how, but I manage to turn the truck around and head back into the town, where there should be lots of people around.

As I reach the town, I frantically look around for someone, anyone. "where are they?" I say out loud in a frustrated tone "everyone in this town usually sees anything and everything" I pass stitch and another blow comes behind me hitting the back left side of my truck causing it to spin, I feel another blow come and hit the driver's side door as I'm spinning and the next thing I know me and my incredibly faithful truck is rolling down through the town, I hear the windows smash around me, and I can hear the metal as it hits the ground. When I finally stop rolling, I can't breathe and start to cough, my wrist is so sore and my chest hurts. Then the next thing I see is two black high heeled shoes walking towards me and then I blackout.

Chapter Fourteen

It's Her

I'm not sure what happened next, everything is black, and my head is all fuzzy, it's making me feel really sleepy. I'm not sure where I am, but I feel so cold and wet. I can feel a heavyweight on my left leg, I'm not sure what it is but I feel trapped like I can't move, and my chest hurts, but I find myself struggling to breathe. The next thing I can hear is panicked voices all around me followed by loud sirens, but I can't feel any pain anymore either, it's like it's just fading away, I'm not sure why but the pain in my chest has gone too and then I black out again.

In the darkness, I can see her standing there, Nana Clara. She's looking at me and smiling. Her light grey hair is short and looks like it had been permed, just as I always remembered it was, she was always a very well-dressed lady and nothing was ever out of place when it came to her appearance, she always use to tell me if you dress good, you feel good. Her smile is very warm and welcoming, I suddenly feel calm and at ease, where am I, I wonder but then looking at her I also find it weird because I know we lost her about twelve years ago. I want to run and hug her but as I take a step towards her, she puts her hand up to stop me and starts to speak.

"Your not ready Baby Bea," she tells me, it stops me in my tracks to hear her speak and even more so that she uses the nickname that she once gave me, This is what people then continued to call me after they had heard her say it once when I was small.

"What do you mean? How are you here? I thought you died" I frantically state

"I did dear... but now is not your time," she tells me and then she smiles a gentle, warm smile again "You have to go back Baby Bea"

"But I don't know how," I tell her

Nana Clara sits smiling at me

"Why are you here?" I continue to ask her

"To make sure you go back"

"Kind of like a guide?"

"You could say that yes," she tells me "I've been watching over you lately Beatrice and I know what's been going on"

"Do you know what's happened to me?" I ask

"Yes, you've been in an accident....... But you need to fight...to wake up, I know how special you are to my Bow" she pauses and says nothing and then finally says "he loves you, you know"

I can't help but smile as i take a seat beside her on what looks like an invisible bench, I look around and my surroundings are white, and I can see things floating around us in the air, things that relate to the life she once had.

"So, how's Grandpa Bill?" I ask

"He's doing well, wishes he could come to see you too dear but only one of us could come…for now, I need you to focus Baby Bea, close your eyes and try and go back"

I do as I'm told; I close my eyes and try to calm myself.

A while later, I'm not sure when but I'm aware of my surroundings again. I can't see anything, and I try hard to open my eyes, but I soon realise I can hear but can't move and I try with all my might, and I can distantly hear a beeping of a machine, "What is that?" it's so annoying, I wish it would stop and then I hear panicked voices that I vaguely recognise.

The first one I hear, I instantly recognize to be my mothers, I can hear her crying, why is she crying? What's going on? I'm so confused, what could be happening that would cause her to be so upset?. I try to open my eyes, but I can't. I try to speak, it's okay Mama I'm here, I try to say but I can't move my mouth and my words are non-existent. I just lay there listening.

"She's a tough cookie, she'll pull through" I hear the voice that I know to be my fathers "Plus we've been in this hospital enough lately to know how good the staff are" his voice says

Pull through, pull through what? Hospital, who's in the hospital? could it be me? This is all so confusing and I'm struggling to understand, I try hard to remember what had happened for me to be in the hospital, but I can't, I have no idea. I feel someone grab my hand and squeeze it.

"I'm so sorry Bea I should have done more, I should have been there with you, got in the truck and drove you there myself, I'm so sorry Beatrice this is all my fault" it's Dawson, I would recognise that voice anywhere his sobs are just heart-breaking. I want to hug him, tell him I'm here, that I'm okay but I can't it's almost like I'm paralysed, I try hard to move my arms and hands, to speak, but I can't move at all or even get the words out "I'm here and I'm okay" I try to say but no words leave my mouth. I don't understand why everyone is here or why there so sad or even what's going on. I try to think back to what happened and I get a slight flashback of a woman walking towards me in black heels, she bends down to look at me and all I remember is seeing a devilish smile on her lips that were painted a bright red colour and then I blackout once more again.

When I come back around, I wonder how long I've been laying here for, but I hear Dawson's voice every now and then telling me about the ranch, our parents and of course Bow, I love hearing about how he's doing and he sounds like he's been doing well, he goes on to tell me that Sienna, Bow's sister has been to visit him and that he's definitely on the mend according to the Doctor anyway, A little while later I hear footsteps and then I think I hear Ruth

"Any change?" she asks

"None yet," Dawson tells her "but hopefully it won't be too long"

"I miss her," she says as she takes my hand "I miss her sass"

He lets out a little laugh "Yeah so do I, Darlin"

"How's her head?"

"Doctor Avery has said that she's doing really well and that her head injury was pretty bad, there not sure if she will have lasting effects, like memory loss or if she'll have knowledge of the accident, her wrist is broken and she's lucky she gets to keep her leg, it was pretty damaged when they removed her from the truck."

"Hmm, she'll get frustrated over that..........what, what if she can't remember who we are Daw?" she starts to cry

"That won't happen she will always remember me; I've annoyed her since the day she was born and she's never had a friend like you"

I hear Ruth laugh "You annoy everyone you meet......me included," she says under her breath

I wish I could laugh at her joke. Just then I hear footsteps enter the room and a deep voice I don't recognise starts to speak "Mr Coleman, a word if you please" says the man

"It's okay doctor you can tell me here, I'm happy for you to tell me any information in front of my fiancée Ruth, she's practically family" I hear him say "and Beatrice would want her here with me"

"Very well, I want to inform you that your sister's condition is improving very well, her brain activity is increasing by the day, but I also need to inform you that Mr Bow Tanner is awake and is asking for Miss Coleman and yourself," he says and I can only guess that he's gesturing towards me because there's a long pause between Miss Coleman and the word yourself "I must warn you he's very confused and doesn't remember much about what happened to him but sometimes that can happen, and his memory will resume in time"

I hear Dawson sigh "Okay, I think I should be the one to tell him about his and Beatrice's accident, it would probably be better coming from me"

"Very well" I hear Doctor Avery tell him

I then hear him scrape the chair along the floor, as if he's pushed it back and has got up, then I hear his heavy footsteps walk across the floor (he was never very light on his feet, I can vaguely remember Mama saying he was like a fairy elephant when entering the room) but I can only guess he's got up, left the room, and gone to speak with Bow.

Everything's quiet, I then hear a voice that I almost forgot was here beside me "Please come back to us Bea, we need the light back in our lives" I hear Ruth's strained voice beside me as she takes my hand again and then the darkness consumes me once more.

I'm back again sat with Clara; she looks peaceful and content

"Are you my guide?"

"Sort of my dear, yes"

"So, what do you do?"

"Well, when we all pass we always have someone there to greet us, someone we have known and loved… you see our loved ones never really leave us"

"So……. I'm dead?"

"No not quite, but your very unwell dear"

I nod "So if it's not my time then what can I do to get back?" I start to freak out as I realise how weird this is "I need to see Bow, my family, Willow" I tell her

"Well dear you need to concentrate on getting better then"

"But how?" I ask as I start to cry"

"Just close your eyes and take a deep breath"

And I'm back to what I can only assume is a while later, I'm not sure when but I have a feeling it's a few days possibly weeks, I've been trying to keep track of the dates people say around me but it's so difficult to remember where I am with them.

Today, I can hear a sound that is very unfamiliar to me, almost like something is being wheeled across the floor, could it be the bed I'm lying in, but I don't feel like I'm moving or maybe it's a cart or maybe there moving equipment around the room, I try to focus on the noise that was now coming towards me and that's when I hear him.

"Oh, Sweetheart…. what have they done to you?" I hear that sad husky tone followed by his muted sobs, I just want to reach out and hold him, tell him that I'm here, that I'm okay and most importantly that I love him. "I'm here Darlin, I'm so sorry this has happened," he says, and I feel him gently take my hand.

I so desperately want to tell him I'm okay, but I can't……oh god I'm so frustrated, I need to wake up, I need to speak to him, I need to know what happened to me, I mean I vaguely remember I had been in an accident and that's what people keep saying around me too so I can only assume I'm right, but I can't remember how or what happened before it. The last thing I remember is being up at the ranch by my truck, I concentrate on the memory hard for a moment and then a woman's voice shifts my focus and I now listen carefully to what Bow and this woman are saying, But who is this woman and why is she in my room?

"It's okay Bow, the doctors have already said she's going to be okay, and that her brain activity is improving by the day," it says in a monotone voice

That voice I recognise it, but I can't place it, who is that? Could it be Willow?....No, it's definitely not Willow, I can't hear her Californian twang, grr why do I know that voice and I can feel it, I'm about to blackout again, I try to hold on, I need to know who that is, but the darkness takes me once again.

Once again I find myself sat with Clara. She places her hand on top of mine this time and says "Dear do me a favour when you go back to our house, get bow to look in the large green heavy box that was in the big cupboard in the kitchen, I know you both moved it"

"Okay….. I will….. but what's in there?" I ask

"Well, there's lots of things… things of his mothers and fathers and when he opens it he will find a smaller box inside that was once ours, it's containing the one thing he's going to need"

"Okay, well I'll make sure to mention it to him, I know he loves your house, we've found lots of hidden gems there, we've really enjoyed making it a home"

"I know I've been watching you both, you see we're never far away, always by your side" She pauses again "You have to go back now, he's waiting for you," she tells me as she gives my hand a little squeeze.

When I come back around I can hear Bow's voice once more, at first I think he's talking but then I realise he's reading aloud and I quickly notice that he's reading the Beatrix Potter book the tales of Peter Rabbit, one of my all-time favourites, I would recognise that book anywhere, I briefly wonder where he got that from and for some reason I think of Clay. I love listening to him read, its really calming and soothing, once he's finished reading to me, he begins to tell me "That today's the day the hospital is discharging him and that he can finally get rid of the awful wheelchair that he had to use in the hospital as a precaution" I can tell he's been really unimpressed by this by the way he's told me, he then goes silent for a brief moment and when he speaks again I can tell he's crying

"Please wake up sweetheart, I need to see that cheeky smile on your face, life just isn't the same without you, you don't have to even go to New York with me, we can discuss that together and make a life together wherever you want to..... just please wake up Bea..... I need you..... I can't lose you too" I can hear his voice break and I just want to hold him. He must have placed his head on the bed beside my hand because I can feel the bed move slightly and I can hear his muffled cries, then my hand is suddenly wet in what I can only guess is his tears. "Please Bea, I need you to wake up…. I miss you…. I'll be waiting here until you're ready" he cries

"It's going to be okay Bow, I promise" that voice I vaguely recognise again speaks. I concentrate hard on it as she continues talking "She's just how I remember her, she was always a tough cookie she'll pull through, but she just needs time, you really mean it when you say you want to stay here for her?"

"Of course, I do, there isn't much I wouldn't do for her, I want to be with her, through the good, the bad and the ugly and I'm pretty sure this experience has had all of those, I'm not going anywhere without her and if this terrible experience has taught me anything it's that life is far too short and that you should treasure every moment and everything you are blessed with in life"

"But what about Dawnwood Manor?"

"Well, I was going to ask her if she would move up and into Dawnwood with me" I hear Bow finally say and honestly to hear this news has really blown me away and left me shocked, he always said that he'd go back to New York to run the business and that his life was there, then we would see if we could do it long-distance and just see what happens, that was always the plan, I think to myself, I'm sure that was always the plan.

"But you said you'd sell it for profit," the voice says

"I did yes" and he's silent for a few moments "…but she made me look at life a different way, she makes me happy, and I'll do anything to be with her, even if that means staying here, plus the house has grown on me, especially all the sentimental treasures and secrets it contains and now that I've had the builders in the last few weeks the house is really starting to look like a home again, it has so much charm"

"Charm? You're keeping it because of the charm? But.... But what about the profit?" the voice says as if shocked and very frustrated, angry even

"That….. that doesn't matter anymore" he stutters telling her

"So, let me get this straight your throwing all that away for some girl? Everything you've ever worked for" the voice says in a furious tone

"That's not your decision" Bow snaps back and then pauses before saying "I'm in love with her"

"But what about your career? the business? New York?" she asks him

"I've looked into it, I spoke to the board the other day and they think it's all possible that I could run it all from here, keeping the main office in New York, plus Dawnwood already has an office room," he tells her

"And what if she doesn't want you? Or if there's someone else? What if she wants to go back to Chicago? Back to that little Italian restaurant?"

He goes silent for around a 30 seconds and then says "I don't think I mentioned she lived in Chicago or anything about her working in an Italian restaurant"

"You told me….. the other day," she tells him

"Funny, I don't remember mentioning that," he tells her in a quizzical tone

"You have been so exhausted or maybe it was Dawson that told me then," she says brushing it off

I'm instantly determined to move, wake up or even speak. I have so many questions to ask now, like is what he's saying true? Does he really love me too? if he's sure about leaving New York? And more importantly who is this woman? And how does she know that I live in Chicago or what I do for a career?..... but I can't. I suddenly feel him take my hand in his again which brings me back from my thoughts and all my questions. I lay there willing my hands to move just to let him know that I'm okay and that I'm still here, I focus hard, but nothing happens. I can hear Bow and this woman continue to have a heated discussion, I want to but in and ask her what it's got to do with her, but I can't, I just lay there willing myself to do something, anything…..but I still can't manage it, maybe I'm not strong enough and it's terribly frustrating, C'mon! I think to myself and yet nothing happens. Okay, Bea, I say to myself, you can do this, relax, and think hard about what you're willing yourself to do, I try to shut out the voices around me and concentrate hard and that's when I manage just a small squeeze of his hand and then I move my index finger and that's when I hear him.

There's silence, the conversation stops dead and then I hear "She moved! She just squeezed my hand, she just squeezed my ruddy hand!! and moved her finger! quick get the doctor!" he says excitedly "Bea, Bea, it's me, come back to me sweetheart" and with that, I start to feel exhausted and slip back into the darkness once more.

Clara is with me once again and when I look up at her sat beside me. I can see Grandpa Bill is standing behind her with a hand on her shoulder.

"Here again Beatrice" I hear the man's voice say

"Bill!" I yell

"Hello Beatrice"

"But I thought you'd said that only one of you could come at one time"

"Well, I had to look after ma boy didn't I," he tells me

"I suppose you did" I smile up at the both of them "He really is something"

"He certainly is" Clara smiles at me "Now dear its really important, that you go back.... somethings about to happen, don't be scared we will be here every step of the way, but you really need to make sure that you fight this"

"What do you mean?" I ask them feeling slightly alarmed, and I think they can sense the panic in my voice "I don't know how to fight"

"There's a plan for you, but don't panic ma dear we're always here remember that," Bill tells me

At that statement, I'm a little confused but nod and just accept it "You know we all miss you guys and Bow talks about you all the time"

Bill smiles then looks down at Nana Clara and they smile together "We know" she tells me "We hear Bow talking to us sometimes"

Bill walks around Clara and comes to me and pulls me up to stand, then wraps me in a warm hug, I place my head on his chest "Close your eyes now baby Bea and with that, I realise that I'm back once more

---

A little while later, I hear that tapping on the floor again, it sounds like someone walking on the hard floor in high heels once more. I'm beginning to wonder if it's just my imagination or maybe I'm dreaming.

"I won't have you ruining things for me again Beatrice Coleman"

That voice, I've heard it recently, who is this woman? and then it comes to me. Bow I suddenly think, she was sat with Bow the other day in this very room discussing me and him but who is she? And why would she want to hurt me? I then hear the click of what sounds like a briefcase opening or is it. It's her! It has to be, I think to myself, she's the reason I'm in here, the woman that ran me off the road, the person who left the note on my car and did the damage to it, and the person that found me at the Ambitious hotel, that day after my wonderful date with Bow. What is she doing here? She's going to kill me, I know she will, I'm terrified and frozen. What could I have possibly done for her to want to hurt me? I need to move, to alert someone, I don't understand why someone would hate me so much. Panic fills me and then she starts to talk.

"You took everything from me seven years ago and I won't have you doing it again" she pauses as if she's distracted, concentrating hard on something and then continues talking to me. "Nathan was my world, the guy who was going to look after us, give us a home, a secure future and everything we could ever want and need, he was my someone to build a future with and YOU took that all away, We were going to be happy.....oh so happy….. yes and I was going to be so successful but after your little outburst on that night, on the 23rd of November all those years ago, oh and don't I remember it well, I watched it unfold right in front of me. How his lies made you lose your temper, how you screamed at him and how you then went on to punch the window to his BMW" I hear a smile playing on her lips "You see I saw it all from the car….. yes, yes that was me in behind those blacked-out windows of his. You see I knew about you, but I was honestly in way too deep to walk away being pregnant and all, of course, I gave him the one thing that you couldn't. After that little incident it caused Nathan to become distant, he drank a lot and was often violent and was basically never there, it's like you caused him to look at things a different way, almost caused him to change his mind about me and the baby. And I would have thought you would have least had the decency to let him keep the house you had together, but you took that from him too and when it sold I would have thought you would have let him take all the cash from the sale but I guess that's how selfish you are" she pauses again for a short while, takes a deep breath and then continues "Then when he got discharged from the Navy due to not only an injury but also a problem with drinking, he just lost it. He became a guy I no longer knew and we lost everything, then he found some little young tart, and then it became clear that I was just a way out of your trashy, sham of a relationship but he was just in way too deep with, he told me he didn't want me or the baby anymore, my poor Benny nearly grew up without a proper dad" she raged on "but I guess I got to find out how it felt, how much it hurt, just to be thrown aside like you mean nothing to someone, you know kind of like just what we did to you" she pauses and says nothing for a moment as if she's concentrating hard on something, then I feel a sharp prick in my left arm "I then hit rock bottom you see, I mean who really wants an unemployed, married, seven-month pregnant woman? But after a while I was saved by my now husband and then built my business from nothing, nothing!, then one day Bow was telling me about Dawnwood Manor, and we spoke about splitting the profits when it sells but I would have no say in that, I mean unbeknown to him the house was never left to me, my twisted grandparents only left that to their precious grandson, but I wouldn't be telling him that anytime soon, I had too much to lose, I wanted my share of course. Then we got talking about his life insurance policy one night too and how it runs out soon and that he needs to make time to do a new one and as soon as I found out that I would receive everything it was a no brainer, but you had to go and get in the way didn't you" she rages

I start to feel funny, all dizzy and weird, I start to drift, and my mind goes blank, what's happening to me? Has she done something? And its like the sun has come up and I begin to put the pieces together and I realise who this is, and it hits me like a ton of bricks like I've been slapped hard in the face. It's her………… it's Bow's sister….. the woman in front of me is….. Sienna.

Chapter Fifteen

Conscious

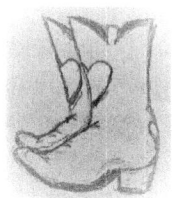

I'm greeted by Nana Clara and Grandpa Bill once more, who are now sat together on the odd-looking misty bench.

"What happened?" I ask them

"You had a visitor and your in critical condition Beatrice," Bill tells me calmly

"Your blood pressure went up through the roof, nearly causing you to have heart failure"

I slowly nod taking in all the new information "But how could this have happen?"

"Not everyone you meet has the best intentions for you I'm afraid ma dear," Bill tells me "Sometimes sugar turns out to be salt"

Then there's silence which is once again broken by Bill

"You're going to need to go back Baby Bea, Our boy needs you," He tells me

"I need him too," I tell them "I love him, and I've never felt this way about anyone before" I admit

"We know," Clara tells me "We've watched you both together, you need each other, and it's clear that you're his missing puzzle piece, no one has ever loved him the way you do" and her words make me smile and almost cry.

Suddenly panic fills me "I need to go back, I need to see my man, I need to tell him everything I've heard, what you've told me, that he's in danger and its Sienna," I tell them in a hurried voice

"You do but… whoa slow down there baby bea" the smile and then there both on their feet

"Thank you for being here for me and being so reassuring," I tell them as they both wrap me into a warm embrace

"Just remember to close your eyes and take a deep breath, and please give our love to our boy" Bill tells me

"And tell him that we love him dearly and that we're always with him…….. oh, and Beatrice please tell him when he thinks someone is touching his face at night, that it's me," Clara says with a big smile

The next thing I know they have wrapped their arms around each other and have turned and walked away into the white. I stand there, close my eyes, and take that deep breath.

I'm conscious of my surroundings again and my right-hand feels warm, I can tell someone's holding it and I can once again hear the beeping of that oh so annoying machine that has become oh so familiar to me. I want to know who it is that's holding my hand, I focus hard, concentrating and try hard to wake up, I can't, I feel so weak again, what happened with Sienna? Where is she now? what did she do to me? Is everyone else safe?

Then I can hear Dawson and his heavy footsteps that I know so well as he walks across the room and say's "Any change?"

"Nothing" I hear Bow's low croaky voice say beside me, it must be him sat beside me holding my hand, it's warm and I've missed the sound of his voice and that southern drawl but mostly I've just missed his gentle touch.

"Black coffee" Dawson then says

"Thanks" then there's silence for a little while which is broken by Dawson

"How could her heart rate just go up like that? She could have died; I just don't understand" I hear Dawson's angry tone

"I know," Bow says and he's briefly quiet "I'm so scared to lose her Daw, I've never been scared to lose anything or anyone before but with her…..she makes me look at life so differently………. and I love her, if I could swap places with her right now I would"

"I know man, we're all scared, I just don't understand it, Doctor Avery said she was doing really well with her recovery"

"I know, something just doesn't seem right, maybe they changed her medication or something"

"Maybe but usually that's something they'd keep us informed about, but I can double-check and ask them," Dawson says as he gets up and leaves the room.

And then there's a long silence, it's not long before he's back and I hear his voice again "No they don't think so, but we will have to speak to Bea's Doctor, When he's back on shift tonight, just to make sure, plus I'm sure he would be able to tell us why this happened"

Silence fills the room once more and for the longest time no one says anything

"How is everyone at home coping?" I hear Bow ask

"Well, Ruth feels like she's lost her best friend and feels completely lost, as you know Mamas not doing so well, she kept breaking down, I would find her most mornings crying over the kitchen stove, Pops is coping and trying to stay strong and positive for everyone as usual and is currently with Mama. Spencer feels terribly guilty and keeps saying that he should have just dropped her to you here at the hospital and is now working around the clock to try and find the bastard's that have done this to her, Willow feels terrible because she didn't come with her and she that she was with Spencer instead of being here with her and Clay doesn't really know what to do with himself but he's refusing to go back to work until there's a huge improvement in her condition, not to mention Mama"

There's silence between them and the beeping of the machine continues.

"And you Daw?" I finally hear Bow ask

"Well……I ……. I mean….. well….." I hear him take a deep breath and then breathe out slowly "I feel awful, like I've let her down, all her life all I've ever tried to do is protect her and stop her getting hurt, but I really fucked up this time didn't I"

"This.... this isn't your fault Dawson" I hear Bow say "If it's anyone's its mine, I shouldn't have taken her away and should have taken her seriously when she said about that person she was speaking to at the hotel, I should have listened and protected her, but I didn't or maybe I should have just listened to you and stayed away from her, like you told me all those years ago, maybe you were right"

Dawson is quiet for a moment "ahhh Bow... man...I mean...I wouldn't say that...... because I do know ......that no one has ever treated her as well as you do, I honestly couldn't wish for someone better for my little sister than you, she just adores you and I don't think she's ever been treated as well as you treat her...... Plus she loves you, she told me"

Everything's quiet for a moment "Thanks..... I think I needed to hear that" I hear Bow say, "and it means a lot coming from you" suddenly my hand feels cold, and I hear their hands slap together and I can only assume he's pulled Dawson into a hug, and I hear him sniff "You know I'd never hurt her on purpose or let her down Daw"

"I know, I know you wouldn't man" Dawson reassures him

It's quiet again for a few minutes so all we can hear is that awful beeping of the annoying machine and then I hear Bow say "So, this wedding huh?"

"Yeah, it was originally going to be the 12th of March this year and that's only just under a month away but Ruth has said she won't do it without her, and I agree it wouldn't be the same without them both, so we're postponing until she can guarantee Bea will be okay and well enough to stand by her side"

I lay there hearing this makes me sad, they shouldn't have to postpone the biggest and happiest day of their lives because of me. I need to wake up, I need to tell them that they can't postpone it, that they need to carry on, I need to tell them all about Sienna being here, I need to tell them none of this is anyone's fault and most importantly that I love them all dearly.

I strongly will myself to wake up…C'mon, I can do this, I just need to open my eyes, C'mon Bea focus I say to myself, I focus hard and the next thing I realise is I'm laying in the most uncomfortable hospital bed, I struggle to open my eyes and my head is pounding, my throat is sore and it's hot and stuffy in this room. I look down and then realise my left wrist and my left leg are in casts, and I can't help but notice my body hurts everywhere. I look around the room and the first thing I notice is the bright sunshine beaming through the large window to my left, it's beautiful and I realise how much I've missed seeing it, I turn my head slightly and notice Dawson's sat in the left-hand corner of the room, next to the large window. he's on the phone talking to someone, I'm not sure who it is but it sounds like a woman's voice, and I can only guess that it's either Mama or Ruth. On the right-hand side of the room, I can see the wooden door with a window within it that's next to that a small sink, and then I see him right beside me, head on the bed next to my hand that he's holding, my man, the guy I love with all my heart. He's asleep, he kinda can't of looks like a small child, a little broken, the dark shadows under his eyes tell me he has had very little or no sleep, he still has a few bruises and is still a little swollen in places and he has a few faint scratches to his face, but he still looks like the same strong, gorgeous man that took me to the hotel that night.

I briefly wonder how long ago that was, then I think to the wedding and overhear Dawson say to Ruth "No Darlin, No Change, were waiting on Doctor Avery to come in and speak to us about what could have caused her to nearly have heart failure.........Yes, yes I know, I know....I was just telling Bow about that... we will postpone everything until they're better and recovered......"

"No, you can't postpone it because of me" I croak

"BEA!" I hear them both say

"I'll call you back Darlin, I need to get a nurse" I hear Dawson say as he drops the phone and gets up, rushing out the room.

"Oh, Bea I'm so pleased to see you" Bow cries as he leans up, places his hands on either side of my face as if examining me and first he kisses me on the top of my head, then on my lips, his lips are just as soft and gentle as I remember. "Oh, I've missed you so much Sweetheart, I didn't think I'd ever see you open those beautiful eyes again" I look at him and notice his eyes are all bloodshot, the dark circles are worse than I thought, and the tears are running down his face, he's lost more weight than I thought possible, how long have I been out for I wonder.

The tears are streaming down my face now too, I didn't think I would ever see him again; I start to cough.

"Water….. yes water" I watch him fumble around the room looking for the jug of water and a glass, he finds it beside the sink and pours me a glass then brings it to me, lifting it up he helps me drink it, the waters cool and refreshing in my mouth, it feels like forever since I last tasted it and after I drained the cup quickly, I realise how thirsty I was. When I've finished Bow places the cup down on the bedside table and I can sense him gazing at me.

"Oh, Sweetheart you don't realise how much I've missed you, I thought we were going to lose you, you gave us all such a fright," he tells me as he kisses me on the lips and brushes my hair back from my face "I'm so sorry I should have believed you about that person at the hotel, I just didn't think it would lead to anything this serious"

"I've missed you too Bow," I tell him in a croaky voice as the tears are running down my cheeks "…..but I need to speak to you about something…..somethings happened" I croak at him

He looks at me with a confused look "What do you mean? do you not love me anymore?… has something changed…do you remember our time together?" he questions

"No, of course, I still love you, I don't just say that to anyone, I say it because I mean it, but someone was here" I tell him "and yes I remember our date, oh and your Nana Clara and Grandpa Bill have told me to tell you they love you and you need to go through the big box that we found in the cupboard, you know that really heavy one that had that date that related to your parents"

He looks at me with a quizzical expression, but as soon as I open my mouth and try to tell him more, a doctor which I can only assume is Doctor Avery, and a nurse that I quickly notice by her badge she's called Madeline, have entered my room shortly followed by Dawson who's on the phone again to who I can only assume is to Ruth or Mama and Pops.

"So, Beatrice, I'm doctor Avery I've been looking after you for the last few months, you gave us a real scare there a few days ago and you've been in a coma for a little while now, so I'd like you to tell me how your feeling?"

"Okay, Thank you…. a little sore in places…. but I'm okay…. I'd just like to see my family please" I croak

"Madeline here will get you some painkillers and we can certainly arrange for you to see your family, but first can you tell me your full name?"

"Yes, Beatrice Louise Alice Coleman"

"Very good, and can you remember how you got in here?"

"I think I was in some kind of accident. It's all a bit fuzzy"

"Okay, and can you tell me what the last thing you remember is?"

"Umm, it's a little fuzzy…..I think I remember being upside down in my truck and seeing a woman in heels walking towards me"

"Okay, very good," he says as he checks my eyes and my vitals I see Dawson and Bow exchange a confused look "Well we'd like to keep you in for a few more days just to make sure your okay and then we can look at getting you back home, but it's going to take you a while to get back to normal, you've had a really nasty accident and you hit your head so there is a chance that you might have some memory loss, we think it'll eventually come back but just see how you go" I nod to him and Bow takes my hand once more "Now there are a couple of officers outside that would like to speak to you, should I send them in?"

"I'd like a couple of minutes with her Doctor if you don't mind?" I hear Dawson say "I know Spencer is waiting outside with officer Jon Daniels, but this won't take very long"

The doctor nods "of course, Nurse Madeline will be back in a few moments with some painkillers for you" he says nodding to Madeline then he and the nurse leave the room, leaving Bow and Dawson with me.

"How you doing baby Bea? Someone in heels huh?" Dawson asks as he pulls me into a tight hug

I nod "Yes I saw her walking towards me when I was in my truck I think, but I'm okay, I just feel exhausted," I tell him "And I'm a little sore" my truck I suddenly think "how is my truck Daw, please tell me we can fix it?" I ask him in a worried tone

I see him put his head in his hands and rub his face "I'd love to be able to tell you that Bea, but she's in a real bad way, I don't think we're going to be able to save her after this, I mean every panel is dented and the damage from where the car rolled is pretty extreme, your lucky to be alive"

I begin to cry, she's been so loyal and reliable, I'm absolutely gutted, I've had that truck for years, she was the one thing that I had to my name, and she never let me down.

Bow's silent and then says "Oh, Sweetheart please don't cry…..we can replace the trucks, but we can't replace you"

"Bow's right you know Bea," Dawson tells me "there's only one of you but millions of trucks"

"I know" I cry "But I really loved that truck, she got me out of some really sticky situations"

"I know, I know" Bow is up again beside me ready to fill up my cup to get me to have a drink to calm down as he does Dawson gets up and takes his seat next to me "Listen I've phoned everyone to let them know you're awake, do you remember anything else about what happened?"

"In bits yes," I tell them as I wipe my face and then look over to Bow, which causes me to remember what happened when I had a visit from his sister, that must have been when I had been in the coma and that I'd seen his grandparents, but now I'm starting to second guess myself maybe it was a dream, maybe she wasn't really here, maybe I need to ask Bow and Dawson things that were said at my bedside while I was unconscious that way I would know if those events actually happened. "I think need to ask you both a few questions" I state

"Okay," Dawson says as they both look at me with a little confused, but worried expression

"I can remember when you woke up" I state to Bow "Dawson came and spoke to you to tell you about my accident and Ruth was here too"

"Yes that's right but how could you possibly know about that?" Dawson asks

"Stop Bea if were doing this I think you need to have Spence and officer Daniels in here too" Bow tells me

"I heard y'all talking, the things you said, you said about moving into Dawnwood Bow and I heard Ruth here with you Dawson, I saw your grandparents Bow, they warned me before I had the heart problem......they knew it was going to happen…. This sounds crazy but they told me it would happen"

"That's pretty impressive," Bow says with a smile playing on his lips and I can tell he thinks I'm taking the piss "Okay Sweetheart….what did they say?" Bow asks as his cheeks glow bright red

"They said when you think someone's stroking your cheek when things are all quiet at night, it's Nana Clara and they can hear you when you talk to them when you're up at Dawnwood Manor, also they've told me to tell you to open the large heavy green box we found in the cupboard, there's a small box inside you need to open, everything you need is in there"

He stands there gobsmacked – smile now gone

"Could you hear anything else?" Dawson asks

"A few other things but I don't want Bow to hate me"

"Why would I hate you?" he says with a slight laugh

"Because I think something happened to me while I was out, I heard it and it was someone close to you doing it," I tell them both as I avoid Bow's gaze

Bow looks very confused and Dawson slightly alarmed "I think you need to get Spence in here," Bow says as he turns to Dawson. He does as he's told and carefully gets up to leave the room.

"Sweetheart, why would I hate you? I could never hate you, quite the opposite actually"

I begin to cry again, this is all so stressful and I know this information is going to hurt him but he deserves to know the truth "Because the other day I heard a woman's voice in here, a voice I vaguely recognised, I've heard it before coming in with you, and then a few days ago I heard her again, this time she was on her own and she must have opened some sort of briefcase or something, she then went on to tell me why she was here, and it involved you and me, and my past experiences"

"Right……but sweetheart why would I hate you? And a briefcase, how do you know it was a briefcase? Hey, I could never hate you, but what do you mean involving me and you?"

"Because the woman's voice was someone I know is very dear to you, but she has other plans, she told me, Bow, she's dangerous" and even I can hear the panic in my voice now

"Dear to me? Beatrice what are you saying? What do you mean she's dangerous? Who are you talking about?" I can hear the slight panic in his voice too

Dawson enters my room with Spencer and officer Daniels in tow

"I'm saying the woman that was here, you know her well, but she's the same woman who tried to kill me…… and you, she's the reason we're both in here"

"Who? what do you mean Sweetheart? Your starting to scare me"

"It was your sister…..it was Sienna,

Chapter Sixteen

Answers

They all stand there looking at me dumbstruck, Spencer who had just entered the room is the first one to speak

"So, what you're saying Beatrice is that Bow's sister...Sienna was here with you a couple of days ago"

"Yes, but everything went fuzzy, and I felt funny and then everything went black again"

Bow stands up and walks over to the large window and looks out at the beautiful morning sky, after a few moments he finally says "And your sure about this Bea?, your sure it was her?...........I mean, well, she left about a week ago" he sighs

"Certain, because I can tell you about all the conversations I overheard while I've been in here, Ruth told Dawson she missed my sass, I heard the doctor when Bow woke up and you Dawson went to tell him about everything, I heard it all" they all stand there looking dumbfound.

"We can always check the security cameras in the hospital. What else did you hear?" Spencer asks me as if testing me "It sounds like to me you were drugged, a blood test would tell us if that's true though" he turns to officer Daniels "Go and speak to that nurse and get her to order bloods for Beatrice, Jon" he does as he's told, silence fills the room and then he's back again within seconds

"All arranged sir, they'll be in in about roughly ten minutes" and Spencer just nods to him

"Well…I heard Mama crying and Pops saying I'm a tough cookie" I look to Bow who is still standing in the large window looking out, who seems to take a deep breath and then his shoulders start to droop, Spence has nudged officer Daniels to get him to start writing this all down. "I can remember most of what happened during the accident…….: and what happened before it….., I remember speaking to you on the phone Spence….., telling you that someone was following me…..then I remember taking all different directions…. and being followed everywhere I went" I'm silent for a moment and then the thought of my truck comes to me " I remember my truck being rammed too and a vague memory of it rolling comes back to me" I focus hard, trying to remember everything that happened.

"What can you remember, while you were in the coma, Bea?" I hear Bow say his tone much sterner now

"Well, I can remember you sat here, I think you were holding my hand because it was warm, I can remember you having a heated discussion with Sienna, over Dawnwood Manor…..: That you were staying and running the business from a new office here….. I think then she mentioned me living in Chicago and working in the restaurant and you said you hadn't mentioned the restaurant" then everything goes quiet for a moment as if no one knows what to say "Then you told her you were in love with me" I say and the room falls silent once more, I suddenly feel terribly uncomfortable like all eyes are on me, and they are, Bow is staring right at me, and I struggle to hold his penetrating gaze and then he says

"I did, yes" everything is quiet again "That all happened"

"It did, we've seen your accident on all the local security cameras in town, but the woman was definitely in heels and a black baggy top, a hoodie I think and black slim trousers too," Spencer tells us

"She…… I mean Sienna then went on to tell me that she was the woman in the car on the night that I found out about Nathan Parker all those years ago" the room is silent once more " You know…..the other woman, that night he turned up at the hideaway, and then she told me how she lost everything because of me" I tell them

"But wasn't the woman he went off with pregnant" Dawson asks

"Yes," I tell them "It turns out that was Sienna"

"I don't believe it… after all these years I had no idea," Dawson tells me

"Oh Sweet baby Jesus … I ….I had no idea" he's silent again "I'm so sorry Bea" Bow suddenly says "So….. this must mean that little Benny isn't Liam's" he says and it's as if he's mentally putting the pieces together "He's nearly 7 years old" he adds as he paces around the room running his hands through his beautiful dark hair

"She also targeted you Bow, because she knows you had your life insurance policy and that you would have left everything you own all to her.....:" silence fills the room once more "Oh and she's not really entitled to anything to do with Dawnwood but with you out of the picture she'd get everything"

"Which would explain why she was so mad when I said I wasn't going to sell it for profit and that I was going to live there with you" the room is quiet again. Looking around I can see the shocked and confused expressions on everyone's faces and when I turn to Bow I can see the frustration on Bow's face, then suddenly it's like a switch has been turned on and he's figured it out "So she tampered with the breaks on my truck"

"It sounds like she's the reason your both in this hospital" Dawson finally says, "So what do we do now then?"

Silence fills the air once more and everything has become rather awkward as if everyone knows what needs to be done but no one wants to admit it or even suggest it.

Bow is the first to break the silence "I need to talk to her" He says looking to me and then to everyone else around the room

"Okay," Dawson says "Do you want me to come with you?... listen man I don't think you should be doing that on your own"

"Please, I could really do with the support and back up"

"I mean we could arrest her, but I've got to admit tracking her down is going to be a bit of the problem, we've tried to track her down a few times already and she just keeps slipping through our grasp. I mean the truck that was used to put you in here Bea was found about eight miles from here, all burnt out" Spencer tells me "So we have no fingerprints and the only proof we have of the accident ever taking place is the security cameras in town, we traced her truck, but it was bought at the dealership in Nashville about three days before the incident from a place called Andy's car dealership and the paperwork they have on file states that it was paid for in cash but that's nothing, we couldn't use to track her down"

Silence fills the room again and no one really knows what to say, as I look around the room at them all it's becoming rather awkward, kinda like we all know what needs to happen but no one wants to admit it.

After a short while, I turn to look at Bow who finally says to Spencer "She's going down for this isn't she" And it's more of a statement than a question

He nods at him "I'm afraid so, never wanted it to be like this though man"

Bow nods and then says "Let me call her"

"What will that do?" Dawson finally cracks and I can hear the angry tone in his voice "She tried to kill you both over unfortunate past events and money, what are you going to say? Because we all know that'll be a jolly conversation – oh hey sis how are you? and oh I was just wondering did you try killing me and my girlfriend lately" he says his tone now very sarcastic

Bow shoots Dawson a dirty, I'm not that stupid look and then says, "Just trust me a second" Bow picks up his phone and dials a number "Oh hey Liam, it's Bow, yeah how ya doing man!....... good, good……. Listen I just wondered if my sister had made it back home safely after her visit here…. Oh, Okay…..she said she was visiting me and then travelling on business….. Oh okay, she said something about a manor house, Ohh yep…. Yep…. Okay well get her to give me a call man, I'd like to thank her personally for checking on me and perhaps take her out for lunch soon… yeah okay…. Thanks, Liam" and he hangs up the phone "Well she's not home, she must be still around here somewhere"

"Sounds like she might be up at Dawnwood staying," I tell him

"But I don't see how, there are builders everywhere, I instructed them to start doing work to the house a few weeks ago sweetheart, so there's no way she could be there" his voice is now soft as he talks to me.

"Then where could she be?" Dawson says getting louder and more frustrated

The room is silent for a short time which is broken suddenly by Spencer "I'm really sorry Bow but I need to radio this through, We need to find her, she's a possible danger to anyone who encounters her"

Bow turns to me "Are you really sure that this is what was said, Bea?"

"Yes I'm certain, I wouldn't lie about this, she said that your life insurance policy was about to come to an end and if they lost you, she would get everything, she even said that Dawnwood was supposed to be left to you and only you, but she wouldn't be telling you that because you had agreed that you would split the profit with her, but if something was to happen to you she would get everything"

"I'm going to have to check this with the company, I know we were the ones that dealt with this for Nana Clara and Grandpa Bill, I need to check that this is right and that it's true, not that I don't believe you, Sweetheart, I just need to check for my own peace of mind..:you know, Can you give me an hour before you do anything? I know that our probate team would know instantly"

Dawson looks to me, then to Spencer, "One hour" Spencer agrees

"Can we keep everything that's been said in this room private for the minute please too?" Bow asks

"Of course," I tell him but I'm not sure how long I can hold off Spencer, when I look around the room I can see some angry faces looking at me, Spencer especially as I know he really needs to follow protocol and radio it through, who I give a pleading look to and looking over at Dawson I can see he's absolutely furious.

Bow then gets up, kisses my forehead, and tells l my me "This won't take long Sweetheart, I'm so sorry, so sorry for everything, this whole thing is such a mess but don't worry we'll sort it… I wont be long" and with that, he turns and leaves the room.

Spencer comes over and gives me a very gentle cuddle "I'm so sorry Bea, you had us all worried sick, thought you were a goner for a while there"

I let out a little laugh "Thanks" I tell him, he always was the bluntest human being I know "How are you doing? Things with the case going okay?"

"Well, this ones been a bit tricky, she's been real slippery, there were no clues at Bow's crash site because his truck exploded, then there were no clues on your truck either because before your accident, this numb nuts over here," he says looking over his shoulder at Dawson, who looks guilty as sin but is rolling his eyes "Cleaned your truck so well when he fixed it for you that it wiped away any trace of fingerprints"

"Hey in my defence it was filthy" Dawson smiles

"Doesn't help my case though does it Daw"

I can see officer Daniels standing by the door wearing the biggest grin and it makes me smile too

Spencer follows my gaze "Go take a break Jon, come back in an hour" he tells him

Jon turns to look at me, almost frightened to approach me "I'm so sorry about the arrest Bea, I was only following protocol, but I'm really glad your okay" he tells me as he turns and leaves the room. As he does a nurse quickly comes in and takes my blood samples and tells us that we should have them back in no time. When she's finished I turn to my two of my brothers.

"So how is everyone?" I ask them

"They're all okay Bea, very worried about you if we're being honest," Dawson tells me

Then there's a knock at the door, Dawson stands there shaking his head and starts to laugh "I thought I told him he had to wait at home" he goes to the door to answer it, stood in the doorway is Clay, "I thought I told you to wait at home"

"You did....... But I needed to see for myself that she was okay" Clay tells them as he looks down at his feet and it's a real funny sight, to see such a masculine, tattooed, bearded guy like Clay look shy and intimidated by the other two, Clay kind of looks like he belongs on the back of a Harley Davidson in a biker jacket with his very manly beard and stocky build.

I start to laugh "I'm okay Clay" I say as I watch him as he stands in the doorway, Dawson looks over to me and then back at Clay "Oh for the love of god Dawson, let him in will you" he does a big sigh the stands aside, Clay swiftly walks past him and it's as if he's expecting a clout around the ear, I can tell because he's lifted his shoulders up to almost his ears and then he makes his way towards me, when he reaches me he wraps me into a big, warm hug and when he stands back and looks at me I can see the tears in his eyes.

"How you doing baby Bea?"

"Much better now thank you, how ya been?"

"Honestly?"

"Yeah?"

"Not great if I'm being really honest with you…I've been so worried about you, I thought we'd lost you Bea…. I feel like everything's falling apart, I've told the company I can't work for them at the moment and plus I've not been getting on with Florence either but that's entirely my fault, I think I've been neglecting her….I've kinda just hidden away since your accident" I just sit and look at him and I can tell he's really hurting, it's very unusual for Clay to open up and actually talk about his feelings like this, usually he just hides away and doesn't talk about anything like that, he's kind of a closed book.

"Well maybe you need to start with Florence, go and speak to her, explain, tell her how you feel, you obviously like her or we wouldn't be having this conversation, plus she's

British and I like the way they talk," I tell him wearing a big smile.

"I know your right," he says "but everything's so messed up at the moment"

"C'mon Clay you can do this, she's a real stunner and if I didn't have Willow I'd have definitely tried my luck," Spencer says

"Spence! You can't say things like that" I tell him

"What?" he says "just voicing my opinion"

Dawson lets out a little laugh and rolls his eyes, which makes it hard for me to contain my laughter too, I look around the room at all three of my brothers, I've missed this, and I've definitely missed them, I have lots of questions that I'm not sure I should ask but the curiosity gets the better of me.

"Soooo……." They all turn to look at me "Who wants to tell me how long I've been out of it?" they all look around at each other to see who wants to tell me first

And it's Dawson who speaks first "Around two and a half months now" they all look at me to gauge my reaction

I nod slowly "That's a while then, have I missed much?"

"No, no not a lot," Dawson says quickly but I can't help but notice he looks to the other two suspiciously as if he's trying to stop them from saying anything to me and then he looks at the floor and I know somethings up.

"What's happened?"

"Nothing," Dawson tells me

Silence fills the room and it's Spencer who speaks next

"We will discuss it later," Spencer tells us all; I look to Clay, and he can't keep eye contact with me

"Clay?, What's happened?" I know he would be the first to crack, he's never been very good at keeping things from me

"I don't think I'm the right person to tell you, Bea," he says as he looks to the other two for help

Dawson takes a deep breath "Now's not really the time"

"we weren't going to tell you yet," Spencer says in a frustrated tone looking at the other two and I can tell he's slightly annoyed that they've even mentioned this much.

"Tell me what?" I say my voice full of panic now as I look round the room at all of them

"Well, there has been some really strange goings-on around here lately" Dawson finally says

"Right, like what?" Both Clay and Dawson look to Spencer "Spence like what? What's happened?" I ask

"Well, just after your accident, I was called into the station… you know around a month and a half ago," he tells me as he waves his hands around "And there had been reports that a guy in Chicago was found shot three times in the chest and was killed…… I was questioned because that guy was Nathan parker" I'm suddenly speechless I don't know what to say and the room is filled with silence once more "and remember the little visit we gave him a while back, well that was picked up on, he was extremely intoxicated when they found him, the police came to question you but obviously, you couldn't have done it because you're here and you were in a coma"

I gasp then look down into my lap and I don't know how to feel, I feel slightly numb and hurt, we didn't really end on the best of terms, but no one deserves that, and was he all bad probably not, I mean he made some shitty choices, but he didn't deserve to go out like that, and I can't believe he was right under my nose in Chicago all this time and I had no idea. Why didn't I know this, I sit questioning myself, did my family know this too and then I think it's the wrong time for that question right now "Right, but why? Why would someone do something like that?"

"No one knows, that's the problem, they've put it down to him owing money or drugs or something"

"Hmph" is all I can manage and then the room is silent again, all I can think is the guy I know would never have touched drugs, he was very against people taking drugs as his mother was an addict when he was small and from what Sienna was saying he was low on cash, but I don't think he'd ever borrow any or dabble in any of that stuff and then it hits me hard.

"Hang on…Do you think all this could all be connected……. Connected to Sienna?" I sit and think again in silence "I mean she would have a motive"

"It's a possibility, We would have to question her to find out any more information," Spencer tells us

"But do we really think she's capable of doing that?" Dawson asks

"Anything's a possibility in this game," Spencer tells us

"You know, we we're all really worried about you baby Bea," Clay says, "Thought we were going to lose you, Mama and Pops are totally terrified"

"Talking of Mama and Pops where are they? I thought they would have been here by now"

They all look to their feet, when Clay looks up, he can't keep eye contact with me again and then he looks to Dawson for help, who looks back at him and then says "Well, it's like we said there's some strange things going on lately but…" They all look down to their feet again, when Clay looks up he can't look at me anymore and then looks to Dawson once more, who looks back at him and then to me "Bea there's something else we think you should know….. it's Mama, Bea somethings happened"

Chapter Seventeen

Mama

I look at all three of them and it's like no one wants to tell me.

"There's….. there's been an accident" Dawson continues

"What's happened and when? And why on earth has no one told me before now" my voice is suddenly full of panic

"We didn't want to worry you…" They all stand there looking at me and they all look so guilty "Well it was a few days ago, maybe two…. or three" Dawson tells me then he looks at the floor and I can tell that he's struggling to speak and hold himself together, but I sit there looking at each of them waiting for someone to give me the information I so desperately need to hear.

"It's Mama…..she's been shot….. twice….. in the chest," he tells me and I'm speechless hearing this and raise my hand to my mouth, how on earth could this just happen in our little town and how could they not tell me, I'm furious with them for not telling me the very moment I woke up.

the anxiety washes over me and I feel like my world has fallen apart once more.

"Is…..Is she okay?" Is all I can muster "What Happened?"

And nobody answers me

"WHAT THE HELL HAPPENED?" I shouted looking at the three of them

Dawson finally continues "She…. she was found slumped down in her car outside of Rose's café, she must have stopped in for a coffee after her usual weekly shop"

The tears are now running freely down my face and I'm trying hard to catch the lump in my throat.

"Rose was the one that found her" Dawson takes a deep breath and continues "It all happened a few days ago, Rose is just a mess," he tells me then looks at the floor, I sit there staring at him and the tears roll down my cheeks.

"WHAT THE HELL HAPPENED DAWSON!" I say suddenly realising I'm yelling "why the fuck did she go alone?"

He looks to the other two for help, but they just sit staring at the floor

"She was getting in the truck after going to the Grocery store and she must have popped into Roses for her usual coffee, She always goes alone Bea, you know how independent she is"

Spencer buts in "The security cameras show that she was approached by a tall stranger in dark clothing, and they talk for a little while, but we all are led to believe this person to be…."

"Sienna" I finish his sentence before Spencer can.

"It looks like Mama was able to get herself back in the truck after it all happened"

The tears are now streaming down my face, and I feel like I can't breathe "Where is Mama? Is she okay?" I sob and none of them know what to do, Dawson comes over and wraps me into a big warm hug, he always has a way about him where he knows just how to put me at ease, he always has done but this time as he wraps me into his arms, and I just break.

"Shhh….. Bea, it's okay….. she's okay" Dawson tells me as he strokes my hair

"Daw, man, don't lie to her……She's in here now Bea, Pops is with her at the moment, she's in a pretty bad way, they went through her main artery, so she lost a lot of blood" Clay tells me

Dawson is the next to speak "she's really unwell Beatrice…… to be honest with you…… we don't know if she'll make it, its pretty much…. touch and go right now"

"Hence why there not here with us at the moment," Spencer tells me as he puts his face in his hands "But they've been here every day to check on you before this all happened"

"Will she be okay?" I croak as I try to contain myself and notice this is the one question none of them have answered

"Honestly, we don't know," Clay says as he makes his way to the other side of the bed and hugs me too

We stay like that for the longest time, and I've really missed being surrounded by my brothers, they always have a way of making me feel so safe, protected even, and put at ease, But I know it's her that's done this, who else would have a motive, just like I know deep down that she'd taken out Nathan.

As much as they try to convince me and I try not to think the worst, I just don't know if Mama will be okay.

A short while later Bow comes back through the door holding five cups of coffee and some paperwork. He starts to hand out the coffee cups and then comes over and kisses me on the forehead.

"She knows," Dawson tells him in a dull tone

And he looks guilty as sin "Oh, Bea, Sweetheart I'm so sorry, We will get this sorted, I popped in to see her this morning and she's doing okay, I wanted to check up and see how Pops was doing too. Listen we will get through this together just like this family always does…together. Sweetheart I wish there were something more I could do to help"

"How is Pops?" I ask

"Honestly Sweetheart, not so good"

"And Mama?"

"She's doing okay but, there's no change yet"

I nod "Hmm……..It's okay……. She'll be fine, she's pretty tough our Mama, She'll get through this" I tell them as I try to be strong for them all and make a silent wish that she will be but looking around all I can see is the glum faces of my brothers and their uncertainty at my words.

"What ya got there?" I ask turning to Bow, noticing his crinkled paperwork in his hand.

"Well, it's the last will and testament of my grandparents, I found it in the box you were talking about when you woke up. Then I sent it to the guys on my probate team, and they confirmed that this was indeed an original and final copy of their will, they have an original copy to match that they have to keep on file. I never bothered to read the one we have on file at the office because I found it too upsetting, but I let Sienna read it after Grandpa Bill died and it states that she's not in the will at all, all she was left was some family jewellery"

"And your life insurance policy?" I hear Spencer ask

"It expires at the end of the month" he informs us

"Well, I'll be Damned" I hear Dawson say "That sly fox"

"So, What's our next step?" Bow asks looking at Spencer

Just then the door is flung wide open and its Pops, looking at his face we can tell he's in absolute bits, he's followed by Ruth who looks at Dawson and just shakes her head, she's been crying too, her eyes red raw and it's like I already know.

"No, no, no," I say as I start to sob

"I'm so sorry guys" he starts "she's......she's gone"

      Spencer is the first to walk up to him and wraps him in a tight hug and Pop's just collapses in his arms. I look to Dawson who has wrapped Ruth in his arms and is holding her as tightly as he can, I watch as they both sob into each other. I then look to Clay, who is sat staring into space and I can tell he's just breaking inside. Bow is beside me now and I didn't even realise it, I can't breathe, I feel like my heart has just fallen from my chest, the tears are down my face and I feel so broken, like my whole world has fallen apart, I've felt hurt before but nothing quite like this….. it's like a piece of me has been taken, I break in Bow's arms and even he's a mess. My mother was always the kindest and softest woman I've ever known (until it came to my father that is, who she would naturally boss around and tell him how it was, but he absolutely loved that about her) my mother would never cause harm to anyone, and she would never dream of causing any pain or hurt to anyone or anything for that matter, she just didn't have it in her, so why would somebody do this to her, to our family, she didn't deserve this. I have so many questions for my brothers, but I don't know where to start and I feel it's the wrong time for me to ask them, I want to know, do they know who could have done this? Why was she left alone? Did anyone see anything? Do they know where the gun is and what it is? Could this have anything to do with Nathan Parker? and could all this be connected? And deep down I know they are. Thoughts run wildly through my head as I look around the room at my now broken family, I briefly wonder how we will cope without her….. mainly how Pop's will cope, who will look after him? What will we all do without her? Who will I call every Sunday evening just because I've had a bad day or to talk to about the books I've read or even just to discuss what she would make for the local fates and just generally chat to her, I look up at Bow and he's in absolute pieces too, if anyone would know how this feels he would know it all too well, seeing how he lost both his parents when he was just ten years old due to a car accident caused by a drunk driver who collided with them at high speed, causing their fancy corvette to be unrecognisable, it was reported that they were pronounced dead at the scene and we were always told they were killed on impact but that has never made it any better. Bow and Sienna were at the scene because they were in the car behind with Clara and Bill. I don't think any child should have had to see that, I mean they were so young with Bow being just ten and Sienna being fourteen. Bow has never mentioned what happened to his parents or spoke about it to us, I think it hurt too much, but I just remember it being terrible, we didn't see them for months after the accident and they kept themselves to their selves, occasionally we would knock the door and sometimes they would come out to play but it was never something any of us mentioned to them and they never mentioned it to us either, that was always the way it was, we just treated them like we always had.

We all sit and for the longest time no one says anything, but we are all absolutely devastated like the light has gone out in our lives.

A while later, Spencer has taken Pop's and Clay back to his place just outside of town, who will be met by Willow, as nobody can bring themselves to be up at the ranch at the moment. Spencer has informed us that he will be back tomorrow because he needs to get his head straight and to be there for Pop's tonight. It's dark, I look around the room and I can see shadows of Ruth and Dawson both asleep in the armchair in the far corner of the room by the window and Bow has been sat on the bed beside me with an arm draped around my shoulder for the last 3 hours, it's now 3.45 am and the room is silent. I want to get out of here, run away from all of this, go back to Chicago, and have a stiff drink, I mean I didn't even get to say goodbye, who on earth would do such a thing to a family, my family and most importantly why would someone do this?

"Still awake sweetheart?" I hear him whisper beside me

"Hmm….Yeah, can't seem to switch off" I tell him "I just keep thinking it all over in my mind"

"I know I'm so sorry this has happened, she was such a wonderful woman, when we were growing up I always wanted a mother like yours….. a very special lady….. you know I once asked her if I could call her Mama too and she said yes, I mean of course she did, she was always so accepting of me and Sienna, even treated me like I was one of her own. she said to me one day you know your always going to be part of this family, whether you have the Coleman surname or not"

And hearing this makes me smile because I can vaguely hear her saying it. The room is silent again for a moment and then he says "Your Mama was always so caring, so loving and she just loved having the house full of children, we were always welcome at the Coleman household" he pauses and then speaks again "You know we'll catch whoever has done this Sweetheart if it's the last thing I do"

All is quiet for a moment and then I say "Do you really think it could have been her? I mean all have been Sienna's doin? Do you really think she'd be capable of doing something like this?"

"I honestly don't know Bea, If I said no I'd be lying, the thing is you think you know someone and then one day you realise you didn't know them as well as you once thought you did"

All is quiet again, I don't really know what to say so I snuggle in closer to Bow as he wraps his arms around me and pulls me in tighter, we both just sit there for the longest time looking at the grey coloured room, and I keep thinking things over in my mind once more, I keep thinking about the conversation that she must have had before she was shot, I think about memories I'd had with Mama, things like being a child and her brushing my hair, dressing up in her clothes and laughing, cooking meals with her and the thing I'll miss most is her gentle hugs, the laughter qand our random conversations. I can see the sun starting to come up and notice Bow is fast asleep beside me and it's not long before I join him and drift off into a deep sleep….

The next morning, I wake up to find them all in my room, Bow is still beside me on the bed talking to Dawson, I spit them all dotted around the room, Dawson and Ruth, Spencer and Willow, Clay, and officer Daniels. I briefly wonder how long they've all been here and hope to god I didn't have my mouth wide open while I was asleep.

"Morning Baby Bea" I hear Clay say

"Morning" I mumble and then looking around at them all "Someone tell me it was just one big, horrible, bad dream"

"I wish we could," Ruth says her tone Sympathetic, but I can't help but notice she really does look a mess

"No Pops? I ask

"No, I don't think he could face it," Clay tells me "he's in a pretty bad way, we've all had to pull ourselves together and see to the animals at the ranch this morning too, he just can't face it"

The thought of this kills me. my poor Pops must feel like he's lost a limb or something, I bet he's in an awful state, completely heartbroken…not knowing what to do with himself. Mama was his total world, his everything, they meant so much to each other and I don't think they were ever apart very long, if at all, it's an awful feeling for us all because we know this is just going to destroy him, I start to worry about how he will manage, I mean I know he's a tough cookie and all, but he's never been without her. They had been together since they were kids, I'm pretty certain they met a middle school. I think we're all just going to have to support him as much as we can, I sit and think for a while about what the next step is for him. Just then Spencer brings me back from my thoughts.

"Right first things first, what happens in this room stays in this room, okay"

There are lots of nods and resounding "yeps" and "Okays" from around the room and some confused looks too

"Listen up, We've got a plan," Spencer tells us

Everyone in the room is listening intently but as I look around I can see the gloom written on their faces.

"After a long chat with Bow this morning," Spencer says looking at me and Bow sat on the bed "We have decided that we need to look at this from all aspects, we know that Sienna put you and Bow in here Bea, so she needs to be taken in for questioning regarding those incidents, but we don't really know what she's capable of, we can't pin any of this on her without any evidence. The plan is to get her to come to Dawnwood to "Chat" with Bow regarding selling the house and then we'll take her down there. This could be incredibly dangerous for Bow as we're unsure of what might happen or what her next move would be, but he's agreed to do this for us, we will make sure he wears a wire and a hidden body cam and cover him so he's safe at all times, we have to be careful as she's tried once to hurt him so what's stopping her from doing it again. When we've got her, we can take her in, then we will search her vehicle and find out the place that she's staying and search there too"

"And when will this take place?" Dawson asks

"Hopefully, Friday night if she agrees to meet with Mr Tanner, We need to get everything finalised down at the station but there are going to be only a few officers that know about it," Jon tells us

"Why?" Ruth asks before I can, and even I'm a little confused

Spencer takes a deep breath and Jon looks to him "Because the bullet that killed Nathan was from a Beretta M9 and the very same bullets were pulled out of Mama

We all look at him with confused expressions and as he goes to speak Bow beats him to it

"It's a gun that is commonly used by officers of the law and was one that would only have been used by a SWAT team," he tells us all

"So do you think some foul play is going on somewhere?" Dawson interrupts

"At this moment in time were not entirely sure," Spencer tells us

"But if it were Sienna, how would she get hold of one of those," I ask them

"We're not really sure" Jon mumbles

Silence fills the room once more and there are a lot of confused faces. Madeline my nurse comes into the room and stands in the doorway.

"Officer Coleman, could I have a word with you please? Perhaps outside?" he nods and follows her back through the door. They're out there for what seems like forever.

"I wonder what that's about," Dawson finally asks as he gets up, wonders to the door and looks through the glass panel within it.

"I have a few ideas," Bow tells them

The door opens and Spencer enters closely followed by Madeline "Right you lot go and get some lunch…. I need to speak with Beatrice"

"I don't mind everyone knowing, I've got nothing to hide"

"Oh no, I think this is something we're going to need to discuss on our own," he says his voice suddenly stern, and I feel like I'm in trouble. I look to Dawson for help then to Bow "Don't even think about hanging back Daw this is important" he tells him following my gaze

He rolls his eyes "We're not going to be far" he tells me as they make their way towards the door

"And I'll be just outside," Bow tells kissing me on the head and ignoring Spencer's glare

"You too Jon" who looks slightly surprised, with that Jon also turns and leaves the room, I watch them all leave and that's when I notice that I can just see Bow's head through the glass in the door and I can tell he's not going anywhere.

"Okay Bea, sorry but I didn't think you'd want to share this new information with anyone yet," he says as he takes the blue seat beside me, followed by my hand

"Okay" I look down at his hand on mine with a confused expression, because this is so out of character for him "What's going on Spence your scaring me a little, this seems slightly serious"

"I just need to ask you something"

"Okay"

"Have you ever taken any drugs? Heroin perhaps?"

"What?!, No of course not, I wouldn't touch anything like that"

"Your sure?"

"Of course, I'm sure! I'd never touch anything like that, you should know that I'm not some kind of junkie" I tell him trying to hold back my laugh

"That's what I thought"

"Why? What's going on?"

"Well, there were high levels of heroin in your system and the Doctors and nurses were wondering if you had taken it previously, I've told them of course not because you've been in a coma here for the last two and a half months, but they can't seem to figure out why or how it even got into your system"

"Sienna, she was here, I heard her, she was here Spence, I felt what she did"

"Well, it almost killed you," he tells me "but what if it wasn't her"

"It was…. I can feel it in my bones…. I know it was her….. but Thanks Spence your right I'm not ready for everyone to know, I don't want them thinking I'm some sort of junkie"

"I need to ask you something else"

"Okay ask away"

"Do you love him?" he asks me looking in the direction of the door

I try to hold back my giggle, it's funny how a simple question can make you feel like a schoolgirl "Yes Spencer I really do, he means everything to me, he respects me, loves me in return and most importantly he wants nothing but my time, nothing more or nothing less, he's my rock and the one I wanna spend my life with"

"Okay," he says looking down in an awkward sort of way "Okay well that's good"

"What is it, Spence?"

"Well, I don't know if I'm the right one to tell you this" he hesitates "But Beatrice you're……..your pregnant"

"I'm what?" I sit in total shock "I can't be, there must be some sort of mistake"

"Nope, I asked them if they were certain"

"But I can't have children….. I was told that years ago…… all the tests…… the scans…….I was the problem...... I can't have children....there must be some sort of mistake"

"Well, it certainly looks like you can" he smiles at me "What are you going to do?"

"Hang on.... You're sure about this? And what do you mean, what am I going to do?"

"Certain the nurse, Madeline, has just shown me it on paper and confirmed it, it came back with your blood test, Well are you going to call Bow in and tell him?"

I think for a moment should I tell him; I don't want to mess with his head at a time like this "Maybe I should let him get his meet with Sienna out the way first, I don't want to put this on him at a time like this, I don't even know what he'll say or even react" I tell Spencer

"Okay well it's your call"

I just sit there smiling at him and he returns my massive grin, and he gives me a big hug, he then heads over to the door, wiping the smile from his face and opens it, letting Bow in. who walks in and says "So?"

"Well, the doctors have found high levels of heroin in Bea's system, so they have determined that that was the cause of the heart failure"

He looks at me and I can't contain my delight, with a huge smile stretched across my face

"That would make sense, but she wouldn't ever touch that, you know that Spence," he tells Spencer looking in my direction and returning my smile "What are you smiling about?" Bow asks as he matches my wide grin "heroin's hardly something to be smiling about"

"I'll leave you two love birds to it; I need some lunch," Spencer says as he smiles too and leaves the room.

"Okay, what's the joke?"

"Oh, nothinggggg……. I'm just happy to see your gorgeous face again"

He Laughs "Okay and why are you really smiling?"

"I can't tell you it's a secret, Shhh," I say "Can you help me stand, please? I want to look out of the window"

"You shouldn't really be getting out of bed, you're not strong enough yet sweetheart, the physio will be in soon to help you gain back your muscle strength and you shouldn't put pressure on that cast," he says pointing down at my feet

"But it won't be for long" I state.

Looking at me he then scoops me up in his arms from the bed and then walks over to the large hospital window. The sun is beaming, it's a beautiful morning, I've missed this sight, the heat on my skin and I've really missed his arms around me. He places me down so I'm on my feet and wraps his arms around me so that he's holding me up so I can put the weight on my good leg. We both stand there looking out of the window for the longest time.

"It's so beautiful isn't it"

"It certainly is" he replies looking at me

"I've missed this sight"

"So have I" he states

"Listen Bow….I'm ……I'm worried for your safety; I don't want you to go see Sienna, You could get hurt" I tell him

"She won't hurt me Sweetheart and if I don't go then we won't find out what actually happened will we, plus I need to straighten out a few things with her"

"No I know, but it's dangerous and I can't lose you too"

"I know, I wonder how your Pop's is doing….. he must be going through hell, I can't imagine what I'd do if I lost you, I know I'd be one broken man"

Chapter Eighteen

Grief

It's 4.30 pm on Friday, the sun is still beaming high in the sky, and I can't help but keep thinking that today is the day, the day that it's supposed to happen. It seems to have come round all to quickly, these last few days have flown by, Bow and Dawson have spent the week with Spencer and the small team he's put together, by the sounds of it they have planned everything down to the finest detail. I however have spent this week having session after session of physio with the physiotherapist, her names Carly and she seems really nice although she's very happy to push me past my comfort zones, she tells me I'm doing really well and that I can hopefully go home by the end of the day, and then I can just come back and see her in two weeks so she can make sure I'm doing okay, and I've got to be honest part of me can't wait to get out of this place, I'm desperate to see my Pops and just to check how he's doing, he hasn't been back to the hospital since Mama. I know Clay has been with him and they have both barely left the house (Spencer's place) since he got there on the night Mama died. I'm currently sitting in the chair in my hospital room and the nurse comes into my room.

"Miss Coleman, the doctors are happy to discharge you today, is there anyone you'd like me to call?

A wide smile flashes across my face as I try to contain my delight, I've been so bored in here but now the dread fills me and I can feel the anxiety rising in my chest.

"Umm, yes I think that would be a good idea"

"Shall I get you your cell for you?"

"No, no thank you, I can manage," I tell her as I gently lift myself from the bedside chair and hobble around the other side of the bed to the draws in which my family had filled with things I "might" need.

"Looks like your getting the hang of that, I'll give you some privacy," she tells me as she leaves the room.

I pick up the cell and dial the only number I know off by heart

"Daw, hey, it's me, I know how busy you are with things right now, but they've said I can come home today"

I hear Bow in the background say, "Is she okay?"

"Yeah, yeah," Dawson tells him "Okay baby Bea I'll be there in ten minutes, don't struggle down to the front entrance, we'll meet you in your room"

"Yep, okay, okay thanks," I tell him "Are you bringing Bow?"

"Of course, I am, he wouldn't let me leave him here" I can tell he's walking "just getting in the truck now" and I know he's telling the truth because I can hear the truck doors slam.

"Let me talk to her" I hear Bow say in the background

"Well, gotta go" I hear Dawson say to him "Oh Okay Bea, you enjoy talking to that nice male nurse"

"WHAT?" I say and then I hear Bow in the background mirroring my reaction followed by Dawson's laugh which makes me laugh too "There's no male nurse!" I shout and laugh again

"Be there soon Bea" Dawson tells me through the laughter, and I can only guess Bow has bitten at his little joke and the line goes dead.

A while later, They both come charging into my room and acting like they're trying to kidnap me. Bow puts me over his shoulder in a fireman's lift and Dawson grabs my already packed bags from the bed and they run out of the hospital. Shouting things like "Quick go" and "We're going to take her and hold her against her will" and it reminded me of just like when we were kids, I just remember seeing all the other patients and staff members wearing massive grins across their faces that coincidentally they matched mine as I roll my eyes and start to laugh.

When we reach the truck, Bow has strapped me in one of the back seats, gives me a kiss on the forehead and then climbs in the front with Dawson.

"Hang on, why do you get to sit upfront?" I ask smiling

"Because I'm co-captain Bow" he replies with a wink and that cheeky smile that I love oh so much.

"So where do you want to go, Bea?" Dawson asks me suddenly serious

"Well, what are my options?"

"Well, you can either go back to Spencer's, where everyone seems to be at the moment, or you can come back to the ranch with us"

I sit and think about what I want to do

"But you need to know no ones been back up there in the house since before Mama passed" he continues "I've only been to feed the animals and clean out the stables

"Well, we can't avoid it forever can we"

"No that's very true but it's very hard for everyone to be there at the moment"

I think for a moment "Take me to the ranch please but on the way I'd like to pop in and check up on Rose please and then I'd like to go see my Pops"

They both look at each other and nod "Okay, I could do with a fresh cup of coffee anyway" Dawson tells me "But could we give the ranch a miss today please? I've already been up there once this morning to sort the animals"

I nod "Okay," I can tell he's hurting but trying hard to hide it

And the next thing I know we're heading towards the town and to Roses café. When we arrive it's pretty quiet inside, there are only about three other people in there including Rose herself. I look to her and realise how tired and drained she looks; she just looks totally exhausted. Her hair is a mess and all fuzzy, which is very unusual for her, her eyes are bloodshot and the bags beneath them are blacker than I remember.

"Hi Rose," I say to her softly

"Be right with ya" she tells me in a dull, monotone then she looks up and realises it's me "Oh Beatrice honey, I'm so glad to see your out of that hospital, how ya doing sweetie?" she says in a deflated tone

"Better than I was thanks Rose" I look around the room at the two other customers who are just about to leave "How ya holding up though Rose?

She looks at her feet and when she looks back up I can see the tears brewing in her eyes. "I'm….I'm so sorry Beatrice" she starts to sob "I tried everything I could to save her……. She was just sat in the old truck….door open…. I'll never forget it…. She was such a kind and Caring lady….would do anything for anyone that one……I'm so sorry Beatrice… I did everything I could…..I tried so bad to help her… I did everythin I could" she continues

I hobble towards her and wrap her into a hug, she holds me tight as she sobs into my shoulder, I hear the bell go on the door and can only assume that the two customers that were sat up at the counter, have now got up and left, so that we're on our own with her, I can feel myself welling up too. I can tell the loss of my mother has affected more than just our family "It's okay Rose, we know you did everythin you could….she would have been so grateful for any help you'd have given her" I say as I try to catch the lump in my throat.

"I just don't know how it happened or who would harm such a special person," she tells me through her sobs "she was such a good friend to me"

"I know Rose, you were such a good friend to her too," I say hugging her tighter and all is quiet for a moment "Shall we have a seat?"

"Oh…yes….of course dear…..please choose whatever you'd like," she tells us as she wipes her face with her hands and picks up her note pad ready to take our orders

"No, no Rose…I think you need a coffee, have a seat, I've got this"

She does as she's told, I make my way around the counter to the side that is very familiar to me. I take four different, quirky multi coloured mugs from under the metal counter and place them on top. I then walk over to the old coffee machine, and I'm stunned that it's still here and more importantly that it's in full working order. I begin to press the buttons like I have so many times before in the past and the machine jumps into life. Everything is still in the same place that it always was…. And then I remember, tapping the wooden floorboard below the coffee machine with my foot and remember what was once hidden underneath it, I reach down and gently lift it, reaching in I pull out a bottle of a very old, very dusty but also a very expensive bottle of whiskey, that she always kept here in case of emergencies or special occasions. I open the half-empty bottle and place a shot of it in her drink.

"What ya having?" I ask the three of them, that are now sat at a funky wooden table just in front of the counter. The round wooden table legs have flowers carved into them and the seats match and are just as ornate.

"I'll have a latte please," Bow tells me looking up at me with a serious look on his face

"Just a coffee with extra cream please," Dawson tells me

I look at rose whose tear-stained face looks so downhearted "I'll just have a black coffee; you know the house special one"

"I'm already on it, whiskeys already in the mug Rose"

She smiles "I didn't think you'd remember"

"I'd never forget," I say returning her weak smile

When I've prepared the drinks, I take them over to the table and take a seat in between Rose and Bow who takes my hand. Silence fills the room and I take her hand trying to reassure her and all is silent as we start to take sips of our drinks.

To my surprise, Rose breaks the silence first "How's Jefferson holding up dear?"

I look to Dawson because I honestly have no idea.

"He's a bit of a mess, to be honest with you Rose, a total mess, he's barely got out of bed all week, he won't eat much, it's all a little worrying at the moment" he tells her

She nods and looks down at her feet "I'd expected him to be that way, poor chap, he must be so heartbroken" silence fills the room once more and then suddenly she jumps up from her seat, "hang there" she tells us "I have an idea"

We watch her disappear into the back and she's back within seconds

"Your Mama helped me make these and here are a few that I've made myself, please take them" she comes out holding four frozen trays of all sorts of meals, casseroles, peach cobbler, lasagne, and American chilli.

"Oh, Rose we couldn't"

"Please" she insists, handing them to us all, "I think Jefferson needs them more than the café at the moment"

"Rose that's really kind of you…..thank you," I tell her, and I notice Dawson is beside her utterly speechless

"I had no idea she was making them all for the café….. she never said," Dawson tells her

"Oh, yes…. She came and helped out twice a week, it was a lot more after Beatrice left, she needed to keep busy, so I helped with that and in turn, it was helping me too" All is quiet for a moment "Is there anything else you need dears?"

"No Rose this is more than enough, thank you very much," Dawson tells her, and I can see the tears in his eyes.

"Thank you so much, Rose, you don't know what this will mean to our Pops," I tell her through the tears

She nods "You know where I am should you need anything else okay, even if that's just your old job back" she smiles at me fondly

"Thanks, Rose but I'm going to have to head back to Chicago sometime"

"But do you though" I hear Bow's voice beside me ignoring him the room is filled with that awkward silence once more

"Right come on, you want to get those back in a freezer as soon as possible," she tells us, and we know that's our queue to leave. We stand up push our chairs in and make our way to the door. "If you need anything dears just you let me know okay"

"Thanks, Rose," I tell her as I hug her tightly "and thanks for being such a good friend to Mama" I look at her and she starts to well up again "we'll be back Sunday for lunch okay?"

Dawson and Bow also turn and hug her too, thanking her

"Okay table for three?"

"Four please," I tell her, and she nods and with that we leave with our Mama's homemade meals and head for Spencer's house to see Pops.

When we get there, all is quiet, the house from the outside is all white and modern, it looks so out of place in this little town but then that's Spencer for you, he loves anything to do with modern technology and there are so many mod cons in here that I feel like I've travelled through time to the future. We walk in to find Clay sat on the white sofa with Florence, who gets up and greets us with a tight hug, I walk through to the all white kitchen/diner to find Willow baking a pumpkin pie.

"Hey," I say to her as I place the casseroles and other yummy dishes that have come from Roses on the island that's in the centre of the room.

"Hi," she says looking at me and I can tell she's not really sure whether to hug me or not, so I walk towards her and wrap her in a tight hug, as I do she starts to cry "What's wrong Willow?"

"I'm…..I'm just so sorry Beatrice…..I'm trying everything……I've baked, and I've cooked, and I can't get it right" she sobs

"Hey, it's okay…" I say as I hug her tighter "What are you trying to make?"

"Well….your Pops said he would miss your Mamas pumpkin pie…..so I tried to make it, but it never tastes right….. I just want him to eat" she sobs as I pull her tighter then I look down the counter and see five homemade pumpkin pies that she doesn't think is right.

"Where is he?" I ask slightly cross that her efforts haven't been acknowledged

"Upstairs in the back bedroom"

"Okay, put those in the freezer for me please, I'll be right back," I tell her as I hobble my way back out of the really stylish kitchen and then hobble past the all-white living room containing Clay and Florence, and now also Bow and Dawson.

I make my way towards the very clean white stairs that are made from wood. I start to climb, just as I do I realise that I've never actually been in Spencer's house before and I notice very quickly how white and clean everything is. Almost like a show home. When I finally reach the top of the landing I see there are five doors, I open the first one I come to and inside is a large bed in the centre of the room, and directly in front of that is a beautiful glass balcony, on the far side of the room is what looks like an en-suite, all once again, yes you guessed it, white in colour, I close the door and open the next I find yet another bedroom but it's smaller than the first and white in colour again, the next room I come to is a very stylish bathroom, with white tiles on the walls and black large tiles on the floor, the best bath I've ever seen and a separate shower that's big enough for at least three or four people. I make my way to the next door just around the corner and slowly open it. It's the smell that hits me first and that's when I see him sat in an armchair by the window and he's fast asleep, my Pop's looks so fragile and faded, and in some ways peaceful. I walk over to the chair and bend down so I can look directly at him.

"Hey Pops" I call

He startles and then keeps blinking his eyes
"Oh…hey…honey" he says as he stretches his arms out above his head "I didn't realise I'd fallen asleep"

"No that's okay Pops, I can't imagine that you've had very much of it lately," I tell him. He looks at me and nods "Anything I can get ya pops?"

"No, no I'm okay thank you darlin….wait a minute…. you've been discharged from the hospital"

"Yep, they let me go…….. you know you're going to be okay don't you…….we're all here to help"

He looks up at me "I don't know how we're ever going to be okay without her honey… how will I run the ranch? How will….will I remember to do all the things she use to do" he sobs "I don't do so well without her Beatrice, y'all know that……I don't even know what to do with myself now, let alone the animals up at the ranch" he stops and takes a deep breath in and then continues "she was my total world and now… now she's gone….taken from us like she didn't matter" I can now hear the rage in his voice "well she did matter, she mattered to me….to us…. our family, she was like the sun one a gloomy day, my light in the dark, the sweet to my sour" and I know what he means because that's the best way I could describe them sweet and sour "and what…..what do I do now?" He tells me looking at the white carpet on the floor, looking defeated

"Well, you do what she would want you to do" he looks up at me and the tears are in his eyes "she would want you to carry on Pops…. She wouldn't want you like this, she'd want you to be happy again"

"How will I ever be happy without her Darlin"

I get up and pull him into a strong hug and then take a deep breath "I don't know Pop's…. I really don't…. But you can't stay here for the rest of your life…..I know she was your world, but you need to go back to the ranch…. You need to live"

He turns and looks out the window "I don't think I can face it Beatrice…it's just not home without her there"

"But it might make you feel a bit better being there"

"No…… I….. I just can't" he then pauses for a moment before saying, "I think we need to call a family meeting darling, I need to discuss some things with y'all"

"Okay…. That's fine… but why?"

"Well, I've been thinking about the ranch, and I don't think I can do it anymore and I wouldn't want to do it without your mother there either…. I…. I think it's time to give it up"

"What do you mean Pops? That's your home, our home, we've so many memories there too…. You can't just sell it"

"I know, I know but I think I know someone who will appreciate it and look after it better than I can"

I look at him and know who he means almost immediately "You mean Dawson"

He nods "I just need to sort some things out first"

"Okay Pops…well…. I mean….. I don't know what to say…..but if those are your wishes then I'll back you 100%"

He nods "I think I need to rest Bea; I'm exhausted…… I'm sorry"

"It's okay Pops it's been a rough few weeks for you hasn't it" I give him one more hug and get up "Pops…. Do me a favour?" He looks at me with a quizzing look "Eat… please … you'll feel better if you do….oh and by the way Willow's been baking pumpkin pies all morning for you and Rose has sent over some meals that Mama made for her, that she had frozen in the freezer at the cafe so please eat"

Tears fill his eyes, and he nods, and I close the door behind me, I realise I'd been holding my breath and can finally release it. That was harder than I thought it would be, I feel a little numb after the conversation with my father, I'm trying hard to hold myself together but it's so darn hard at the moment., I walk down the landing, I head down the stairs to the bottom floor, when I hear a phone ring.

I turn to my left by the living room door. I hear Bow Shhh everyone and he must have answered the phone because the next thing I hear is….

"Sienna….. Oh good, you got my text message…..yes, yes, I've decided to sell Dawnwood, I just thought we could meet up there and discuss what it's worth then maybe you could….. sell it for us both, seeing as your in the business…… I was thinking you'd have an idea about what its worth now its almost finished" I hear him say

"Yes, Okay, that would be great 7 pm tonight sounds great to me...as I have to go back to New York tomorrow....yes, yes you were right about her sister...... there was someone else...... oh and hey I think I've found a buyer" at that point I stand in the doorway and stare at him and our eyes lock "Okay great see you tonight, thanks Si" and with that, he hangs up and looks straight to me

"Right about her hey," I say looking him dead in the eye then shuffling a little further down the corridor

he follows saying "Oh shit" and its as if he instantly knows I'm pissed "I had to say that sweetheart, I need her to meet me"

"Hmm, You didn't have to say that," I say, and I certainly feel a little like I've been betrayed

He walks over to me and kisses me gently before wrapping me in his arms "You are and always have been the only one for me Beatrice Coleman" and I'm a little taken back to hear him use my full name.

"You never call me that, cowboy, but mr name is Sweetheart" I tell him with a smile

"That's because your mine, sweetheart"

I smile into his chest "Always and Forever" I tell him

"Hmm, always and forever" and I can hear the smile playing on his lips. He pulls me tighter, and I close my eyes as I place my head on his chest, I then hear Dawson's voice and notice he's appeared beside us.

"We've got to get to the station with Spence and the others," he tells him "I've just spoken to him; they want to go through everything before it's too late," he tells us

"Okay, I've got to go sweetheart"

"I know, stay safe" the anxiety washes over me and I'm suddenly terrified not just for Bow but for Dawson too, I hold Bow tightly before letting go and giving Dawson a big squeeze too I tell him "Please keep him safe Daw"

"Will do," he tells me in a casual tone

"And don't do anything stupid Daw"

"I won't, don't worry" Dawson tells me with an eye roll and a smirk that's playing on his lips

"please remember that I love you both" they nod at me and then I watch them leave

---

Chapter Nineteen

The Plan

I stand there in the glass doorway to Spencer's house with Ruth and Willow watching them leave, Clay and Flo have stayed behind too but have stayed in the living room out of the way, when they're out of sight I notice my phone buzzing in my pocket, its Bow.

"We love you too Sweetheart"

"Come home safe, both of you"

"Of course, we will"

Ruth closes the door and I follow her and Willow back through to the all-white and marble kitchen.

"Coffee anyone?" Willow asks picking up the jug from the coffee machine

"Please," Ruth says, and she looks at me for a response

"Umm, No….thanks"

Ruth sits at the breakfast bar, and I sit beside her, all is quiet for the moment, When I suddenly snap, my thoughts are running wild, what if they don't come back? what if she already knows? what if it's an ambush? What if they get hurt or worse? I can't lose anyone else.

"I can't do this," I say getting up from the barstool.

"What?" Ruth asks

"This…..I can't just sit here and wait to see if they come back" I get up and walk into the all-white living room with Ruth following, it really is like a show home here, the mantelpiece is all white, along with all the modern furniture, there are no ornaments placed around the room, it's so minimal here. I turn to look at Clay who's sitting on the sofa looking back at me.

"Have you lost your mind?" Ruth asks me

"I don't know, but I do know I can't just sit here and wait…..I need to know what's happening……Clay??"

"Err….Yes" he looks at me as if he's a little confused

"Where are the keys to your Mercedes that you use for work?"

"Umm… in my pocket" I can see Ruth beside me looking at him and shaking her head as if to silently tell him no.

"Can I have them please?"

He looks at me then to Ruth unsure of what to do "Umm…..why?"

"Because I need them…."

"For?" he asks

"Because she's going to go after them," Ruth tells him

"Listen Bea I don't think that's a very good idea….." he starts

"I know what you're going to say," I tell them

"How will you even drive it?.... you're not even fully recovered and you can't possibly drive," he asks

"I won't…..Ruth's going to take me"

"WHAT?..... this is totally ridiculous," she says beside me

"Want me to drive it on my own, do you? Because you know as well as I do that I'll crash that beautiful Mercedes of his and there's a high possibility that I'll end up hurt again"

Clay looks at me and then says "Your going even if I say no aren't you"

I look at him and it's as if he knows me all too well before handing me the keys.

"Thank you"

"This is ridiculous," Ruth says again beside me before storming out of the room" then I hear a bang

"What you doing?" I ask her as I follow her out

"Trying to find my fucking shoes…..seeing as your so determined to go after them and be involved" I walk out to her in the hallway "Keys," she says holding her hand out "God Daw mentioned you were stubborn but geez," she says as she struggles to get her shoes on and heads for the door "keys" she says again so I hand them to her.

Willow comes over to us and I can see Flo and Clay stood in the doorway to the front room

"What's going on?" Willow asks looking confused

"We're going after them," she tells her with an eye roll "this idiot won't let it go and is insisting we make sure there safe"

"Oh, Bea…I mean….C'mon…. don't do this….Spencer has it all under control"

I turn to look at them all "Look after Pops… We'll right be back"

I walk out to the brand new, slate grey Mercedes sat on the driveway, Ruth Climbs in beside me "This is utter madness" and I can tell she's somewhere between pissed off and scared of what might happen next.

When we're halfway to Dawnwood Manor I break the silence and turn to Ruth "Thank you for doing this with me, I promise that i'll never ask you to do anything as mad as this again"

"So, you admit its madness then," she tells me

"Well…..yes….. but I can't lose them both too"

Ruth huffs beside me. "What exactly is your plan here Beatrice?" she snaps

"Well…I'm not too sure"

"Please tell me that's a joke!" and I can now tell by her tone she's pissed at me

"Well… I think we could park in the field just down from Dawnwood and walk up through the gardens to see what's happening from there"

"We'll be seen"

"You'd think that wouldn't you but the gardens all over grown"

"And if were put in danger?"

"We won't be…. They won't even know were there"

"For fuck sake Beatrice….you better pray this plan of yours works"

       We pull up into the field and park up beside the hedge, behind a really large bush, so the cars out of sight. We walk down the road and then start to head up the long garden, up towards Dawnwood Manor. I know everything is overgrown and out in bloom, so it works in our favour, we stay low so we're definitely out of sight, it's like I know these gardens like the back of my hand from when we used to play here as kids. As the manor house comes clearer into view, we notice Dawson's blue truck sat on the gravel and a fancy white rental car just beside it.

"She's here… she would have had the rental car"

"Why?"

"Less suspicious, looks like she's travelled to get here then doesn't it"

"Oh course" she whispers

"Who's that up there hiding in that large elderberry bush?" I ask and Ruth notices too

"That's weird, I would think Spence and his team would all be in uniform and out of sight"

"Yeah, that's what I'm thinking too, I would imagine it would be SWAT uniform for something like this" Ruth tells me as we look at each other "What if that one's not part of his team"

"Let's get closer" I whisper

"Oh no you don't, you don't know what's happening up there"

"oh…. c'mon….. don't you want to make sure they're okay"

"I'm sure they're fine, officers will be everywhere up there…hey wait a minute" I hear Ruth say but I've started to crawl up the lawn

"Stop being such a pussy" I tell her as she rolls her eyes and drops down to her knees just like I have

"If we're not killed here Beatrice I'm going to kill you myself when this is done"

Hearing this makes me smile….she's very much like Dawson in this way and I absolutely love her loyalty, we get closer to the house and on the other side of the bushes I've spotted Spencer who looks less than pleased to see me. We sit hidden behind a large red-leaved shrub, and I can see the person who was behind the elderberry bush is now by the rental car and is none other than Christine who works for Spencer at the station and it all starts to click into place. I turn to Ruth and poke her then nod towards

Christine stood by the rental car. The house is even more breath-taking than I remember it, the work Bow's had done to the house is just incredible now that it's been restored to its former glory and I can't wait to see what he's done to it inside, but I push that to the back of my mind.

"She's been in on this the whole time" I whisper "explains where the gun came from and the bullet they pulled from Mama when she was killed doesn't it"

I hear Ruth gasp beside me.

We hear raised voices from inside the manor house and it goes on for a few minutes, I can't tell who's voice I can hear but they're now shouting. The next thing I know, I hear the sound of a gunshot, I get up and run towards the house, but Ruth grabs me by the ankle, and I fall to the floor with a thud.

"No Bea you can't" she whispers "They can't know we're here"

We watch as Christine makes a move towards the house but it's as if from now where we see officer Daniels tackle her to the floor, there's a scramble for the gun she's holding but Spencer soon comes up behind him and helps him pin her to the ground.

"Good job Jon" I whisper

We sit and watch as the team gradually make their way into the house some through the front door others sit right underneath the window ledges.

"They must have her surrounded," Ruth tells me

But all I can think is who's shot the gun and who's on the receiving end, I wait a few minutes as we sit and watch them enter the building, I get up and start walking towards the house not caring who's seen me. I watch as officer Daniels places Christine into the back of the police cruiser that's just come up the long driveway at the speed of light, with the lights and sirens going, as I reach the front door another two officers are pulling a very distressed, very mucky looking Sienna out of the house.

I stand and just stare at her for a few moments, and I can't hide the look of disgust on my face, which I can clearly see the guilt in hers.

"Get her out of here" I hear Spencer's voice and with that I run up the porch and in through the front door and into the entrance hall. I turn to my right and head into the front room and see Dawson sat on the floor with Bow crouched down beside him.

"Oh my god" I gasp and then I notice Ruth beside me who rushes to be beside Dawson in seconds.

"Daw talk to me…say something," she says

"Hey, Darlin…what you doing here?"

"What did she do to you?" I ask

"This idiot took a bullet for me," Bow tells us

"Man, it was nothing….its just a graze" he turns to Ruth and looks her dead in the eyes "honestly Darlin…it's just a graze….that crazy bitch couldn't even aim straight" and we all laugh as Spencer enters the room shouting

"WE NEED SOME MEDICAL ASSISTANCE IN HERE…how ya doing Daw?"

"Fine….it's just a graze…I think Bea did more damage when we were kids" he laughs "But it does sting a little he suddenly admits and that's when I notice the blood coming from his shoulder on his left side.

"And you," Spencer says turning to me, "I thought we had agreed you two would stay back at my place," he tells me in an angry but relieved voice

"Well, in my defence I never actually agreed…. I just listened"

"You could have destroyed the whole operation if you had been seen"

"Sorry," I say "I just had to make sure y'all would be okay"

"Hmm, you should have listened," he says as he starts pulling me into a hug, but I can tell he's more relieved than mad "Not just you to worry about anymore baby Bea" and the words are out before he can stop himself.

The medics have now entered the room to patch up Dawson but all I hear is an echo of "What?"

Spencer releases me and then says "My time to go…. got questioning to do" he winks at me before leaving the room

I turn around and look to Bow who's grinning at me but he also looks slightly confused "What did he mean Sweetheart?"

"Surprise," I say "you're going to be a Pops yourself" he walks over to me and wraps me in his arms snuggling his face into my shoulder. "Your certain?" he cries

"I'm certain, it came back in my blood results at the hospital, which is why Spencer wanted to speak to me privately" a smile spreads across his face as I continue talking and he picks me up and wraps me into a tight embrace, I can see the happy tears in his eyes before he gently places me back on my feet. Dawson try's to stand with the help of Ruth knowing he can't put any pressure on his arm, but he reaches forward to give us both hugs.

"Congratulations guys….I can't wait to be an uncle" then he whispers to Bow "Your going to need to think about putting a ring on it now" he says with a smirk and a wink

---

A little while later, we've headed to Roses cafe to find out what really happened up at Dawnwood. When we enter were greeted once again by Rose herself.

"Back so soon dears, I thought you said you'd be back tomorrow?"

"I think we're in need today Rose could we sit somewhere out of the way?"

She points and we notice Clay, Willow and Flo sat over in the far corner at one of the large tables. As I look around I notice how dead it is in here which makes me wonder if Mamas death has had any effect on the business, there are only around four other people here, three of who are sitting at a table at the other end of the café, old Billy I think his name is, who is sat at the counter reading his daily paper and drinking his coffee. We walk over to them and all start to sit, Bow pulls my chair out for me and sits closer to me than he normally would and then he drapes a protective arm over my shoulder. Once everyone is seated Rose comes over and takes our orders, most of us decide on just coffee for the minute. When Rose notices Dawson's shoulder all bandaged and wrapped up she says, "Need a special house coffee, sugar?"

"You know Rose that's the best thing you've ever said to me" he smiles at her

"You know I think we could all do with one of those Rose," I tell her

"Not you," Bow says with a wink

"Oh....umm....yes I'll just have an orange juice please"

When she comes back with our drinks we all sit there eager to hear what actually happened up at Dawnwood manor.

"C'mon this melon didn't put me in danger for nothing," Ruth says gesturing to me, and I giggle

"What actually happened?" I asked

"Well... we walked in" Dawson starts "Bow walked into the front room first, then around five minutes later Sienna walked in too behind us, you were right Bea, she must have already been in the house, she came in through the back entrance to the front room, you know the one that's direct from the kitchen, she then asked "why I was there too"

"So, I told her, he was interested in buying it from us," Bow tells us

"Quick thinking that was" Dawson replies

"We then walked her around the house as if to show her the work we'd done to it, I asked how Liam and the children were, she said she'd been working a lot lately so hadn't had chance to see them much, I then asked her where she'd been, she then became very shady like she didn't want us to know, I asked if she had been in and around franklin because the rental car she had come in had come from a local firm, but she insisted that she only flew in yesterday"

"I then asked why she had bought Christine with her; she couldn't answer me," Dawson tells us

"When I'd finished showing her around she started to talk figures but seemed very cold, she gave a really unrealistic figure, Dawson laughed and told her there's no way its worth that much"

"I told her that's extortion" Dawson buts in, then looks to Bow to continue

"She got pissed at me because I'd told her that her pricing was wrong, I then told her we knew why Christine was here, what she was up to and what she had done, she looked shocked but then that look turned to smugness. She asked us how we knew, how we figured it out, I told her about Bea in the hospital" he takes my hand and gives it a squeeze "she then asked us to prove what Bea had told us, I told her I knew it was her that tampered with the trucks which caused myself and Beatrice to be hospitalised, to which she replied very good, I didn't think you would figure that one out, I then told her we knew about how she was working with Christine and that we know she had taken out Nathan parker" he stops and takes a slip of his coffee before continuing "she then told us that actually Nathan parker and your Mama was all Christine's doing and that they had agreed to split the profits from Dawnwood and my life insurance policy, just like Beatrice had told us when she woke up"

"When she said about Mama, I lost my shit, but she suddenly pulled the gun out and aimed it at Bow, as if she knew she was in too deep," Dawson tells us

"Let me guess…. The Beretta M9?" Ruth says

"It was indeed," Spencer says appearing from nowhere, walking towards us taking a seat in between Willow and Clay "luckily for me we got it all on the hidden body cameras"

"I then started telling her a few home truths like she was wrong to have done what she done all those years ago and that she's a terrible mother for hiding all that information from poor little Benny, that she was just money grabbing and certainly not the person I once knew."

"Then she turned the gun on Bow," Dawson tells us butting in again

"And I must admit I did shit myself a little, I thought that was me done for," Bow says "if it wasn't for this guy sat right here," he says slapping Dawson on the shoulder, who winces "I wouldn't be sat here with y'all if it wasn't for him"

"Ahhh, it was nothing buddy, I know you would have done the same for me"

"Darn right I would," Bow tells him.

"Okay, let's leave them with there Bro love," Spencer says wearing a big smile "I wanted to come here to tell y'all, we think we've got her. The bodycam footage shows what went on and as these two described that's what happened, we've got a confession from that, we've also taken in Christine too as you and Ruth saw Bea. She has also admitted to assisting in this, she's told us that Sienna was going to split the profits of the life insurance and of Dawnwood, she's admitted to what she did to Mama, but it was all under the instructions of Sienna, you see it turns out that Sienna had some past dirt on Christine too, who was also being blackmailed" he shifts in his seat "we've charged her with first-degree murder and attempted murder because she helped do the brakes on Bow's truck"

"and Sienna?" I ask

"Well, she's not saying anything, unfortunately, she's refusing, but we'll crack her. She knows she's been caught out, but we will be charging her with two counts of attempted murder, one count of first-degree murder and one assisted murder"

"So where does this leave us?" Bow asks

"Don't worry, they'll both be going away for a long time" Spencer tells us.

Chapter Twenty

New beginnings – 7 months later

I find myself walking down the streets of Chicago, walking is said loosely, waddling..... yeah I'm waddling more like. I've just been in to see Carlos and his family at the restaurant, they're all so happy to see me and keep offering to help me as much as they can but as you know I'm pretty independent, they continue to hand me all different Italian dishes that are in heatproof containers, that they have made that day for me to take along with me. waving them goodbye and leaving the restaurant, the cold wind makes my cheeks burn as I continue to waddle down through the wintery streets to my old apartment, I keep thinking about how far we've all come and how much has changed for my family over the last year, as I walk a little further it starts to snow and jeez it's cold here, not really what I'm used to anymore.

So, we buried Mama next to the Nana and Gramps that we never knew (which were her wishes) around six months ago, at the local church in our little town surrounded by all our and Mama's loved ones. The service was just beautiful, and she would have been so proud of the turnout, I must admit it was the hardest day of my life, it was so hard to say goodbye but she's finally at peace.

Which means we were all able to finally take the next step in our lives.

Ruth and Dawson were married a month ago on the second weekend in April which wasn't as planned but they wanted to do it sooner rather than later, the ceremony took place in the local little church, in our little town. It was a beautiful service, which was followed by a very traditional, very southern reception party. which was held in the barn up at the family ranch. Which now belongs to Dawson and Ruth, Pops had given it to them as a wedding present after speaking to us all and no one else really putting up a fight for it. We know it was a hard thing for Pop's to do but like he said he still has his memories, and it really does need a family living there, he seems to be looking forward to not having so much work to do and actually spending time with Rose.

Dawson and Ruth have definitely made the ranch their home, they've redecorated it and given it the much-needed care that it deserves. Clay has finally left home, like he had a choice really, I mean Dawson and Ruth did offer him to stay but he didn't want them starting married life with him in the way and he could have gone with Pop's to live but he thought that would be a way to awkward, so he went to live with Florence in her apartment in Franklin.

Pops is doing much better, seems more relaxed and most importantly he's happy. He's actually working part-time in Rose's quirky café, it keeps him busy and he and rose have become rather close over these last few months, they're seen as more of an item now and she looks after him, and I've got to be honest I couldn't think of anyone else that I would rather be with my Pops…apart from maybe my Mama, but she makes him happy and I know it would make Mama happy because she loved them both so much. I've never really seen my Pop's cook before like the way he does now, I think Rose is teaching him and he says he's enjoying it. Rose herself has been so kind and supportive of all of us, she's helped us in ways that we never realised we ever needed help, she told us when her and my father became an item that she knows that she'll never replace my mother because she knows that that's big shoes to fill but she's there for us if we should ever need her and I definitely thought that was rather sweet of her.

As I mentioned Clay has finally left the ranch and moved into a small apartment in franklin above the hairdressers where Ruth once worked part-time, with his now girlfriend Flo, they seem really happy, and I really like her, particularly the way she talks. Although their apartment is small, it's cosy and I absolutely love visiting them, they've now got a little dog whose name is Duchess, she's a…… well none of us are sure what breed she is, all we know is she's white and brown and fluffy and she's the kindest, sweetest little thing, so friendly and snuggly but also a bundle of energy.

Spencer and Willow have just found out they're expecting a little boy at the end of August and they are both soooo excited. Spencer more so… it almost like he's a changed man, he's already decorated one of what was the all-white bedrooms a baby blue colour and even paid for someone to come in and do a mural on one of the walls of all kinds of zoo animals, its lovely to see the nursery all set up with a crib and other nursery furniture, like a wardrobe, blanket box, changing station and matching toy box, not to mention all the new mod cons that he's had put in there too, like the mood lighting, a motion censored floor and crib and even a rocker that simulates that the baby is in a car. It's all very smart and impressive but I can also imagine it's very expensive too. I'm pretty proud of him, he's really grown up over the last year and it's been lovely to see him all settled down now.

As I walk down the street I come to the place that was once my apartment when the voice that I know all too well startles me from behind.

"Ready to go Sweetheart" I hear his southern drawl

I turn around and wrap my arms around him "Of course…do we have everything?"

"All in the van," he says nodding towards the van "but there is a really miserable older lady in there…..I didn't know what to do she kept telling me off….. and….she's…..she's kinda scary" he whispers as he takes the trays of food I'm carrying

I laugh and roll my eyes "Mrs Moyles" I tell him, he looks at me a little confused and smiles too "forgot to mention her didn't I"

"Yeah must have slipped ya mind" he jokes

"Local busy body, who basically thinks she owns the building and everyone in it"

"Not going to miss her then?"

"Not on your Nelly, god no," I tell him "Can I just take one last look around before we go?"

"Sure," he says with a light laugh and takes my hand and we start to make our way up the stairs, I don't remember it ever being this steep and I'm out of breath in no time. "Take your time Sweetheart" I hear his soft voice beside me.

"Thanks," I say with a smile playing on my lips. I finally reach my apartment, number nine. Looking down I can hardly believe it was ever this high up I always thought it was lower down than this, but then again I wasn't carrying this much weight the last time I was here. Walking in the little red door, I stand there in my dated apartment, it's really empty and walking through I notice the kitchens still yellow, and it makes me laugh to myself.

"I really should have painted this place and made it my own"

I walk through the living room, and I can see the imprints on the carpet from where all my furniture once was. I wander through into what used to be my bedroom and en-suite, I'm still taken back by the emerald colour of the walls

"You know I actually really liked that colour but maybe just not on all of those walls," I tell Bow as he looks at me as if to say you have got to be kidding me. I find it funny how even though I know the apartment is extremely clean, it looks so dated now and tired and I secretly hope the new owners give this little place what it needs. Once I'm finished looking around I tell Bow I'm ready and we head back to the door and down the stairs to the foyer. Heading to my post box I pop the keys inside so no one can get them and then head to the front door.

"Beatrice" I hear a voice that makes me stop in my tracks and turning around I see her standing there in the foyer, it's Mrs Moyles and to my surprise, she's smiling "Don't come back" she winks

I smile at her, and she matches it "Take it easy Mrs Moyles, I hope the new owners aren't too loud for you" I tell her grinning

"They couldn't be any worse than you" she winks and to my surprise, she comes up to me and gives me a cuddle and hands me a gift bag, full of hand-knitted baby clothes all in lemon and white. "I wasn't sure what you were having"

"Thank……thank you, neither….. neither are we," I tell her feeling slightly shocked and thank her again as we leave the building.

When we reach the truck Bow turns to me and says "She's not so bad….. not really that scary" he turns to look at the entrance where she's standing

"No, she's not," I say as he starts the engine

"But she's probably watching to make sure you leave" he laughs, and his comment makes me smile as we pull away.

A few hours have passed and we're still on the road heading to the place that we both once called home, but this time I don't dread it and there's a van in tow. After hours and hours of driving overnight and many rests stops due to this baby using my bladder as a trampoline, we eventually reach our little town in the early hours of the morning, in the distance I can see the sun coming up over the hill and it is absolutely beautiful.

"Can we stop at Rose's? Pops might be there, and I'd really like to see them both"

"Sure, we can Sweetheart" and after a short while, he pulls up outside the café, the streets are empty. We both jump out of the truck and head for the door, as we reach it, he opens it for me and the bell on the door goes as we enter. That's when I see him standing there wiping down the counter.

"We don't open till 8.30 am" his voice calls and hearing it makes me smile

"Hey Pop's, it's us"

He looks up and I can see the slightly shocked expression on his face to see us standing there so early then he comes out from behind the counter wrapping me into a warm, welcoming hug and then does the same to Bow "Oh hey Honey Bea, we didn't expect to see you till tomorrow, how ya doing?"

"I'm fine Pops, thanks"

"Bow its good to see you too, made good time today," he tells him

"We did," Bow tells him with a smile

Pop's looks me up and down "look at you…. your just glowing….Rose….Rose… come see who's here"

Then I hear her "Well blow me, you made good time," she tells us wrapping us both into a big group hug, which makes us both smile "Beatrice… dear look at you," she says standing back and looking at me "You look incredible, just radiant"

I blush "Thank you….we just wanted to pop in and see you on our way home" and it dawns on me it sounds so weird to call it home but there's something soothing about it.

"Well I'm glad you did," Pop's tells me, It's like he's a different guy since he started spending time with Rose, it's nice to see. We were so worried about him when we lost Mama, he was a totally different guy, he was so angry and just wanted to hide away from the world, we were all really concerned about him, he was so lost but now it's like he's got a new lease of life, like he's enjoying each and every moment and treasuring them all. He and Rose have become inseparable and it's really lovely to see him so happy again. I think when Mama died they literally began to lean on each other for support and then soon became an item. I like Rose but she'll never fill the shoes of my mother and she knows that, but I think there's an unsaid mutual respect there, we know she would never ask us to call her anything other than Rose. We stayed a little while, had a coffee, and then went on our way to the place we now call home.

Pulling up the long newly gravelled driveway and looking around the gardens I notice that the flowers are just coming out into bloom and it's so beautiful to see, in the distance, I can see the roses in what used to be Clara's rose garden just coming into bloom, there arc all different colours and the house comes into view and it's absolutely breath-taking, there are shutters either side of each of the windows have been placed back to how they once were in there hay day, they are a lovely green colour which matches the front door, and I notice that the garage door has been restored or replaced and is now a deep red colour.

Getting out of the truck with little assistants, I notice how crunchy the new beige gravel is under my feet and when I look at the house I can really tell how much work Bow has done to it, and we can now call it home.

"Wow," I say, "you really have worked so hard here haven't you" and it dawns on me that I haven't really seen the house since the day that I was here helping to rip it all out and ready to replace things. I hadn't really taken much notice the day Sienna was caught here, it all happened so fast, all I cared about was Bow and Dawson and whether they were safe that day.

Bow comes round and takes my hand "Welcome home sweetheart" he says as he tries to lift and carry me over the threshold and into the house, with much difficulty, I laugh and insist that he puts me down before he puts his back out and then he leads me through the front door, I stand there looking around the large hallway and I start to notice all the changes that have taken place, the walls are beige in colour with a wooden dado rail that goes around the hallway and the wooden floor is very much the same as it was, it just looks like it's had a good sand and varnish, but then I always loved the original flooring that was all around the house, it oozed character, I waddle on through to the living room on the right and I love how light and airy it is, the fireplace is still the same just cleaner, the large red rug is in the centre of the room which has been cleaned too and looks brand new.

"It's beautiful," I tell him "but is that the same rug?"

"It is," he tells me, and I pull a face as if to say I'm surprised but very impressed.

Walking around I notice the exquisite armchairs sat either side of the fireplace and matching sofa, it's a burgundy red in colour, they must be new. the walls up to the dado rail are a deep burgundy red in colour too and above the dado rail is a lovely white colour, its light and airy and I notice the bay windows have been all cleaned and painted looking new, little trinkets that were once in this room have been placed back as they once were, things like the grandfather clock and there is a now a black grand piano to the left of the room and a widescreen tv has been placed to the right of the fireplace.

We make our way across to the dining room, which is just across the hall, and I love how the sunbeams through the large windows, there's another fireplace in there and the wood panelling on the walls have been painted a beige colour and it really compliments the room. The ornate wooden table and matching chairs which have been covered in a beige coloured material are back where it once was, and the vintage dresser has been painted and placed back to where it once was too. Only now containing all the vintage teacups and plates that Bow was once going to throw away. looking up I notice the ceiling that was once hanging down has all been replaced and repaired, I remember I haven't seen this room since I first watched Bow pull it down. The next room we drift off into is the kitchen which is located in behind the living room. I walk into a very modern, cream, country style kitchen, complete with matching island in the centre of the room, complete with oak worktops. The wooden floor has been replaced with dark slate flooring and above the counter, the walls have been tiled with cream tiles, it's all very shiny and new looking and I absolutely love it.

"Have you seen the utility room?"

I look at him with a quizzing expression

"Open that door over there"

"But this was the cupboard," I tell him as he looks at me
wearing a smug but satisfied grin. I open the large door
and when I step inside I notice a washing machine, extra
freezer and a tumble dryer have been placed and fitted
inside along with very nice units that are a deep blue
colour with a walnut-coloured work surface, it also
contains a bell sink and wall cupboards which are dotted
around the room for extra storage.

"This is incredible Bow; I mean look at it in here what a
difference," I say leaving the cupboard and making my
way around the kitchen cupboards

"Open that end one, over there," he says pointing to the
small floor cupboard by the back door.

I waddle across the room and slowly open it up and what I
find is just the best sight "You kept them" I say looking in
his direction "Thank you Bow. I told you it would be
important to keep them" standing right before me I can see
all of Nana Clara's, Handwritten cookery books as well as
some that were once my mothers

"Just thought they belonged to the house ya, no, plus I
knew you d kill me if I got rid of them and Pop's gave me
your Mothers cookbooks with the other ones, he thought
you'd like them"

I head into the next room which is the study

"This one's mine," Bow tells me as he opens the door

Inside he's placed the mahogany desk back where it once
was (in front of the large window) and left the shelves in
the same places they were, there are a few folders within
them and I notice the floor is a lovely oak wood that's

been polished, and it just looks so different. I can't help but notice a brand-new computer system that sits upon the desk.

"So, this will be my office" he informs me

"Well, you've definitely cleaned this up a bit haven't you," I say

"I have and I can access the security cameras that have been placed all around the outside of the house and the entrance"

"Very nice," I tell him "This is Clays doing isn't it"

"Yep, you can never be too careful," he tells me as we leave the room

I smile at him and head across the hallway and down to the parlour, right before we get there I pass some black and white pictures that have been put up on the freshly painted white wall, the first one I notice is of Nana Clara and Grandpa Bill, on inspection, it's one of them stood outside on the front porch smiling and joking in their prime, I can only guess it wasn't long after they got married and bought the house, they look so young and carefree. The next one I come to is a picture of Bow's mother and father and this must have been taken on their wedding day, It's then that I realise I've never seen what they looked like before, his mother was stunning and had long dark hair and the sweetest, kindest face and I can definitely see Bow in her, he has her smile and his father, looked strong, almost like no one would mess with him but you can see the kindness in his eyes which match Bow's.

The next photograph I see is the one we found of Philip and Daphne and it's nice to see it in a frame and back where it belongs, in the next frame is a photograph of my parents from when they were younger, then I notice the fifth and final frame, this one makes me laugh and cringe at the same time. There I am sat in the frame and god this is not a pretty sight.

"Couldn't have picked a better picture then?"

It's a photo of the both of us when we were kids, were both sat out on the porch of Dawnwood Manor

"What?..... I like it" he laughs "It show's that anything's possible and sometimes things or people have a way of coming back to you, in a time when you think your life has fallen to pieces and you're at your lowest point"

I walk up to him and place my head on his chest "I am so lucky to have you" I tell him

"No, I think it's me that's lucky to have you, you picked me out of a black hole," he tells me "but come on I want to show you the rest of the house"

I take his hand and we head on up the large staircase to the bedrooms. We walk around the landing to the room that was once Bow's, when he was a small child, he opens the door and the first thing I notice is the dark blue wall has disappeared and is now a lovely fresh white colour, walking in I notice the carpet is white too and there is a beautiful oval crib in the right-hand corner, a changing station and child's wardrobe both white which are on the far wall next to the window, on the other side of the window is a rocking chair too, he's definitely thought of everything.

"This is stunning, when did you have time to do all this?"

"Well, it was kinda rushed but I want the best for our little pumpkin"

"How do you know it's a girl?" I laugh

"When you know you know," he tells me

"Might be a boy, isn't that right Timmy" I say looking down at my bump

"Timmy?" he laughs "Absolutely not, we are not calling any son of ours Timmy, the poor kid will be picked on" he laughs "Timmy Tanner, geez…. I'm so hoping it's a girl, we will not have a Timmy"

"Yep didn't think that one through" I laugh "Sorry"

"So, I had Spencer come in and tell me about the mod-cons he's got at his place the floor here is also motion censored and the lighting is a mood lighting that you can change with a remote control, Willow picked out the baby furniture, if you don't like it we can change it…."

"No, it's perfect, everything's perfect….thank you"

"Your welcome," he says kissing my forehead as he leads me out of the nursery along the landing and into the first bedroom which was once Grandpa Bill and Nana Clara's bedroom and its so light and airy this room is white and grey, and I absolutely love it, the colours really compliment each other there's wood panelling around the room which has been painted with varnish. The large ceiling to floor windows have white flowy curtains on either side and the bed is one like out of a storybook, the magnificent wooden four-poster bed is stunning, with its white curtains down each side and sitting on the edge of it makes me feel like I'm never going to want to leave, it just cushions to me. Bow pulls me up and takes me through a doorway which I think use to be a storage cupboard, which is now our very own walk-in wardrobe "Your stuff to the left and mine to the right he tells me….I've put a few things away already" he tells me nodding towards one of the doors. I walk over and open the first wardrobe door; inside is a beautiful pair of brand-new cowgirl boots and I get very excited about these "

keep going" he tells me, I open the next set of drawers and inside is a new cowgirl hat

"Thank you" I smile

He then nods towards the next wardrobe door and inside is a stunning knee-length navy blue with floral print wrap-around dress. "ooh Bow you really shouldn't have, it's so pretty…. Thank you I love it"

"Your welcome Sweetheart"

There's a small door to the right of the wardrobe and I head on through and notice that he has turned one of the bathrooms into an en-suite its all been done out really well in white with pink and grey accessories, towels, candles, cabinets, and toiletries. The en-suite is complete with a toilet, built-in shower and a clawfoot bathtub as well as his and her sinks.

"So, you blocked off the door on the landing?"

"Yes, I wanted us to have our own private bathroom, especially as the kids get older"

"I could be wrong but I'm pretty certain you just said the kids"

"I did," he said as he walks further down the landing "we'll want more than just this one" hearing this makes me smile; I love it when he talks about our future.

We spend the next half an hour walking around all the bedrooms, they've all been done really well and kept to neutral colours but all contain double beds, Bow tells me it's just in case we get visitors, but I'm not convinced. He takes me on through to the family bathroom, which also has a roll-top bathtub, a new toilet, built-in sinks and cupboards and a large shower cubical.

We get to the library and it's absolutely breath-taking, I look to my left at the large wall and as I get closer I notice that it's completely covered in books that are my total favourites and others that are very old but timeless classics.

"I've always wanted my own library," I tell him "But where did you get all of these? I would have thought you would have had to throw a lot of the originals away when you renovated"

"I know Sweetheart, I always told you, you will always have what you want, but some of those are yours, some I found in the house, others I bought online and Pop's gave some to me"

I can feel the tears stinging my eyes "Mamas books?"

"I believe so," he tells me

I'm speechless that's so thoughtful, he walks me over to the spiral staircase.

"Ready?.... this is for you"

"Please tell me you haven't changed much up here"

"Of course not," he tells me with a smile

I follow him up the spiral staircase and when I reach the top I'm out of breath but what I see is just the best sight. There are two chairs on either side of the large round window, one a rocking chair which I vaguely recognise and an armchair on the opposite side.

"Is that?"

"Yes it's the original one that we found up here, so yes it's Nana's"

"Oh…Wow… Bow….." I say taking a seat and looking out of the large round window "It's beautiful, look at the gardens"

"I know but it's going to need some work out there, we've done what we can for the moment and it's tidy" I sit there looking around the room and notice that he's carpeted the floor with a deep emerald green coloured carpet and the walls have been panelled with wood and painted a light grey colour, there's a wooden ornate desk is to the left-hand side of the room, housing a laptop and a desk lamp, I notice that some of the panelling has been turned into several shelves where Bow has placed folders, books, documents and of course a printer.

I turn to look at him "So, I've made this your office" he tells me

"I see… it's very cosy up here……I absolutely love it….. thank you"

"Well, I was hoping you would look out for me when I come home"

"I think that could be arranged"

"I've just got one more room I'd like to show you"

"The parlour?"

"The Parlour…yes"

"I did wonder why you didn't take me in there when we were downstairs," I tell him

"Well, let's go and take a look," he tells me as he takes my hand leading me down both sets of stairs and into the parlour, I stand there and it takes my breath away and I know that this is possibly my favourite room in the entire house, it's been restored to the beautiful gold and light blue almost lilac colour it once was, the furniture's all vintage and almost French looking and it's stunning, the long light blue and gold curtains have all been replaced or restored I'm not sure which yet, the huge light blue and gold rug is where it once was and I notice that the little hole in the floor has been covered by the rug once more, the white marble fireplace has been thoroughly cleaned and looks almost new containing the open fireplace. Two new baby blue French-style sofa's sit across from each other with a white ornate coffee table sat in the middle in front of the fireplace and I absolutely love it.

"I thought we could do something fun," Bow says from behind me as he watches me take in the room

"Oh, I bet you did cowboy" I reply with a wink

He laughs "No I've had an idea; you know we found what Philip and Daphne left….. Well…..I was thinking we could do the same….I've taken something out of the last book, and I was thinking we could do our own letter and place some money in the last book" he tells me holding up and handing me the Tess of the d'Urbervilles by Thomas Hardy. I open it and just like the others the first few pages are normal and then about three-quarters of the way in the middle of the book, pages are cut square so you can store things in the centre. "I was thinking we could place in two hundred dollars and a letter," he tells me

"I think that's a great idea, I would love for someone to have the same luck we had and the same nice discovery we did" I say as I sit on the floor by the coffee table, and he sits on the right beside me

He hands me two hundred dollars and a piece of paper and a pen "Well…. What should we write?" I ask

"Umm… Well, I was thinking something like this" I sit and brace myself pen in hand and begin to write what he tells me.

"We hope this brings y'all the same luck it has bought us, we are a young couple expecting a baby in the year 2019.

Should our letter be found, like we have found Philip and Daphne's, we hope this house brings you the same happiness and joy that it has brought us.

we are a fun, loving couple that lives for each other and are very much in love……

please enjoy our home/ your new home…..

Warm Wishes

Mr and Mrs Beatrice and Bow Tanner"

I turn to him and give him a quizzical look "You've really thought about this haven't you" and then I laugh "Mr and Mrs Tanner…. That just reminds me of the restaurant" I continue to laugh at the memory

"You don't understand do you" he laughs too

"Understand….What's there to understand" we both sit there laughing as I finish writing

"Beatrice…. I…… I want you to be my wife….. I love you….. you are and always have been the one person I want and will always want"

I try to hold my tears in but suddenly tears are running freely down my face

"You have made my life so much better, and me, I'm a better person with you in my life and I honestly don't know what I would have done without you these last few months. Not once over the years have you left my mind, I wondered what you were doing and would occasionally ask Dawson how you were, and now I'm lucky enough to be starting a family with you, Please Beatrice marry me?" he stands there and reaches into his pocket to reveal Daphne's engagement Ring and it's even more breath-taking than I remember. The sapphire in the centre of the ring is a deep blue colour and there are eight diamonds surrounding it that are set into the dainty gold band.

"Yes of course I will"

He picks me up and gently spins me around. I don't think I've ever felt love like his, he's gentle, caring, not to mention totally gorgeous and if he's taught me anything it's to never accept anything less.

Five years later

It's been five years since we moved into Dawnwood Manor and Bow proposed and not much has changed, to be honest.

Clay and Florence still live in their small but cosy apartment and have recently got married. They have decided to go travelling around the world for the next eight months and will be going to places like parts of Asia, Spain, France, Germany, the United Kingdom and I think they mentioned going to Russia too, they have taken their much-loved pet dog duchess with them too and are getting in some "them time" before they have to return back to work. Clay still works for a company that no one really knows much about and every time we question him he just still says "Oh nothing much it's just security" Florence has recently become manager of Stitch the clothing store in the town and is doing really well for herself, she also designs the clothes in there too and is working with a designer to get her clothes out there, she likes that she can bring duchess to work too. I think they're going to be the type of couple that never have children because they enjoy spending time just the three of them and having holidays with their dog but that's okay, I know it's not for everyone, Clay has never been the paternal type anyway and always liked his own space.

Spencer and Willow still live here in Franklin, In the same house, Spencer is now head of the station and he's absolutely loving life, I've never seen him so happy, he's in charge and we'll respected within the force and still loves his job and Willow works part-time as a waitress in Rose's Cafe allowing her to look after their four-year-old son Bobby in her free time. Bobby is the spitting image of his dad when he was his age, his hair is dark and he's so loud and cheeky too and that's what we love about him.

They visit us most weekends but nothing for them has changed too much, I'm pretty certain that they won't be tying the knot anytime soon though or having any more little ones. Willow once told me that she'd rather get a dog instead of having another child and plus Spencer is like a big kid anyway so why have more when she has him too, she also told me a dog wouldn't be as messy as another child but I'm not so sure myself. They still live in the white, very up to date house with all the mod cons that I know Spencer loves.

Pop's and Rose are doing so well, and he recently asked for her hand in marriage over a family BBQ, of course, we were all in on it and she was totally clueless about the whole thing. It's really nice to see them both happy. They're never really very affectionate towards each other in public but I think that's just them. They both work at the café now and Pop's is now cooking most of the meals in there as head chef, Roses son went off to university as an adult learner in hopes of becoming a doctor, were all very proud of him, and Pops and how he turned a really awful situation into a better one. He and Rose are living in her newly built bungalow just down the road from Spencer and Willow which seems to work well for them and childcare.

Dawson and Ruth are doing really well for themselves, Ruth has given up being a hairdresser and is now running a riding school and stables full time up at the ranch which she absolutely loves, Blossom takes riding lessons with Ruth twice a week, which I know they both enjoy. Dawson is generally running the ranch with the help of a few guys from town too. We occasionally take the kids up there to explore, see the animals and visit them. Myself, Dawson, Ruth, and Bow are all still really close and they love being an aunt and uncle to the kids, we occasionally have dinner together and take it in turns to host get-togethers for the family at each other's houses, there basically the type of people that make themselves at home in our house and we do the same in theirs by helping ourselves to stuff in the fridge etc, we're always welcome there and they're always welcome here too but that was always how it was. Everyone is always welcome at Dawnwood manor or so Clara and Bill always told us, so it's something we kept.

As for Sienna and Christine, well they both got life in prison and we don't really have much to do with them anymore, Liam occasionally visits Sienna with Benny, but he's recently moved on with his life and has adopted Benny, when he found out what had happened he was absolutely devastated but got full custody of the children, he has recently found himself a new partner…. Tom who he worked with at the hospital, you see Tom is a nurse and helped out a few times and gave Liam advice on certain things, but Liam seems really happy, and Tom seems to love the kids just as much as Liam does.

As for us, we are still very much in love, don't get me wrong no relationship is perfect but were taking on every single challenge head-on and together, We try to forget the past and all the crap life brought us all those years ago, but I believe its what has shaped us into the people we have become. We had Blossom just over four years ago, she is the absolute light of our lives, with her long, dark wavy hair and the biggest, bluest eyes and her mother's attitude, but is the spitting image of Bow. She was shortly followed by Cooper who is definitely a Mama's boy and is now two and a half years old, again he has the bluest eyes and has the softest, darkest curliest hair I've ever seen. He often follows me around the garden, helping dig up various plants and weeds, and we are once again expecting another one, which would take us to baby number three. We got married in the winter after Blossom was born too which we kept a very intimate snowy wedding, in which we only had close friends and close family members attend, we just felt we didn't need or want anyone else who wasn't important to us, the ceremony was perfect, my dress hugged all my curves and we both had the best time at our wedding reception, again that was a very southern very fun experience, but the only one missing was my mother of course but we saved her a chair. We both currently work from our home, in the attic room that Bow converted to an office for me. You see I got the dream job as a publisher in which it means I can work from home a lot of the time so I'm here for the children. Bow is back and forth from the New York office some of the time but he's never away for too long, plus he'd miss me and the kids far too much if he were away too long.

life really seems to have all worked out for all of us…..or did it?

The End…… or is it